I0784691

R.L. RINNE

Sir Lancelot's Scroll

(3rd book in the "Scroll's Journey" series)
By R. L. Rinne

DEDICATION

Dedicated to Mark

Character	Years	Description
St. Martin	316-397	Bishop of Tours
Magnus Maximus	340-388	Roman Emperor during the years 383-388
Magnus of Rau	383-450	Student of St. Martin lifespan
St. Patrick	387-493	Son of Calpurnius and Conchessa
Cynde	385-460	Wife of Magnus of Rau
Bertrona	410-491	Daughter of Cynde, Grandmother of Igraine
Eris	431-507	Mother of Igraine
Igraine	453-516	Mother of Morgan Le Fay
Morgan Le Fay	473-506	Mother of Thaney, step-sister to King Arthur
Thaney	499-581	Daughter of Morgan Le Fay and King Lot
St. Kentigern (Mungo)	518-614	Son of Thaney, born Culross, died Glasgow UK
King Owain mab Urien	499-571	Son of King Urien
Saint Servanus	500-583	Saint of Scotland, Apostle of Orkney Islands
King Uther Pendragon	433-510	High King
King Arthur	475- 505	Son of Uther Pendragon
King Lleuddun (Lot)	457-524	Husband of Morgan Le Fay, father of Thaney
Sir Lancelot	?-?	Knight of the Round Table

Preface

How did Jesus do these things?

- Turn water to wine
- Walked on water
- Healed the sick
- Raised the dead
- Fed over five thousand people with a few loaves and fishes
- Paid taxes with gold from a fish

The same way his followers have through the centuries following his ascension. The religion of Christianity grew because of the healings of sin, disease, and death. The stories of miracles in people's lives are still occurring, although discounted, discredited, and unknown by most people. Primal Christians expected spiritual healings and other miracles. Concepts and possibilities that have been largely replaced by technology in today's world.

"Eye hath not seen, nor ear heard, neither have entered into the heart of man, the things which God hath prepared for them that love him. But God hath revealed them unto us by his Spirit: for the Spirit searcheth all things, yea, the deep things of God." (1)

I began writing this book several years before I found more genealogical evidence on St. Kentigern or St. Mungo, as he was also called. The man led a life filled with miracles from a young age, but this story actually begins with his mother, Thaney, who lived a life of seemingly insurmountable challenges and trials. She was possibly Scotland's first rape victim. She was the only daughter of a pagan king in what is now Scotland. If you read my two previous novels, Thaney was a descendant of Cynde. Her mother had died, and her only connection to a Christian heritage was through her grandmother. I had written half the book before my research took an unexpected turn! I found an ancient pedigree record that said her grandmother was Igraine and her grandfather was Gorlois. They had two girls, Morgause (the older one) and Morgan Le Fay. Gorlois was killed in a battle, and Uther Pendragon, who was the high king, took Igraine as his wife. One of their sons? You guessed it, King Arthur.

Morgan le Fay (Morgan the Fairy) was Thaney's mother. Early writings about Morgan call her a goddess, a fairy, or a sorceress, a benevolent person, and a dedicated protector of King Arthur. They don't elaborate on human failings that appear in subsequent stories, and this tale will concentrate on the original version of Morgan Le Fay.

So, this book takes a turn away from my typical religious historiographer sources for a credible storyline, and I move into the complicated and often contradictory accounts of the legend of King Arthur and other figures of that time. Rest assured, the healings are still real, but the adventure is fiction. A fascinating story that required an intimidating re-write involving a few characters from Camelot.

Chapter 1

England, March 29th, 517 AD

There was no moon, and a cool mist enveloped the moors in a dense shroud of damp darkness. "Pssst… Thaney, over here!"

The king's daughter recoiled for a moment at the sound of the voice. Then she began moving forward again, dragging her hand gingerly along the top of a rough stone fence to maintain a sense of direction. Rounding a corner in the wall, she entered a small gateway. "How did you know it was me?" she asked.

"I heard your footsteps in the leaves. I knew it had to be you walking so lightly. Anyone else would have been louder." The boy's whispered voice replied as he gave her a clumsy embrace. "Come on, the friar is already there." He said as he held her hand and walked slowly down the stone pathway. As he walked, he gently tapped a worn wooden stick ahead of them with his other hand to make sure they stayed on the rocky trail. The countryside was rugged here, and it was dangerous to get lost on nights as gloomy as this one.

Thaney gripped the boy's hand tighter, as she wondered why she was even taking these chances. Her father would be furious if he knew that she had snuck away in the night, and even more livid if he knew of her intentions.

Hopefully, the rolled-up bedding she had arranged would look enough like her sleeping form to fool anyone, and she would be safely back in the castle before morning's light.

"There it is," Owain announced, and Thaney could see a flickering light in the misty darkness. Drawing closer, they heard a chorus of low voices around a small fire pit.

"I tell you it is true!" The old monk's voice announced loudly. "It happened a century ago. Father Melnic was the bishop's trusted clerk and witnessed it all. The evil Bishop of Seaford Downs was murdered by foreign mercenaries he employed to strike fear into the hearts of peasants in his parish. The men turned on him sometime after they were ordered to decapitate an innocent student of St. Martin of Tours.

"Why did he have the boy killed?" A woman asked.

"The young man had a scroll of parchment, supposedly written in the Saint's own hand, which conflicted with church doctrine. The bishop wanted to rewrite it and display a forged copy as a holy relic. That would have helped to support his version of dogma with his parishioners. When the group returned to the Abbey, the mercenaries waited to be paid for their efforts in finding the boy. The bishop was ecstatic that he had finally secured the sacred scroll and was studiously reading and comparing it to an authentic letter of Martin's, dispatched to him by the priest who was awarded Martin's post at the church in Gaul after his passing. Anyway, on comparing the documents side-by-side, the man suddenly realized that it was only a crude copy. The counterfeit signature was blatantly obvious, and the writing styles didn't match at all. At that point, the bishop flew into a rage, refusing to pay the armed men unless they could produce the original document.

The monk visibly shuddered before continuing, "Melnic said the chief of the band just produced a wicked smile, grabbed the bishop by the throat, lifted him up eye to eye, and said in broken english, 'You vanted to see the boy die slow, now I show you how to die slow. You vill vatch as ve destroy dis place, but you vill suffer good und die de last!' Melnic was terrified and rushed out of the bishop's chambers as the little man's screams pierced the air. Desperate to hide, he crawled into the bowels of a latrine while the rowdy band of Saxons lay siege to the monastery. Melnic crouched in the foul excrement, listening to the horrors taking place throughout that terrible night. In the morning light, he arose and beheld utter desolation. The church was in rubble and flames, as were most of the outbuildings. Townspeople began to enter the grounds, gaping at the twisted bodies lying where they had fallen. Making his way to the bishop's chambers, Melnic saw the remains of the little Abbot, sliced into small pieces, and spread across his large desk."

A collective gasp spread through the audience, followed by shocked silence.

"Melnic and six others were the only monks to survive that ordeal, but Melnic was the only eyewitness of the bishop's folly to survive," the friar announced.

"So, was there ever a real Scroll?" A man asked.

"Most definitely, but it may be lost for eternity now," the monk replied in a sad response. "It reportedly contained St. Martin's methods and thoughts on healing. He cured many souls instantly, as did our master Christ Jesus. The church forbade any detailed record of the events, and the story has become less accurate since it has only been transferred verbally. We may be the last generations to remember it at all." He finished.

"Where could the Scroll be hidden?" asked another.

Melnic languidly recounted the chase of the young heretic before he died. "The boy left from Hastell Cenllys, to Clataguay, to Reidrag, then to Kilpatrick just west of here, then down to Craig Intahl, and a little way westward down the coast to a fishing settlement where the boy was killed. The Scroll could be anywhere along that route, or he could have given it to someone else. His girlfriend and another young man escaped the bishop in a rowboat. They may have traveled to Hibernia or been killed in a storm. We have no way of knowing."

"Did he visit any specific people on his journey?" Thaney shocked herself by asking, as all eyes turned toward her.

The man paused as he considered her question. "He visited a blacksmith shop in Reidrag, and a man called Calpurnius in Kilpatrick, he was a decurio, if I recall correctly. I believe the man's wife might have been a distant relative to St. Martin – but enough of this story, I didn't come tonight to spread tragic tales of the church, I came tonight to proclaim the gospel of Jesus!" As the monk began to preach a well-rehearsed sermon. "Jesus, our lord and master, was in Galilee as it was written. **'And seeing the multitudes, he went up into a mountain: and when he was set, his disciples came unto him: And he opened his mouth, and taught them, saying,** Blessed *are* the poor in spirit: for theirs is the kingdom of heaven. Blessed *are* they that mourn: for they shall be comforted. Blessed *are* the meek: for they shall inherit the earth. Blessed *are* they which do hunger and thirst after righteousness: for they shall be filled. Blessed *are* the merciful: for they shall obtain mercy. Blessed *are* the pure in heart: for they shall see God. Blessed *are* the peacemakers: for they shall be called the children of God. Blessed *are* they which are persecuted for righteousness' sake: for theirs is the kingdom of heaven. Blessed are ye, when *men* shall revile you, and persecute *you*, and shall say all manner of evil against you falsely, for my sake. Rejoice, and be exceeding glad: for great *is* your reward in heaven: for so persecuted they the prophets which were before you.' (2) My friends, be courageous in your dealings with unbelievers and you will be victorious."

"He obviously hasn't met my father," Thaney

exclaimed under her breath.

She and Owain sat down in a comfortable clump of grass. Owain listened intently to the friar's stories, but her thoughts drifted continuously to the heartbreaking story of the two lovers. She replayed it in her head, trying to figure out some way to locate the missing scroll.

"So my friends, I hope you understand that: **'Ye are the light of the world. A city that is set on an hill cannot be hid. Neither do men light a candle, and put it under a bushel, but on a candlestick; and it giveth light unto all that are in the house. Let your light so shine before men, that they may see your good works, and glorify your Father which is in heaven.'** (3) Thank you for coming here tonight, my friends."

In a little over an hour, the monk finished his sermon and carried a small leather bag around to each of the attendees to receive an offering. When he approached, Thaney made a show of dropping a large gold coin into it and asked: "Father, do you recall the names of the two lovers in your story about St. Martin's scroll?"

Smiling widely from the large contributions he flushed. "Let me see, the girl's name escapes me, but the boy was named after Magnus Maximus, the emperor of Rome from 383 to 388. He was Magnus from someplace in Gaul." He added, hurrying away, and quickly offering the bag to a few other people who were starting to leave.

"That might be a light for this dark world," Thaney said.

"What do you mean?" Owain asked.

"The scroll of St. Martin may hold some secrets to healing spiritually." She replied.

Owain just shrugged and began carefully leading the way back to the castle, while Thaney's thoughts surged with possibilities. Her mother had a reputation for being a healer before she died. *Could reliable spiritual healing still be possible? How did Jesus and his followers heal, and the prophets before him? Where could the scroll have been hidden for the past century?*

Lost in her thoughts, Thaney was surprised when Owain reached around her with a hug. "What are you doing?"

"I thought I might rate a good night kiss for bringing you home, I'm your best friend, you know." Owain stood motionless in the shadows, frowning.

"Oh sure." As she realized that they were standing outside the castle gate. The courtyard was already bustling with early morning traders. "I'm sorry, thanks for taking me." She gave him a quick peck on the cheek and hurried away.

She paused and gave him a small wave before she walked through the gate. He was still frowning.

Chapter 2

Grandmother's House

Thaney stretched lazily in the mid-morning sunshine streaming through the window. She was tired, but her mind was full of questions from the night before, and she forced herself to rise. After dressing, she hurried across the castle grounds toward the widow's lodge. "Grandmother, it's Thaney." She announced as she pushed the door open.

An old woman, seated in front of a fireplace, crocheting a lace doily, looked up with a wide smile etched on her withered face as the girl gave her a hug. "Are we alone?" Thaney asked, looking around. They had carried on secret conversations about Christianity for years, without her father's knowledge.

"Yes, my maid is at the market. As long as your little brother didn't follow you, we should be safe," Igraine replied with mischievous eyes. "Did you hear another sermon last night?"

"I did, but more importantly, I heard a story about a lost scroll." She blurted.

The old lady's eyes widened noticeably, and she whispered. "Of Saint Martin?"

"Yes, but how did you know?"

The elderly woman took a deep breath as she wrung her hands nervously for a few moments and again whispered.

"It is part of a legend in our lineage, but your father, the king, demanded that I never speak of it after your mother's death." Tears began to blossom in her eyes as Thaney sat down and enveloped her in a tender hug. Thaney didn't know why, but she was crying too, thinking about the mother she had barely known and the daughter that Igraine had lost. "Your father would have me killed if he knew we spoke." Igraine finally said, drying her eyes on the unfinished doily.

"Why did my mother die? Wasn't she good?" as a tear dropped from her chin.

"She was more than good." Igraine dabbed again at her own eyes before continuing. "I taught her everything about the one true God that my mother taught me, but Morgan somehow had a clearer view of Spirit than anyone else. It takes more than just being good; your mother used to tell me that you have to understand what God sees, not what man sees. The Bible says: **'Is any sick among you? let him call for the elders of the church; and let them pray over him, anointing him with oil in the name of the Lord:'** (4) I tell you my child that our little band of Christians prayed day and night for your mother to recover, and she was healed for almost a year after your Uncle Arthur's death in the Battle of Camlann near Hadrian's Wall. She had always prayed for his protection, and many times he was saved from certain harm, but that dark day, Arthur succumbed to a sword strike from his own son, Mordred, who also died in that fight. She had always considered herself Arthur's spiritual protector and was heartbroken afterward. She felt she had failed to pray enough to save him. There was a spark in her eyes that died, and I never saw it again. No matter what I said, she seemed fixated on depression or agitation and wouldn't let it go, until she eventually became ill. Your father, the king, was dubious of the power of prayer, but grateful when she seemed to become healthy again for a while. Then she slipped back into depression and sickness as the cold winds of winter approached. She grew weaker, and King Lot grew more sullen. When she passed on, he had the other Christians whipped and driven out of his kingdom with threats of death if they ever returned. I was the only one allowed to remain and take care of you."

"Why do you think she died after feeling better?"

"I don't think we saw God clearly enough or knew how he views us with unconditional Love. The good book says: **'So God created man in his *own* image, in the image of God created he him; male and female created he them.'** (5) We tried, but I don't think we had the depth of knowledge to comprehend how she was healed and the fact that she was always a perfect spiritual image of God, untouched by the sadness or ills of mortals. Understanding God is supposedly what Martin wrote about in his scroll. I'm sure he tried to record how and why he was able to heal and resurrect people from death. He knew God and the power of God. I wish we all had been able to read his scroll."

"Where could it be hidden? You know I will never tell," the girl replied, wiping stray tears from her eyes.

Igraine swallowed and spoke after a long pause. "Mind you, there may be no truth in any of this tale, but it has been passed down through our generations for over one hundred years. My great-grandmother, you're great-great-great-grandmother she added, was Cynde of Kilpatrick. I remember her clearly because I was seventeen and had just given birth to Morgan when she passed away. She had the bluest eyes and a joyful demeanor tempered with a tinge of sadness, but there was expectation too, as if she was waiting to see someone again. My mother told me the story of the scrolls a few years after Cynde passed."

"Scrolls as in plural? The monk only mentioned one."

"I'm sure he didn't know another one existed. It was a story guarded by our family through generations. It began with Cynde."

"Where is she buried?" Thaney asked in a hushed voice.

"In the old Kilpatrick church yard, I think. That is not where the story begins, though."

"I know," said Thaney, as she recounted the monk's story. "He also said that the boy's name was Magnus, but that he was killed by the bishop."

"Yes, that was his name," Igraine answered with wide eyes. "He wasn't killed by the bishop, though. Cynde wore a large golden torc and traded it for his life, moments before he was beheaded. He was my great-grandfather. They escaped and were married. That was a family secret. No one spoke about the vengeful bishop or the missing scroll, to anyone outside our family ever again," she winked.

"Magnus was her husband?" The girl asked.

"I'm certain of it. Their love lasted until his death about ten years before Cynde died. Maybe that was who great-grandma was waiting to see." Her grandmother added with a soft smile.

"So where are these scrolls hidden?" Thaney asked.

"Scroll my dear, the second scroll I mentioned was a poor copy that Magnus gave to the bishop to try and make him stop chasing them. It didn't work. The real scroll was hidden by Cynde before that and has never been found. Magnus and Cynde were basically adopted by Calpurnius and Conchessa of Kilpatrick and spent the rest of their lives with them. Calpurnius was a decurio in Kilpatick."

"I remember the friar said that the bishop found out that the scroll was a copy and flew into a rage. That's when his mercenaries killed him and looted the abbey. Was Conchessa a relative of St. Martin's? Thaney asked, remembering the monk's story."

"Indeed, she was his cousin. St. Martin had sent another copy of his scroll to her for safe keeping, but it was destroyed in a barbarian raid. Do you know who her son was?" The older woman beamed.

"No idea."

"Saint Patrick." She announced. "Their village was

attacked, and their copy of the precious scroll was destroyed when their house burned. Patrick and his sister Darerca were kidnapped in that raid and enslaved in Hibernia. He escaped to Britain some years later, became a priest, and returned to that hostile island to preach the gospel to the savages. On his departure, Conchessa supposedly gave him Magnus's scroll to aid him in surviving the anticipated trials and to heal others. He was very successful in his ministry, although no one can verify that he had the scroll." She finished.

"Where is Magnus's scroll now?" Thaney asked.

"No one knows. Time changes things." Igraine replied thoughtfully. "Here, help me up." She demanded suddenly.

The girl took her wrinkled arm and pulled gently until the old lady was on her feet. Igraine grabbed a walking stick and tottered off toward her bedroom. Reaching a heavy wooden chest, she began rummaging through the contents. At the very bottom, she found what she was looking for. "Here!" She announced, as she stood up slowly and handed a stained and faded rag to Thaney. "This was Cynde's needlepoint. It's very fragile, so be careful with it."

Thaney looked down at the sad piece of ancient cloth in her hands. Color had drained from the threads, leaving a limp mass with varying shades of gray. She carried it to a table and carefully smoothed it flat. She could see letters stitched into the cloth, but some were missing.

"That was Cynde's own hand that stitched those words. The only message she left." Igraine announced proudly.

"But what are they?" Thaney asked, perplexed.

"Let me see, I remember having to learn the saying from my mother: The greatest gift lies beneath the soul's shower. I think," she added.

Thaney squinted at the battered fabric. "I see a 'T' and an 'H' and that could be…"

"What are you two doing?" A coarse voice demanded.

Thaney looked over her shoulder to see her father and little brother at the door. "Nothing, Father! I was just checking on grandmother; she was showing me her doilies." Thaney replied as she shoved the small wad of material under her bodice, before turning and facing him.

"You need to tell me when you're going to visit here. I've wasted half the day looking for you!" He said grumbling.

"Sorry, Father, bye, Grandma, I love your lace." She said, giving Igraine a quick kiss, and hurrying out the door with Gawain following.

The king stared at the old woman with scorn as he lowered his voice. "You said nothing?"

The woman returned a haughty glare, raising her chin high. "You are the king. Would I dare?" As the man slammed the door behind him, she grinned.

Chapter 3

The Riddle

Thaney spent the rest of her day with her father and little brother in a myriad of trifling duties. Inspecting the gardens, archery practice, and a dinner meeting with his lieutenants about threats to the kingdom. Finally, a pagan priest arrived for entertainment after dinner. He was introduced by Oberon, the king's resident wizard, and began reciting tales about the struggles between ancient gods and a few unbelievable human heroes. She struggled to stay awake through the mind-numbing monologue, but finally gave up. A sharp prod from her father woke her up, and she begged forgiveness.

"I just don't understand you." He moaned. "You should relish the rich history of your people. Instead, you fall asleep!" Oberon nodded silently, his dark eyes flashing brightly.

"You sleepy head," her little brother Gawain retorted.

Thaney shot him a look of disgust. "I'm sorry, Father, may I be excused? I don't feel well."

He made a disgusted flick of his wrist. "Resume your story." He commanded.

Thaney made her way back to her chambers, her

sanctuary in the castle. Once there, she removed the wad of cloth from her bodice, grateful that it hadn't fallen out during any of her day's activities. That would have caused an incredible onslaught by her father. Smoothing it out on a table next to a candle, she tried to read the pale stitched letters and tried to remember the words that her grandma had recited, but couldn't. Finally, she rolled the cloth up, found the loose stone in the wall that hid all her valuables, and carefully pulled it out. Inside were four items: a purse filled with coins, a lock of blonde hair tied with a pink ribbon, a small scroll with the Lord's prayer written in longhand, and an ornate silver dagger. All of them had been her mother's. She added the roll of cloth to the stash of items, replaced the rock, and had just turned around when the door burst open.

"Thaney girl, why did you leave our party?" The man announced with slurred speech.

"What gives you the right to invade my room. Get out. I'm not feeling well." She answered.

"All I desire is a delicious kiss from my sweetheart." As he wobbled toward her.

"Get out, or I'll have you beheaded this very night!" She said with a vicious hiss.

Percy of Winthrop, one of her father's knights, suddenly stopped his advance. "You wouldn't."

"One more step, and I'll scream. Percival"

"But I love you…" He said, as Thaney drew a large breath into her lungs. "All right, all right I'm leaving, I'll call on you tomorrow, after you've rested.

As the door closed, she released her breath and dropped a large oak board into the iron braces mounted on either side of her door for security. Then she crawled into bed and tried to fall asleep.

Thaney was standing beneath lush foliage on a stunning seashore. The sun was blinding as it glistened off the tops of rolling ocean swells. Waves broke gently across a soft, sandy beach with a warm breeze blowing in from the sea. Where was she? Looking around, she saw a lone figure striding toward her. The woman's long golden hair erupted in plumes as the wind caught it.

"Mother?" Thaney asked in a quivering voice as the lady approached.

"No, my dear, but your mother is fine, in fact, wonderful."

"But who are you?"

"Just a distant relative with this message: Remember that the greatest gift lies beneath the soul's shower. Remember, the greatest gift lies beneath..."

Thaney awoke from the dream and immediately went to the table and wrote down the words that she hadn't been able to recall earlier. Satisfied, she crawled back into bed and fell asleep thinking about the beautiful woman.

Bam, Bam, Bam… "Thaney, open this door!" Her father's voice bellowed.

She rolled out of bed and muttered. "Just a minute." Shoving the oak board aside, she turned and again dove under the covers.

With a look of exasperation, her father entered the room. "Why did you block the door? Why are you still in bed? Are you sick?" Looking around, he strode to the table. "What's this note?" He demanded.

"Nothing, I thought I'd try to write a poem."

"A POEM? By the gods if you weren't my daughter, I'd, I'd… Dash it all, get up. The old woman is feeling poorly and asked for you." He said, turning and leaving the room.

"Grandma?" As she rushed to grab her clothes.

She arrived breathlessly at the widow's cottage and rushed through the door without announcing herself. A servant girl sat next to her grandma's bed as Thaney charged up. "Are you all right?" She gasped.

"Fine, fine, my dear. Lorna let Thaney stay with me for a while. Take a break now."

"What's wrong?" She asked, sitting down and noticing dullness in the old woman's eyes.

Her grandmother waited for the servant to exit before replying. "Nothing is wrong, it is just my time, honey."

Tears welled as her grandma continued. "Now don't cry, don't make my advance a dreary occasion. I have lived a full and wonderful life, and you are one of my greatest treasures in it."

Thaney's voice was choked with emotion. "If you leave me, I'll be alone." Hot tears began to streak her cheeks.

"You are never alone, dear; God pervades every portion and thing in this world. Look for His guidance in all things, and you know that no matter where I am, I will be praying for you."

"But Father…"

Igraine fastened her gaze on her granddaughter. "You know why he hates Christians so much? It is the pain of losing his wife, the love of his life, a few short years after you were born. She told him that God would sustain her, and I'm sure he has. However, he is still feeling the personal loss and pain of Morgan Le Fay being gone from this world. He blames God and Christianity, even as he ignores all the healings and miracles she experienced in her life with him and the prayers of protection for her stepbrother, King Arthur. If Arthur hadn't passed, I feel she would still be alive. I know your father loves you, but be careful that he doesn't transfer that load of hate onto you in his desperation. Even if he does, you will be victorious with God, dear." She smiled weakly and spoke. "Now I am going to take a nap. Remember, I love you."

"I love you, too." Thaney said quietly, as she reluctantly released her grandma's hand.

She sat quietly, praying for God to make her grandmother live another year, or another ten years! Yes, by then she would be married and have a family started. Grandma could pass then, when Thaney was ready for it. A sudden loud sigh from Igraine announced that the battle was lost, and Thaney cried beside her until the servant girl returned.

Chapter 4

Pagan Burial

Thaney stood quietly and stared at the mound of fresh stones that had been added next to her mother's grave as her tears mingled with heavy raindrops. Her father hadn't listened to her impassioned pleas for a Christian burial for her grandmother and had interred Igraine in a pagan mound next to her mother. He knew of Igraine's wish to be laid to rest in a churchyard, but his smoldering anger against the Christians and their God made him determined not to allow it. Thaney made a vow never to forgive him for that decision. This was her first chance to be alone at the gravesite, as she replayed the events of the past week in her mind:

First, they had washed and dressed the body in an Eslene or death shirt and laid it on a table in the cottage. Burning candles surrounded the corpse for seven days as an endless parade of people traipsed around it, wailing and proclaiming their condolences. She felt sorry for Gawain and spent many hours trying to comfort him as the throngs passed by the viewing. Three days after Igraine first lay on the table, there was a feast held in her honor, but Thaney couldn't bring herself to eat anything. A large bowl was placed on her grandmother's chest, into which people put food and coins for the woman to use in her next life.

On the morning of the burial, a Druid arrived with a fey rod and measured the body to ensure a proper fit in the resting place. He then whispered instructions to Igraine on how to find the next world, before they carted the body off to be interred with the bowl of offerings.

Thaney had navigated the whole week in a dream state; her grandmother had passed, yet she still felt Igraine's strong presence. Many people had tried to pursue conversations with Thaney, but they all seemed meaningless and were quickly forgotten. Owain and Percy had shadowed and pestered her relentlessly with their concerns for her well-being. She wished they would just leave her alone. Percy was older and handsome, but a bore, and she suspected a narcissist. Owain was cute, but not much older than herself, and still childish in many ways. His father was also a king on the West coast of Scotland, but he grew up mostly in nearby Yester Castle with his older uncle. That had made it easy to be friends. The two kingdoms had a peace pact with each other that had fortunately survived almost a century. She didn't want to be bothered by anyone now, except her grandmother.

Gradually, her thoughts before the burial had grown to include the missing scroll of St. Martin, and she realized that a quest for it would make Igraine proud, wherever she was. Thaney hoped she was watching over her now as a guardian angel. It would also make Thaney's father furious. *It would serve him right,* as she stared at the rain-soaked mound in gathering twilight. Making a firm decision, she turned and stomped back to the castle.

Entering the north gate, she stopped and stared up as water streamed from the moss-covered stones. This was her favorite side of the fortress, because it was soft and alive as she ran her hand lightly over the lush, spongy green vegetation. Alive, like her grandma should be, and perhaps was somewhere. What had the lady in the dream said? "Just a distant relative…"

"Thaney, by the gods, I've been looking all over for you," Percival said as he wrapped his cloak around her shoulders. "My word. You're soaked through and through. Did you get caught in this downpour?"

"No, I was just walking."

"You need to take better care of yourself. I want you to be around for a long time, you know." He said with an affectionate wink. "Go get dried off, and I'll meet you for a drink in the pantry."

"I really would love to, but I'm going to rest awhile. It was a really long walk," she replied, smiling, as she handed his cape back and hurried up the steps toward her room.

"All right, I'll see you at dinner."

"Certainly." She said, inadvertently turning and blowing him a kiss. Once out of view on the next floor, she hurried to the far end of the corridor. The large wooden door protested on rusty hinges as she forced it open and entered her father's seldom-used library. Dust-covered books and papers were strewn about on a haphazard collection of tables and shelves. She rummaged around until she found several old rolled-up maps and a collection of blank paper. Taking them in her arms, she peeked out the door. *Oh no, Oberon is walking this way.* She watched as her father's dark wizard finally turned and walked down a stairway toward his lair in the dungeon. Then she rushed toward her room.

"Where to begin." She whispered out loud as she carefully straightened the rolls out and spread the brittle pages across her bed. She studied the faded lines and notations, rearranging them several times until she had a rough representation of the British Isles.

She found the town of Seaford Downs on the southern coast. That is where the chase began, but where had it ended? She examined the maps, looking for other towns that the old monk had mentioned, until she noticed the light growing dimmer in the room. She suddenly realized the sun was setting and that she would be late for dinner. Peeling her damp clothes off into a pile, she hurriedly dressed and rushed off to the dining hall while dragging a comb through her hair. She slowed as she approached the last doorway and walked in, nodding vague greetings to the assembled guests.

"Daughter!" her father beamed as he saw her threading her way through the crowded benches, toward the head table.

She curtsied deeply and quickly sat down between her father and Percy, who were just finishing their appetizers.

"You missed a delicious first course," Percival said, smacking his lips loudly.

"I'm sorry, but I fell asleep," she lied and averted her eyes.

"Well, at least you won't miss the main course," Percy replied as he touched her hand and smiled.

Thaney sat quietly throughout the rest of the dinner, thinking only of the maps as Percy, her father, and even Gawain tried in vain to engage her in conversation. Oberon was the only one who sat silently, but he never tried to talk to her anyway. *Thank goodness, he scares me enough, even being quiet. I wish Father would banish him; he's creepy. Even Mother seemed uncomfortable in his presence.* Finally, the others seemed to have given up, and Thaney asked: "Can I be excused? I have a dreadful headache."

"No doubt because of the drenching you had today." Percival blurted, as Thaney cringed.

"What! You were out in that deluge? Why, young lady?" her father demanded.

"I visited Igraine's grave."

"What… in the rain? You should have more sense than that!" he retorted.

Tears suddenly filled her eyes as she stood and rushed out of the hall, ignoring her father's protests. He would never understand. She knew he cared for her, but his warrior heart was too coarse for empathy. She ran through the corridors as the sounds from the dining hall faded.

"Thaney, wait."

Slowing her pace, she heard a boy's footsteps as she turned around. "Owain, I didn't see you."

"I saw you run out. What's wrong?" the boy asked earnestly.

Instead of answering, Thaney asked. "Do you remember the monk's story about St. Martin's scroll?"

"Somewhat," Owain answered.

"Well, I'm going to search for it. Will you help?" Thaney stated.

"Sure," he answered too quickly.

"Follow me," she said as she turned and flitted down the hallway.

"What is wrong with that girl?" the king growled at Percy as he scowled at his guests.

"Just that, Sire, she is just a girl and needs a strong hand to guide her into being a woman. I think sometimes you are too gentle with her."

"Perhaps you are correct. I've tried to spare the rod ever since her mother died," the king answered with a thoughtful groan.

"I will be glad to assist in any way I can." Percival smiled as he slapped his own leg loudly, and Oberon emitted a wicked smile.

The king offered a troubled grin but said nothing.

At that moment, Thaney reached the door to her room. "You must never utter a word of this to anyone."

"I swear," Owain replied breathlessly.

Thaney pushed open the door, revealing the old maps strewn about. "I've located Seaford Downs, where the monastery was, and I'm trying to find the other towns now."

They searched for several minutes, and Thaney decided that Hastell Cenllys either wasn't listed or had disappeared as a village. Owain suddenly pointed. "Here is Reidrag."

"That is almost halfway to Kilpatrick," Thaney answered. "Where should we start?"

"Where did they spend the most time?" Owain questioned.

"Or what was their destination?" Thaney corrected. "It was Kilpatrick where St. Martin's relatives lived.

"What was their name?"

"Calpurnius and Conchessa," she answered quickly

"How do you know her name now? The friar didn't know."

"Never mind, right now we need to concentrate on where the scroll might be hidden."

"So could it be where they lived?" Owain asked.

"Yes, and Kilpatrick is only a few days' journey to the west," Thaney smiled as she took a few minutes and scribbled a quick map of the route to Kilpatrick from Lothian atop some loose sheaves of paper. Then she and Owain gathered up the charts and returned them to the library.

She had just started to close the door when she heard her little brother say, "What were you guys doing in there?"

Chapter 5

The Quest Begins

"We were looking for a treasure map."

"Real treasure? Can I help?"

"You could if we had found one – but we didn't. If we do, I'll let you know. Isn't it your bedtime now?"

His gaze suddenly fell, "Guess so," as he padded across the stone floor toward his room.

"What excuse could we use to visit Kilpatrick?" Thaney whispered on the way back to her room.

"Do you have any relations you could visit there?"

"Not that I know of, I'll have to ask Father," she stated, suddenly stopping as Percival stepped out of her room.

"Well, I guess you were tired of our adult conversations, but not too tired to traipse about the castle with this 'little' boy," he smirked.

Thaney glanced at Owain and noticed he turned beet red. "Shut up, Percy, I go where I want, with who I want," she shouted as she stepped between the two.

"Oh, so this 'little' man is my competition for your hand."

"There is no contest for my hand. I will decide who holds my heart and no one else," Thaney stated defiantly.

"You might want to check with your father before

making such bold statements, dearest. He is of the opinion that a man's strong guidance may be needed in your life, and he has just accepted my offer for your courtship."

Thaney opened her mouth but was speechless as Owain stepped around her and piped up. "Thaney can decide for herself. You keep your hands off of her."

Percy grinned widely and backhanded the boy's face so hard that he spun into the rock wall and crumpled to the floor.

"Stop it!" Thaney screamed as she reached for Owain, but the man grabbed her wrist and pulled her upright.

"Remember this: if I tell you something, I mean it. I'd hate to hurt you like that," he said, pointing to the boy. "You are the love of my life. My betrothed," he said with a wicked smile as he released her and strode away.

Thaney seethed as she stooped again to help Owain up. *That beast thinks that I'm his property now!* She didn't know how, but she was going to show him how wrong he was.

Owain wobbled to his feet, trying to hide the hot tears running down his face. "I'm sorry," he mumbled.

"You stood up for me. You're my hero," Thaney replied as she clasped his hand and pulled him into her room. "You go home and change into old, ragged clothes. We don't want to stand out as we travel."

"To Kilpatrick?" Owain asked, surprised.

"Yes, I'm not staying here another night with Percy around. Kilpatrick is where we will start looking. Meet me behind the castle at midnight," she answered as she shooed him out of the room and went to her desk to write a short note to her father:

Father,

> **Percival just declared that he has your blessing for my engagement to him. I do not love him; he views me only as a piece of property, and I will never marry him. Because of his advances,**

I made a decision to leave at once on a quest to find a historic relic, a valuable scroll that has been lost for nearly a century. Please understand that I love you, but I have my own ideas about life, religion, and what comprises happiness. I am of age and am going to pursue this challenge.

Hoping to return home soon and victorious,

Thaney

Then she pulled the loose stone out of the wall and collected her treasures. She started to put the lock of hair, the Lord's prayer, and Cynde's fragile needlework back inside, but then paused. What else should she do to prepare for this quest? She carefully smoothed out the roll of parchment and began to study the Lord's prayer in the flickering candlelight, trying to understand how God's loving kingdom could be expressed in this coarse world. **"Our Father which art in heaven, Hallowed be thy name. Thy kingdom come. Thy will be done in earth, as it is in heaven. Give us this day our daily bread. And forgive us our debts, as we forgive our debtors. And lead us not into temptation, but deliver us from evil: For thine is the kingdom, and the power, and the glory, for ever."** (6) An hour later, she felt a warm sense of peace about the coming journey. Thaney replaced the items in the recess of the wall and carefully fitted the stone back into place. Then she lay down on her bed until the moon rose high enough to be nearly eleven o'clock. Getting up, she dressed in her oldest clothes beneath a worn, heavy wool cloak and strapped the purse and dagger on beneath them. Grabbing an old leather satchel, she headed to the kitchen and gathered food for the journey. Thaney carefully made her way through the darkened courtyard. Sleepy guards were on duty, but she snuck by them easily as they made their repetitious rounds. Once outside, she ran to the backside of the castle.

"Owain," she whispered.

"I'm here behind the big oak," he answered quietly.

She trotted over to the tree, and together they began their grand adventure.

Chapter 6

The Chase Begins

Beating on the wooden door with his fist, the King suddenly lost his composure and burst inside. "Thaney! By the Gods if you weren't my daughter, I'd…" He stood with his mouth agape, wondering if she was visiting Alma's grave again. Seeing the parchment note lying on the desk, he picked it up and read it again and again as his face transformed into a mask of anger. He crushed the note in his hand as he roared out the window, "Guards, arrest Sir Percival and bring him to my throne room now!"

A few minutes later, Percival was led into the throne room. "Where did you find him?"

"Sire, I protest…" a wave of the king's hand silenced him, as the guards pushed him roughly onto his knees.

"Sir Percival was just finishing a large breakfast when we tackled him at the table and bound his wrists behind his back. We led him through the castle, as he yelled expletives and demanded that we take him to see you," the captain replied with his face barely masking a smile.

"Leave us." The king uttered in a low growl through a mask of hatred, and the guards abruptly vacated. To his credit, Percival remained silent with his head bowed.

A great feat for a man like you who enjoys hearing

yourself talk. The king began speaking in a strained voice just above a whisper. "I went to Thaney's room this morning, and I found this." He said, smoothing out the note and holding it in front of the prostrated man's eyes. "Read it." He commanded. Percival tried to concentrate through his confusion. "Out loud!" the king yelled.

Percy began in an unsteady voice, "Father, Percival just declared that he has your blessing for my engagement to him. I do not love him. He views me only as a piece of property, and I will never marry him. Because of his advances, I made my sudden decision to leave…" and the man fell silent.

"Just what advances is she referring to, my dear knight? Why do you view my daughter as only property? What did you do that was so egregious that my child left the safety of her home, this castle, for some ridiculous quest?" the king hissed as he bent down and stared at Percy in the eyes.

"I, I don't know my liege, I was just being myself. I slapped her little friend in the hallway, but I didn't think that…" The man's normal bravado fled from him as he now grasped how precarious his situation was.

"You didn't think! You worthless knave. Now my daughter is gone to who knows where, but I know where you are going." He spat out the words. "Guards heat the oil cauldron to boiling!" Sentries rushed into the throne room and surrounded the kneeling man.

"Please, sire, I can find her. I know how she thinks. I apologize for this, but I can find her, I know I can. Please let me try!"

The fury in the king's eyes softened slightly, and he replied. "You have been faithful throughout your years of service to me, but my daughter is my only living relative besides Gawain. All right, I shall give you a final chance at redemption, but if you fail, rest assured that a vat of boiling oil will be your fate." Motioning to his guards, he said.

"Captain, take a few volunteers with you and accompany this prisoner on his 'Quest' to find my daughter. After a week, deliver word to me on your progress, and I'll send back your orders," he spat as he leered at Percy.

—————•●•—————

The man's spirit appeared broken when his hands were cut free, and he shuffled out of the room with his eyes downcast and his shoulders slumped as his mind pondered. *Where in the world could that stupid wench be?*

"When will we be leaving?" the captain asked as he motioned for a guard to accompany Percy as he gathered his belongings. "Stay with him," he said.

"Give me a chance to gather my thoughts and pack. I'm sure that I will be ready by noon." With a nod, the captain left him. "Follow me to the princess's room first," Percy said to the guard.

"I'm not sure you should..." started the guard.

Percival announced loudly. "I am trying to save my neck and the life of her highness. I know what I am doing." As he turned and marched off, perspiration filled his eyes. *I hope I know what I'm doing.* He entered the small bedroom and began to search for any clue as to the girl's destination. He upended the bed and mattress, opened a wooden box and emptied its contents across the floor, thumbed through the blank papers on the desk, and started to run his fingers across the mortar joints in the walls when he stopped, and turned back toward the desk, where a few pages of paper lay. The top one had a few light indentions on the page. Grabbing a small piece of burnt wood from the fireplace, he lightly rubbed it across the paper. He held the sheet up, shook it slightly, and said, "Nothing as far as a destination, curses."

Just then, Gawain looked into the room. "Are you looking for treasure too?"

Percy forced a gentle smile to slide onto his face.

"Why, I sure am, young man. Did Thaney say where the treasure is?"

"No, she didn't have a map yet, but she said I could help her search when she found one."

"Did you hear her mention a name or a town?"

"I heard her tell Owain a name, Kilpatrick."

"Why, thank you, Gawain, you're a great help," as he tossed a gold coin to the child. "Guard, follow me to my chambers. I know where she is going."

Sir Percival strode out of the castle with an erect posture; a self-assured smile once again etched across his handsome face. He mounted his horse with a flourish and rode out of the castle as the small group of guards struggled to match his pace.

———•●•———

"Hmmm, maybe I should have made him travel in irons," the king said to Gawain as he watched the group's rapid departure from an upstairs window.

———•●•———

The captain whipped his steed and finally rode alongside Percy, demanding, "Where are we going?"

Percy ignored him for a few moments and then decided to answer. "We are going to Kilpatrick. It will take us less than two days to reach it," as he spurred his horse back into the lead.

The captain frowned as he dropped back. "I may need to cut your ego down soon," he yelled.

They had been riding hard for several hours. Percival expected to ride up on Thaney at any moment, but after every hill, every turn in the road, he saw nothing but a few peasants who scattered out of the way of their galloping horses on the narrow roadway. He abruptly pulled on the reins as his horse slid to a stop in the muddy road. *She must have that boy with her, and they would be dressed as farmers. I probably rode right past them.* With fury etched across his face, he spun his horse around and raced back up the path, with the confused guards in close pursuit.

Chapter 7

The First Night

Thaney and Owain had barely escaped being trampled by the horses as they slid across the mud toward the protection of a nearby tree. "Did you see him?" Thaney gasped as she held onto the rough bark.

"Yeah, and he looks mad," Owain answered quietly, remembering his last encounter with the man.

"They're searching for us," she replied. "We need to get off this road."

"Head for that stream, it's fairly deep, and we can hide among the rocks," Owain said, sprinting toward a nearby depression in the hillside.

They had just tumbled over the edge when they heard the sounds of horses' hooves approaching again. "We need to get away from here; they may return with more horses and search the whole area," Thaney said. Owain just nodded and began creeping down the rock-strewn waterway.

"Keep looking for anyone on foot," they heard Percy

yell loudly as the riders thundered past once more. The soldiers spent the rest of the afternoon chasing and interrogating dozens of pedestrians. Hours later, the captain finally urged his lathered horse next to Percival's mount and asked with a good-natured grin. "Enough exercise for today. We should camp now. Where are we off to tomorrow, genius?"

Percy seethed at the comment. "Kilpatrick." He rasped through gritted teeth.

————— • ● • —————

Thaney and Owain had kept up a steady pace throughout the rest of the dwindling daylight hours, despite their lack of sleep the night before. The stream bed had gradually widened as they traveled. When twilight fell, they found a small ledge that had been formed by the water rushing through a limestone corner in the bank. Crawling beneath it, they lay on the smooth flat rock, eating dried venison, apples, and drinking handfuls of water from the stream. "Good place to hide," Owain said as water dribbled down his chin.

"Unless it rains, then we'll have to move out of here quickly." Thaney added.

Owain scooted over close to Thaney and casually draped an arm over her.

"Hey, don't get too familiar," she said, roughly pushing him away.

————— • ● • —————

Owain said nothing but smiled as his fingers caressed the smooth metal flask in his pouch. He was too tired tonight, but maybe tomorrow or later on.

Chapter 8

A Friend Found

In the morning, Thaney unfolded her map and tried to determine the safest route to Kilpatrick. "I was planning to follow the Antonine Wall but I think it will be safer to travel a zig-zag course and avoid the main roads," as she drew her finger across the paper. Owain just shrugged; he really didn't care. "Do you know anything about the Dunglass Castle?" she asked.

"They aren't on friendly terms with my uncle, something about poaching deer," he answered quickly.

"What about Bothwell Castle?" she added.

"Don't know, never heard of it. Where is it?"

"Probably two full days west-southwest of here, it will take a lot longer, but we should avoid Percy and his soldiers on that route. If we stay well clear of the castle grounds, we should be safe," she decided as she refolded the map.

Owain said nothing as he fell into step behind her.

———•●•———

Percival had wrestled with various strategies throughout the night to locate Thaney. *Did I pass her on my rush down the road? I probably could have.* He realized that hurrying had been a huge mistake on his part. He wanted to be done with this foolish chase and back in the king's good graces. Knowing what her final destination would be, he finally decided to travel directly to Kilpatrick. If he continued searching the countryside, it could add days to the pursuit. *Best to let her come to me,* he thought with a sly smile while touching the full money belt hidden under his clothes. *Besides, I can have a lot of fun while I'm waiting.* As soon as he had finished breakfast, he readied his horse. "Mount up, we'll head North and take the old road next to the Antoinine Wall." he announced as he swung his leg over his horse and took off without a backward glance, as the armed knights scrambled to mount their own horses.

Percy laughed as he watched the captain lean low over his horse's neck in a wild sprint to catch up. The scowl on the man's face left no question as to what he was thinking.

"What took you so long, Captain?" Percy asked good-naturedly as he sped down the road. Resigned to the King's orders, the commander reluctantly grimaced as he eased his reins and let his horse fall behind.

———•●•———

Thaney yawned continuously as they walked up and down the hills in the morning sunshine.

"Didn't you sleep last night?" Chided Owain.

"I did, but I think I'm still tired from staying up the night before," she smiled and stretched her arms wide. As she did, she caught a faint odor of smoke. "Do you smell that?"

"I don't smell anything."

She paused to determine the direction of the light breeze. "It's coming from over there," she said, pointing at a small cluster of trees and rocks on the banks of a creek in the distance where she could just see a thin wisp of smoke.

Thaney strode straight ahead while Owain was looking for an alternate route. "Wait, let's go a different way."

"Might as well be fearless," she announced over her shoulder without hesitation.

Shaking his head, Owain hurried along behind her.

As they drew closer, they could see an older man in a simple brown robe dipping a bucket into the stream.

"Hello!" Thaney yelled loudly.

The man was startled and dropped the bucket, as he stared at the two interlopers.

"I didn't mean to scare you," she apologized.

His worried expression faded as he suddenly recognized the girl. "I remember you, my child. You were at my sermon near Hogsdale a while back."

Thaney's face brightened. "I really enjoyed your stories," she said as she hurried toward the wrinkled old monk. A toothless smile spread across his face as she clasped his hand in hers.

"What are you doing here? How did you find me?" he asked.

"We weren't looking for you; I just smelled the smoke," she said, pointing toward the trees.

"Nothing happens by chance, my dear, there is some reason you are here, but follow me and share some vittles. I don't have much, but I don't need much," he said, smiling as he quickly gathered up water in his bucket and hobbled away.

Thaney quickly caught up with him and said, "Let me help you," and took the bucket out of his hand.

"Thank you, daughter." The man croaked as emotion lit up his face.

I wish my father would respond to me like that, as she followed him on a narrow path through banks of thorny bushes. Behind her, she heard Owain cursing as the barbs caught in his clothes.

"Why do you live in this god forsaken place?" he muttered.

The old monk turned around with sadness in his eyes. "There are no places that God forsakes. Besides, where else can I go? I'm too old to be of use at any abbey, and I have difficulty following their rules anyway. It is better that I try to spread God's word as a hermit waiting to pass from this world."

The man's words tore at Thaney's heart, but she didn't know what to say. Suddenly, she blurted, "We are on a holy quest to find that lost scroll of St. Martin."

The monk's eyes widened, but he stayed silent as he walked into a little clearing surrounded by large boulders, a small fire was burning beneath a pot of beans. "This is my home," he said, motioning toward a small cave that had been dug into the hillside. Grabbing a long-forked branch, he pressed it into the prickly bushes and pushed until they closed off the narrow entrance. "These barbed plants are my security system," he smiled. "Now let's sit and enjoy what God has provided. Let us pray," he said, bowing his head as he sank to the ground. "Thank you, God, for this food you have provided to nourish us and enable us to continue to express you in our daily work and deeds. Thank you for providing friends for me to share your bounty with."

"I have some food, too." Thaney said when he had finished, and before Owain could stop her, she opened the bag and dumped the entire contents out onto the grass.

"Thank you, my child, you have the heart of an angel," the monk smiled gratefully. "But from your friend's expression, you had better save those items for your journey."

Thaney quickly glanced at Owain, who threw her an apologetic grin. "No, we all share in the Lord's bounty. He will supply our needs," she announced firmly.

"You are a remarkable young lady; do you think there is a chance of finding the scroll?" the monk asked as he handed her a steaming bowl of beans.

"I think so," she said as her brow wrinkled in thought. "After you told us the tale, my grandmother said that Magnus was actually my great-great-great-grandfather, he didn't die at the hands of the bishop, and she gave me a clue. His wife made a needlepoint with the words, 'the greatest gift lies beneath the soul's shower. '"

"A riddle?" the monk asked.

"Maybe, or just a location, I don't know," she admitted.

"But we are on our way to Kilpatrick, where that decurio lived," Owain interjected, wanting to be included in the conversation.

"Calpurnius," the monk said, smiling. "How did the boy escape the bishop?"

"Grandma told me that Cynde traded a golden torc to the bishop in exchange for Magnus' life. Then they traveled back to Kilpatrick and stayed there," Thaney said.

"Marvelous!" the monk exclaimed and clapped his hands. "I hated the idea of the boy being killed by the bishop every time I retold that story. So, you think the scroll could still be hidden after all these years?"

"We hope so, or else our journey is pointless," Owain said as he ate an apple.

Thaney glared at him before turning back to the friar, "What is your name?"

"Call me Ezra, Brother Ezra," the man repeated. "Where are you from?"

"Nice to meet you, Brother Ezra. I'm Thaney, and this is Owain. I live in Hailes Castle close to Hogsdale," she blushed as she shook the man's hand again.

"A princess? You're a real princess?" the monk gushed. The girl remained silent, and Ezra felt her unease as the monk continued: **"But ye *are* a chosen generation, a royal priesthood, an holy nation, a peculiar people; that ye should shew forth the praises of him who hath called you out of darkness into his marvellous light:"** (7)

"Thank you. sir," as she flashed him a humble smile.

"Not only a princess, but the niece of King Arthur!" Owain said proudly.

The monk's eyes widened, as Thaney snarled and quickly shot a fist into Owain's ribs.

"Your secret is safe with me," the monk suddenly said as he raised his hands with his fingers spread wide in surrender.

Chapter 9

The Second Night

"Now what?" the captain grumbled as the group rode along the main road through Kilpatrick in the early evening.

Percival turned toward him with a carefree smile and said, "What else? We enjoy all the various distractions that this village has to offer, until Princess Thaney shows up. Then we take her home to the king. Now let's find an inn with decent food and bedding." as he spurred his horse. Exasperated, the captain looked back at his men, shrugged, and followed suit.

They recklessly galloped down the crowded cobblestone street until they heard music and laughter emanating from a sagging building. Slowing his horse, Percy read aloud the weathered sign hanging outside. "The Drunken Chicken, this should do nicely for a start." He dismounted and wrapped the reins around the hitching post. He paused as he waited for the captain and his men to assemble, and they strode in as a group. "Barkeep, a round for the house!" he shouted.

Cries of joy erupted through the room as the middle-aged bartender and a scrawny young barmaid hurried to refill forty flagons of ale.

When the decibels had lowered enough and all the

patrons had full mugs, he winked and motioned the barmaid over. "What kingdom is this?" he asked.

"'Tis the Kingdom of Stewart of Dunglass Castle."

"And is the castle near here?" He asked, stepping closer to her.

"No, sir, it lies toward Glasgow to the Southeast. They leave us be for the most part. We do have a town sheriff who runs the grinding mill, though," as her face flushed.

Gently taking her hand, he raised it to his lips and gently kissed each of her knuckles. "Thank you, my dear, and you are?"

"Amelia, sir."

"So pleased to make your acquaintance, my name is Percival. I hope to see more of you," he said as he turned her hand over and slowly dropped several gold coins into it.

She smiled widely through her reddened cheeks and stumbled quickly back to the bar. *Percy, you have a way with women.* He was confident his plan would work now that he knew there was only one local officer representing the kingdom.

— • ● • —

Thaney and Ezra had kept a continuous conversation going the rest of the day while Owain listened dispassionately and tended the fire. Thaney had asked a myriad of questions as Ezra struggled to explain the answers with his religious knowledge.

"I know the Lord's prayer," she announced proudly.

"That is good, very good. I repeat it to myself many times throughout the day, trying to understand all that it means." Ezra replied as twilight began to invade the clearing.

"I think it is directly speaking to the goodness that is God and knowing that his commands for harmony will be expressed in our daily lives."

Ezra's face brightened. "I see that, remarkable. You are not of this world, my dear."

"What do you mean?"

"I mean as our master said, **'Jesus answered, My kingdom is not of this world: if my kingdom were of this world, then would my servants fight, that I should not be delivered to the Jews: but now is my kingdom not from hence.'** (8) (John 18:36) You have a spiritual insight that escapes most people."

"Oh? What would my father think of that? she asked Owain.

Before he could answer, the monk said, "Lord Jesus said, **'And call no *man* your father upon the earth: for one is your Father, which is in heaven. Neither be ye called masters: for one is your Master, *even* Christ.'** (9)

"But what is the Christ, was he speaking of himself?" she wondered aloud.

"Yes and no," the monk answered. "Jesus was the Christ, the Messiah chosen by God to show the world how to defeat the limits of materiality, and he overcame lack, disease, physical laws, and even death. Prophets before him and disciples after him also performed miracles, so the understanding of God was not limited to him, but it was fully expressed by him. Christ was his divine essence."

"So, everyone can express the Christ?"

"If they follow Jesus' teachings, they can. As it says in the good book, **'Let that therefore abide in you, which ye have heard from the beginning. If that which ye have heard from the beginning shall remain in you, ye also shall continue in the Son, and in the Father. And this is the promise that he hath promised us, even eternal life. These *things* have I written unto you concerning them that seduce you. But the anointing which ye have received of him abideth in you, and ye need not that any man teach you: but as the same anointing teacheth you**

of all things, and is truth, and is no lie, and even as it hath taught you, ye shall abide in him. And now, little children, abide in him; that, when he shall appear, we may have confidence, and not be ashamed before him at his coming. If ye know that he is righteous, ye know that every one that doeth righteousness is born of him.' (10) You are anointed with the Christ spirit if you follow Christ Jesus," he added.

"And that is what St. Martin's scroll must be about. His understanding of Christ is the essence of God. We must find it," she said emphatically.

"Would you allow me to accompany you?" the monk asked humbly.

"Of course, we would be delighted to have your help," Thaney said as Owain frowned.

"Let's get a good night's rest, and we'll begin in the morning. You are welcome to squeeze into my cave if you want to," Ezra said as he yawned loudly.

"I think we should sleep out here where I can tend to the fire," Owain replied suddenly, and he was happy when Thaney agreed.

"Whatever, call me if you need anything," The old monk ducked down to enter his burrow.

Owain smiled as he piled more branches onto the fire, and Thaney spread the hides and blankets on the ground to sleep. "What did you think of Ezra's information?" she asked.

"There was a lot of it, I guess he didn't make it up," Owain replied.

"I thought it was exciting. He gave me so many ideas to work with to see a different reality than this world. I think I'll be up all night thinking about them."

"Would you like some cider? I brought some along," Owain said offhandedly.

"Sure, that would be nice," Thaney smiled, considering how thoughtful Owain was, the opposite of Percival, she decided.

He rummaged in his bag and removed a small flask. "Here you are."

"Why, thank you, sir," she said with a flourish as she took a long swig and offered it back to him.

"No thanks, you enjoy it."

"Thanks, it's delicious," she said as she sat down on her bedding and watched contentedly as bright flames licked the wood.

Chapter 10

Stories Of Devastation

The captain gazed at his men in the early morning light, all sleeping at odd angles and snoring loudly.

"They don't make soldiers like they used to," Percy said.

"No, they don't," the captain agreed with a sad smile. He found that he was beginning to like Percival, especially after he had paid for their festivities the night before. "What be our plans for today?"

"None for you," replied Percy. "Just take care of your boys today while I pretend to be Thaney's uncle and get eyes looking for her throughout this city."

"But I can't let you go off on your own, you're still under arrest."

"You have to. How would it look if I said I was her loving uncle, worried about her well-being, while I led a group of mercenaries with weapons around the town? They would think that I was going to arrest her."

"But the king said…"

"My plan won't work with you or the others tagging along. Look, I promise that I will meet you here at the Drunken Chicken at least by six o'clock, all right? Then I'll pay for another night of frivolity while we wait for her to turn up."

"If you put it that way, agreed," the captain said with a wide smile.

Percy began by first riding through the town. He made mental notes on the roads, markets, and popular gathering places. Then he visited the grinding mill. The large stone wheels turned slowly as water from a stream outside cascaded into the wooden pockets of a massive wheel that powered the mill. Entering the door, he smelled the dust in the air and felt the vibration of the millstones as they ground the grain into flour. "Hello, is the sheriff about?"

"What do ye need, sir?" A large man lumbered into view, coated head to foot in flour dust.

"My name is Percival of Edinburgh. I am here searching for my niece, who ran away from home. I wonder if you might have seen anyone answering her description, or might be able to pass the word to have your villagers on the lookout for her?"

"Is there a reward?" The man asked as he stifled a sneeze.

"Certainly, twenty gold pieces for her safe return. Have you seen her?" Percy asked wide-eyed.

"No, but we will be watching for that price. What do she look like?"

———— • ● • ————

Thaney awoke slowly, to the loud sounds of birds tweeting in the trees, and struggled to wipe the sleep from her eyes.

"Good morning, my dear, my but you are a sound sleeper," Ezra's gravelly voice said.

"I don't know how. I guess I was exhausted and didn't know it," she said slowly. Her clothes were twisted around her, and she struggled to her feet while trying to straighten them.

"Whoa, you almost fell into the fire," The monk said, quickly grabbing her arm.

"I don't know, I feel funny this morning," she said, rubbing her head.

"Here, maybe you're just hungry," Owain said, trying to hand her an apple.

"No, I need to fix my garments," Thaney announced as she wobbled out of the narrow trail, pulling at her dress.

"She'll be fine in a little while," Owain said as he noticed the worried look on Ezra's face.

Thaney knelt by the creek and splashed cold water on her face. Then she stood up and slowly rearranged her clothing. A few swallows of Owain's cider last night and all my clothes are twisted, she thought. No more cider for me! When she returned to camp, Ezra handed her some fruit and flatbread.

"Owain told me that you plan on traveling to Kilpatrick by way of Bothwell Castle."

"That was our plan. Why?" she replied as she nibbled on the bread.

"I have ministered throughout that region for years and believe that I can suggest safer and shorter routes," The monk said sincerely.

"We are open to any suggestions you have. In fact, lead on and we will follow," she announced as Owain shot her a questioning look.

"The monk took a moment to wipe gratitude from his eyes. "You remind me of the story about our Lord. **'And when Jesus was entered into Capernaum, there came unto him a centurion, beseeching him, And saying, Lord, my servant lieth at home sick of the palsy, grievously tormented. And Jesus saith unto him, I will come and heal him. The centurion answered and said, Lord, I am not worthy that thou shouldest come under my roof: but speak the word only, and my servant shall be healed. For**

I am a man under authority, having soldiers under me: and I say to this *man*, Go, and he goeth; and to another, Come, and he cometh; and to my servant, Do this, and he doeth *it*. When Jesus heard *it*, he marvelled, and said to them that followed, Verily I say unto you, I have not found so great faith, no, not in Israel. And Jesus said unto the centurion, Go thy way; and as thou hast believed, *so* be it done unto thee. And his servant was healed in the selfsame hour.' (11) You have that same strong faith, my girl. Are you sure you feel well enough to travel?"

Cynde nodded.

"Let me gather my satchel, and we can leave," as Ezra entered his cave to gather belongings Owain whispered, "Are you sure we should trust him?"

"Of course. He knows the lay of the land, and we don't. It will be safer traveling with him, and he can teach us more marvelous things about the Bible on our journey," she said with a weak smile as she slowly gathered up her bedding.

They left the clearing, and Ezra carefully pulled his gate of brambles into a closed position. "I don't want to get close to Dunglass Castle. King Stewart reminds me of your father, Thaney, extremely pagan and not very keen on Christian concepts. It will be better for us to travel toward Glasgow."

Ezra led them through the countryside on side trails and deer paths, successfully avoiding any other travelers. Around midday, they passed through a towering mass of ruins slowly succumbing to growing vegetation. "What was this?" Thaney inquired.

"This was Gifford Abbey. I visited here before this destruction," the monk said with emotion choking his voice. "It was beautiful."

"What happened to it?" Owain asked in awe.

"The bad blood between two kings caused this devastation. King Stewart and King Ilslip fought bitterly through the years. King Ilslip's castle was located a few leagues north of Kilpatrick. He and his warriors came south to attack King Stewart's troops, but they were lured into a trap. A decoy contingent skirmished with the interlopers and led them into this abbey, while the rest of King Stewart's men surrounded the monastery and set fire to it, closing all the possible escape routes. King Ilslip and his men were slaughtered, along with many of my brother monks who could not escape the terror." Tears filled the man's eyes as he fell silent, making the sign of a cross and leading them slowly through a maze of naked flying buttresses.

Thaney and Owain followed the monk, lost in their own thoughts. Each felt a sense of despondency at the carnage that had erupted and destroyed the tranquility and beauty of the holy cloister. It was shameful that harmony was so fragile in this world. They trudged along in silence for most of the afternoon.

"There is Glasgow," Ezra finally announced as he topped a small hill in the twilight. Thaney could see a large city spread out in the valley before them.

"Are we going there?" Owain asked.

"No, we will take the road less traveled, and we will be in Kilpatrick tomorrow afternoon," the monk said as he turned and led the way down toward a river. "Thaney, what were the words about the hidden scroll again?"

"The greatest gift lies beneath the soul's shower."

"I must remember that," Ezra mumbled as he walked the narrow path toward a small hovel on the riverbank. "Brother Caleb, are you about?" he shouted.

"Ezra, is that you?" A short, pudgy man emerged from the hut and peered at the group.

Thaney and Owain watched as the two friars embraced. "I need your ship again, Captain," Ezra snapped a salute.

"She is at your disposal, mate," Caleb grinned as the two went inside and returned carrying an

ungainly long wooden frame stitched and wrapped with oiled animal hides. They set it down next to the river.

"What is that?" Owain asked with disgust.

"That sturdy craft will ferry us across the river. Caleb invented it himself. It is lighter than a wooden one, but bigger than the coracles that most of the people use." Ezra smiled.

"Where are you headed?" Caleb asked.

"We are on a quest to find a sacred scroll of St. Martin," Ezra announced with undisguised pride.

Caleb only hesitated a second before he asked, "Can I come?"

Ezra looked at Thaney, who just as suddenly acquiesced, "Sure, you can."

Beaming, the short friar rushed back into the hut and returned with two rough-hewn oars. "Then let's be off."

"Owain, help me set her in the water," Ezra said, grabbing and lifting one end while Owain carried the other end into calf-deep water. "That's good, now climb in."

The two friars sat abreast of each other and pushed on the oars until the ungainly craft pulled free of the muddy bottom. With Owain in the bow and Thaney in the stern, they began their voyage.

"Hey, there's a lot of water coming in here!" Owain shouted as he stared at a small geyser at the base of the bow.

Craning his neck to see, Caleb replied, "Oh, bother, I need to fix that sometime. Move back toward us, young man."

Owain quickly scooted toward the rear of the craft as they all shifted their positions back and the bow tilted up above the waterline. "There, no more leak," Caleb grinned as he and Ezra rowed in unison.

They ran aground next to a large rock on the opposite shoreline, carried it ashore, and quickly covered the boat with some brushy limbs.

"In four or five more hours, we should be at Kilpatrick," Ezra announced as he led the group forward at a fast-walking pace.

"As they traveled Thaney asked, "Can you tell me the story of Jesus' birth? Grandma re-counted it often, but I would love to hear how you tell it."

Ezra cleared his throat and began, **"Now the birth of Jesus Christ was on this wise: When as his mother Mary was espoused to Joseph, before they came together, she was found with child of the Holy Ghost. Then Joseph, her husband, being a just *man*, and not willing to make her a public example, was minded to put her away privily. But while he thought on these things, behold, the angel of the Lord appeared unto him in a dream, saying, Joseph, thou son of David, fear not to take unto thee Mary thy wife: for that which is conceived in her is of the Holy Ghost. And she shall bring forth a son, and thou shalt call his name JESUS: for he shall save his people from their sins. Now all this was done, that it might be fulfilled which was spoken of the Lord by the prophet, saying, Behold, a virgin shall be with child, and shall bring forth a son, and they shall call his name Emmanuel, which being interpreted is, God with us."** (12)

"Just imagine, she gave birth to a child of God," Thaney said dreamily.

Ezra continued, "The prophet said in Isaiah, **'Therefore the Lord himself shall give you a sign; Behold, a virgin shall conceive, and bear a son, and shall call his name Immanuel. Butter and honey shall he eat, that he may know to refuse the evil, and choose the good.'"** (13)

"Maybe that is what is wrong with the world, we should all just eat butter and honey," Owain said with a sneer.

Ezra ignored him and continued, **"Now when Jesus was born in Bethlehem of Judaea in the days of Herod the king, behold, there came wise men from the east to Jerusalem, Saying, Where is he that is born King of the Jews? For we have seen his star in the east, and are come** to worship him. When Herod, the king, had heard *these things*, he was troubled, and all Jerusalem with him. And when he had gathered all the chief priests and scribes of the people together, he demanded of them where Christ should be born. And they said unto him, In Bethlehem of Judaea: for thus it is written by the prophet, And thou Bethlehem, *in* the land of Judah, art not the least among the princes of Judah: for out of thee shall come a Governor, that shall rule my people Israel. When they had heard the king, they departed; and, lo, the star, which they saw in the east, went before them, till it came and stood over where the young child was. When they saw the star, they rejoiced with exceeding great joy. And when they were come into the house, they saw the young child with Mary his mother, and fell down, and worshipped him: and when they had opened their treasures, they presented unto him gifts; gold, and frankincense, and myrrh." (14)

"Gifts to the son of a virgin," Thaney repeated to herself. *What gift would I give to my son?*

Chapter 11

Capture

"Evening, Captain," Percival announced cheerily.

The captain had been dozing at a table and straightened up suddenly. "What did you do today?" He grumbled.

"I have met with nearly a hundred people. I have eyes watching throughout this village. I'm sure we will hear something the moment Thaney arrives in town. Barkeep, bring drinks for my friends," Percy smiled as he draped a roving arm around the barmaid. "Don't run off, honey, I want you to bring me all of my drinks tonight," as he tried to remember her name. She wasn't beautiful, but she was cute, he decided as he lifted the first mug to his lips.

Several hours later, Percy noticed that he was a trifle past drunk. He had tried to dance with the barmaid as the minstrel played, but his feet didn't respond well, and he finally sagged onto a bench next to the captain.

"Your attempts at dancing made her laugh."

"My dancing efforts made me laugh," Percy said good-naturedly as he lifted another drink. He noticed a man was talking to the bartender, who turned and pointed at him. As the guy shuffled over, Percy tried to sober up.

"Are ye looking for a blonde girl?" the fellow mumbled.

"Yes, have you seen her?"

The man responded by holding his hand out, palm up.

"Here, here," Percy said hurriedly, dumping twenty gold coins into the fellow's hand as the captain stood to gather his guards.

The man grinned appreciatively. "There be a group of four strangers who just entered the town's east gate. One is a girl with blonde hair."

"The others?" Percy asked.

"A young boy and two old monks," the man replied as he left.

"That's them, I'm sure," said Percy as he rose on unsteady legs.

"Assemble," the captain slurred as his men struggled to stagger into a line.

"Follow me," Percy cried as he led the way down a narrow street toward the stables. The barmaid watched from the open door. He thought she looked grateful that he was leaving.

They mounted their horses in a haphazard fashion and galloped out into the crowded street. People screamed expletives as they carelessly rode past, nearly trampling several pedestrians.

Percy pulled his cloak over his head and reined his horse into a walk as they approached the eastern edge of the city. He steadily scanned the throngs of people crowding the street. Then he noticed a small group buying food at a vendor's cart. He held up a fist and dismounted, as did the captain and his men. Dropping the reins over a nearby hitching rack, he began walking toward a flash of golden hair.

Thaney had just taken a large bite out of a sweet roll when she felt a strong-arm wrap around her waist and lift her from the cobblestones. "What!" she blurted with a full mouth. As Owain turned, he caught a studded-glove fist full in the face and fell unconscious to the pavement. The two friars watched what was happening for only a moment before they turned and ran for their lives. Luckily for them, the soldiers were too inebriated for a long pursuit, and they were able to lose them quickly in the clusters of shabby buildings.

—•●•—

"What are we going to do?" Caleb wheezed from beneath a splintered table.

"Shhh. Nothing for now, just be quiet," Ezra commanded, watching as Owain and Thaney were both bound and trussed securely to horses. Ezra watched as Percy led the group out of town and committed the man's face to memory. Then Ezra and Caleb carefully followed them to the city's edge and clambered up the old Antoinine Wall. They sat hidden in the brush atop the crumbling earthen wall, praying and wondering what to do as the group ride eastward.

"Caleb, what could be a Soul's shower?" Ezra finally asked.

"I don't know, maybe rain, waterfall, fountain, dew," Caleb ran out of ideas. "Shouldn't we try to rescue them?"

"But the Soul part. What could that be?" Ezra continued.

"I know." Caleb clapped his hands. "What else could it be but a baptismal fount, saving the soul with a sprinkle of holy water!"

Ezra's smile shone through the gathering darkness. "Caleb, my friend, you are a genius."

"My Father in heaven is the genius, I just try to express his ideas," Caleb blushed.

"True, my friend. Now we must finish Thaney's holy quest and deliver St. Martin's scroll to her. Do you know where the church used to be here?"

"The one that King Stewart's father demolished? No, I

don't. Why did he destroy it?"

"I think the local priest refused to pay tribute to the king. The story is that he was locked up in the bell tower as his church was torched beneath him. I know a few of the faithful still meet in secret, but they are too afraid to rebuild the church."

"I'd be afraid, too. I don't want to be torched." Caleb shivered.

"I think it was in the northwest part of town. I can't imagine that a paper scroll could have survived that inferno, but let's rest and resume our quest in the morning. If we are fortunate enough to find the scroll, we'll decide how best to deliver it and free Thaney," Ezra said as he sank down into the soft grass and closed his eyes.

Chapter 12

Where Is The Church?

"I think it could be behind these houses." Ezra said as they walked through the winding city streets.

"But the houses are built so close together, I don't see a path to the backyards." Caleb said as they circled a large city block looking for any opening.

They finished the second circuit and Ezra decided to knock on one of the doors. After several minutes of sustained pounding, he finally heard a voice. "Hold your pants on, I'm coming." The door opened slightly as a dubious eye peered from the crack. "What do ye want?"

"Ma'am, we are hermit monks, and we wanted to pray at the site of the church ruins here, but we can't find them. Do you know where it was located?"

The door swung completely open as the old woman urged, "Inside quickly." Only hesitating a moment, the two hurriedly stepped inside as the door slammed shut behind them. "Where are you from?" her voice asked in the gloom.

"Southeast of here in the open countryside, madam. Why did you slam the door?" Ezra asked.

"Never know who might be watching," she answered abruptly.

"So do you know where the church ruins are?" Caleb

asked.

The woman sucked in a long breath and spoke. "I do, and my neighbors do also. If you noticed, these homes are built side by side with no other egress."

"To protect the church grounds," Ezra suddenly gasped.

"Yes, it was the only way to conceal and shield it from vandals. A group of the faithful began building this community the day after our church was razed and our priest killed. It was twenty years ago this spring that the tragedy happened. We still hold lay services in the ruins," she added tearfully.

"But we couldn't see the towers or walls of the church; surely they didn't fall."

"They were disassembled, in part to construct these homes and also to hide their location from outsiders."

"Ingenious," Caleb said with delight. "Can we see it?"

"This way," the woman replied, wiping her eyes and leading them out a small back door into a large meadow. Sheep meandered around, keeping the grass short around the low stone walls that had once been a church. A short distance away, tombstones were visible. "The church cemetery," she announced when she saw them looking. "Let me show you Father Leo's tomb." They followed her to a small stone crypt.

Ezra read the inscription, "Father Leo, death 9-11-494 AD, Faithful servant who died trying to protect the Lord's church from heathens. He fell through the flames of this world's hell, but resides safe in the arms of God now."

"He is a hero to us," she said, turning and walking toward the remains of the church.

They followed her up stone steps to where large double doors had once stood and carefully walked across the fitted stone floor. They strode past the rows of large stones which had replaced the burnt pews. Soft green moss had begun to grow over the walls. As they walked, Caleb nudged Ezra and pointed at a large carved stone baptismal fount sitting in what had been a transept of the church.

"This is now our altar," she said, kneeling and crossing herself before a stack of stones with a roughly carved image of a man on a cross perched atop it. "My husband carved that a year before he passed."

"He did a good job," Ezra said.

"Not so good, but he tried," she laughed.

"So, who conducts sacraments now?" Caleb inquired.

"John, the butcher, why are you available?" the woman asked.

Caleb looked shocked at the notion. "I... don't know, I haven't held an official position in a very long time."

"We would love to have you. You'd eat well, and maybe we could even start rebuilding the church someday." She wore a hopeful expression.

"You should consider that offer, my friend," Ezra said, and Caleb just nodded. "Brother Caleb and I would like to spend some quiet hours in supplication, if you could excuse us for the afternoon?" With assurance that they would both return to her house for dinner, the woman left them and hurried off to gossip with her neighbors.

They crossed themselves and knelt for several minutes in front of the makeshift altar, praying earnestly that they would somehow find the hidden scroll intact and unharmed. Ezra arose first, and with Caleb close behind him, went to the fount and pushed. It didn't move. "Too heavy, we'll need to find another way."

Caleb walked around the bulky stone bowl, studying its construction, and then pointed. "Look there, a pry point. Hallelujah, we have a chance." Caleb said as he folded his hands and mouthed a silent prayer.

They spent the next few minutes collecting items to lift the basin. Ezra gathered various rectangular-shaped stones, while Caleb found a pile of charred wooden beams behind the altar. He pulled a sturdy-looking one out. "Let's try this."

Ezra knelt and shoved the largest stone into place, while Caleb slid his blackened lever into place under the fount. Using all his weight, he pressed down and watched the fount tip up slowly. "Hurry, it's heavy." He said quietly through gritted teeth.

"All right, let it down easy," Ezra said after he had stacked small stones on either side.

Dust ground off the rocks as the weight of the basin pressed down on them. "Whew, good thing I ate a big breakfast." Caleb quipped as Ezra lay prone and stretched his arm under the base. At first, he only felt dust and cobwebs, but then he reached up into the hollow base and felt a stiff cylinder.

"I think I've got it!" he said excitedly as he crawled back and sat up. It was a rolled pouch covered with a thick coating of wax. His hands shook as he carefully scraped the thick layers of wax off with his knife and gingerly pried open the old leather. They could see a roll of parchment inside.

Chapter 13

Chained To A Tree

"What's going on here?" Both Ezra and Caleb turned to see a large, menacing man holding a wooden pitchfork. Caleb suddenly diverted the man's attention.

"We are just doing some overdue cleaning, my son, I am Brother Caleb, I plan to be ministering to your flock here."

"What's he got there?" the man demanded, still holding the pitchfork.

"Trash hidden beneath your baptismal fount for decades, my son. This whole place needs some tending to." As Caleb walked forward, ignoring the weapon, and stretched out his hand with a smile. "And who might you be?"

"They call me John. Who let you in?"

"John the Butcher, is it? I've been wanting to meet and thank you for conducting services for these folks." Caleb said conversationally, while shaking the man's hand and guiding him away from Ezra. "You know I didn't catch the woman's name, but she lives in that house." He said, pointing across the field.

"The widow Mary?" John said as his eyebrows lifted, and a smile crept across his face. "I'm surprised she even talked to you."

Ezra blew a sigh of relief as he concealed the roll beneath his habit and got to his feet.

"This is my friend Brother Ezra. He was kind enough to accompany me on my search for your church. Come and meet layman John." Caleb said, motioning to Ezra.

John reached out to clasp Ezra's hand and let the pitchfork rest upright on its handle. "Sorry if I scared you. We don't get many visitors here."

"No problem at all. I applaud your resourcefulness in protecting this sanctuary," Ezra said.

"It must be time for supper. Ezra, we don't want to be late," they hurriedly said goodbye to the butcher quickly and shuffled down the hill.

"So, you accepted the position?" Ezra asked with a smile.

"I didn't know what else to do; he was going to catch on to us. It just came to me."

"A God idea, my friend, and I thank God that you were receptive," as Ezra placed his hand on Caleb's shoulder.

"When are we going to examine the scroll?"

"When it's dark, and we're alone, so we can make copies for ourselves to protect and study," Ezra declared quietly.

<hr>

Percy had led the group a few hours east of Kilpatrick so the soldiers could sober up. Reaching a small hamlet, he dismounted and made arrangements with the locals to camp near their village. He dismounted in a small clearing, pulled the two prisoners off their horses, and removed their gags.

"Let me go!" Thaney screamed.

"Not going to happen, my dear. Last time I let you go, I nearly got myself boiled in oil by your father," Percy quipped. "I did, however, bring along a sturdy chain and padlocks so that you can enjoy some privacy," he said as he wrapped the heavy iron chain around her neck and snapped a lock shut. Then he led her away to a large tree surrounded by smaller bushes. He drew the chain around the trunk and secured it with another padlock. "Now, Princess, you shall have your privacy and freedom, for a scant few steps anyway," he laughed.

I wish he had boiled you. She thought angrily as the cold iron links pressed heavily against her neck. It had been a long day, and she was exhausted and dejected as she lay down next to the tree. In a few minutes, she fell asleep.

The beautiful woman was alongside her, in a forest this time. "Don't fret, my dear. Stay the course, and you will still win the prize. Others are helping you."

"Who?" Thaney asked and then remembered Ezra and Caleb. "They are searching?"

"Very diligently," the woman replied with a wide smile. "I have no doubt they will be successful."

"How is my mom? Is she still all right? Does she know about my quest?"

"Your mom is fine, and yes, she knows about your search. We all do, and you are always in our loving thoughts."

"Who are you? Are you Cynde?"

"Ow!" Thaney opened her eyes to see Percy prodding her with a stick.

"Wake up, darling. It's time to travel and see your daddy," he said as he reached down and unlocked the chain. "Get something to eat. We leave in a few minutes."

Thaney realized that there was nowhere to run, so she plodded over to where Owain was still chained and eating some dried beef and apples. "How about sharing?"

He wouldn't look up but held the food out at arm's-length.

"Hey, what's the matter? Look at me," he turned slightly, and she could see that his eyes were glistening, one was also black and swollen. She dropped to the ground, ignoring the food, and hugged him. "It's all right, it's going to be all right. Ezra and Caleb are still seeking the scroll," she whispered as she rocked him back and forth.

He stiffened and asked. "How do you know that?"

"A dream."

He looked away. "Great, a dream, I wish this whole thing was a dream. I couldn't protect you. I didn't even see…" a sob escaped his throat as his eyes closed tightly.

"What's wrong with the little man? Does he miss his mommy?" Percy laughed loudly.

"Stop it," Thaney cried, jumping to her feet and aiming a slap at Percy's face.

She never connected because the man hit her in the chest and sent her sprawling. "Tie her up and put her on a horse," he growled to the soldiers.

"I need to finish my quest. It's important," she pleaded.

"So is my life, to me," he added. "Captain, please gag my future wife so that we can enjoy a pleasant journey back to the castle."

Chapter 14

Return To The Castle

Thaney had given up trying to scream at Percy. The dirty rag the captain had muzzled her with was tied so tight that her jaw ached from trying to bite through it. *What had happened to Ezra and Caleb? Would they return to their hovels and forget about the scroll?* She prayed earnestly to know that their hearts were pure and receptive only to right thoughts, God-inspired thoughts. She was feeling stressed and dejected when a passage came to her mind, **I can do all things through Christ which strengtheneth me.** (15) God will give me strength when I need it. She repeated to herself. Finally, she relaxed and dozed in the saddle for most of the day, and into the night.

She might have been asleep when the castle came into view the next day when the men shouted loudly. Turning around, she saw Owain staring at her with reddened eyes. He probably watched my back this whole trip. He still wants to protect me, a boy surrounded by men. She thought sadly.

In another hour, they reached the castle gate and rode in under the watchful stares of its occupants. The King stood red-faced with his fists resting on his hips. "Sir Percival, bring my daughter to the throne room. Captain, you and your men take that poor excuse for a young man to his uncle's

Yester Castle and kick him off that horse. Boy, you are hereby banished from my lands, return here under penalty of death!" With that, the king turned and strode into the castle.

Thaney tried to scream, but the sound died in her parched throat. As soon as Percy cut the rope on her wrists, she threw her arms out and spun herself out of the saddle. Then she reached toward Owain, but one of the guards had already grabbed the boy's reins and pulled his horse around. Owain twisted in the saddle and gave Thaney a longing look as he was led away.

Percy growled as he grabbed her hair and marched the girl up the steps into the castle. "Forget him, missy, I'm the only man you'll ever need in your life from now on,"

Her father looked nervous, upset, and relieved as she was roughly pushed into the room. "That's enough, Percival! Let her go and leave us," he shouted as the man released his hold and began untying the gag in her mouth. As it dropped to the ground, Thaney remained silently seething as she rubbed her aching jaws.

— • ● • —

Her father waited to speak until Percy had exited the room. "Daughter, I've been beside myself with worry for your well-being. I never thought you would rebel against me. Haven't I given you everything?"

Thaney's voice croaked with emotion as she replied with moist eyes. "Not everything, Father. My love for God came from Grandma."

The king was suddenly filled with indignation, but he was not a stupid man. He knew that his little girl was extremely agitated and that anything he said would inflame the situation. "Eat and rest, we can talk later," he said in a tired voice as he sat down heavily on the throne.

———•●•———

Thaney was suddenly ashamed but quietly turned and left. She went to the kitchen, where she drank several glasses of water and ate some fruit. Then she tested her voice; it was hoarse, but better than before. Then she returned to her room and spent several hours tossing and turning until she finally fell asleep.

It was a dark night with a light wind as something fluttered and tickled her nose. She brought her hand up and realized it was someone's hair. "I'm sorry, I'll step back," a woman's voice said.

"Cynde?" Thaney asked as a cloud moved away from the moon and revealed the woman.

"Yes, my dear one. Cynde of Hastell Cenllys, but I'm much more than that now."

"You're a spirit?"

"No, my little one, not a spirit, but spiritual. You yourself are not a mortal being trapped in a material body. You are a spiritual creature experiencing a mortal nightmare."

"But I'm flesh, I bleed, the rocks and earth..."

"Are just as real in this dream, my dear, but are they Reality? What if I told you that everything you've learned about your earthly, limited life is a lie?"

Surely that couldn't be true. What kind of ludicrous dream was this?

"It isn't ludicrous; it is spiritual consciousness dawning in your thoughts. You see material items as real through your five senses. You don't see them for what they really are – spiritual concepts of God. For instance, a house, what does that typify spiritually?"

"Shelter, beauty, a gathering place for loved ones, safety," Thaney said.

"That's right, and there are many more qualities that a home should express. Those are the features of it that are Real. Like the Bible says, **'Now we have received, not the spirit of the world, but the spirit which is of God; that we might know the things that are freely given to us of God. Which things also we speak, not in the words which man's wisdom teacheth, but which the Holy Ghost teacheth; comparing spiritual things with spiritual. But the natural man receiveth not the things of the Spirit of God: for they are foolishness unto him: neither can he know them, because they are spiritually discerned.'** *(16)"*

"So I need to be spiritually discerning about everything I experience," Thaney stated haltingly.

"Yes, it will help immensely to see through the lies of material existence and open the portals of Heaven in your thought. The Lord's Prayer states, **'After this manner therefore pray ye: Our Father which art in heaven, Hallowed be thy name. Thy kingdom come. Thy will be done in earth, as it is in heaven.'** *(17) You can glimpse heaven on earth if you are attuned to God's thoughts, and I can see Truth in your consciousness now. Spirit will teach you all things," Cynde's smile was brilliant in the moonlight.*

Thaney suddenly came awake in her room, awash with bright sunlight. Lying in bed, she pondered what Cynde had said, realizing that she was cheerful for the first time since being abducted by Percy. She once again felt the presence of good in the world. She knew that she had to speak to her father, and although she initially resisted the thought, she dressed and went to find him.

"I don't want to quarrel with you," he said as she walked up to the throne.

"I want to apologize, Father."

"Really?" he said, looking surprised and relieved.

"I should never have run away without talking to you first, and I promise not to do it again."

The king got up and buried his daughter in an affectionate hug. "Thank you, I admit I was terribly afraid for you."

Thaney noticed that his eyes were moist as she replied, "I was just so frustrated and mad about what Percy said and did. I don't ever want to see him again. It wasn't true that you promised my hand to him, was it?"

"Er, we did discuss marriage, but I will talk to him. I'm sure he will understand your feelings and call it off."

Thaney's blood suddenly turned cold. Somehow, she knew Percival would never release her from her father's vow. Not because he loved her, but to gain power in the kingdom by marrying the only successor to the king. "He wants to be king," she heard herself say.

"Over my dead body." She heard her father reply harshly as Thaney silently prayed. **"Thy kingdom come. Thy will be done in earth, as it is in heaven."** (18) She suddenly wondered if heaven was a place, or a state of mind where thought was receptive to God's thoughts and completely attuned to spiritual concepts. "I'll see you at dinner, Father." She said absently as she exited the room and concentrated on the new ideas presented.

"Guards! Bring Percy to me now!" the king barked.

Moments later, Percy marched into the room with half a dozen guards following him. "Sire, what do you desire of me?" he said with a flourish and deep bow.

Before answering, the king dismissed the guards with a wave of his hand. After they had closed the door, he spoke in a subdued voice. "I want you to release my daughter from my promise of her hand in marriage."

Shock showed on the man's face, but he quickly answered, "Of course, my liege. My only wish has been to serve you and return your daughter safely to your arms." After a moment's hesitation, he added with a choking voice, "Might I inquire why the only woman I have ever loved is to be denied me?"

The king still held deep feelings for his dead wife and couldn't bring himself to answer harshly to a man professing love to his daughter. He finally said, "My daughter is not ready for marriage, and she may never grow to love you."

"But will you allow me to try and change her mind? To show her that my love is true? I will drop the subject of matrimony until she is ready."

"I suppose that will be satisfactory, but never pester or harm her, or I'll have you horse whipped!"

"Of course, sire, you know I would never go against your wishes. I remain your loyal servant,"

Percy bowed deeply to hide his red face and exited the throne room seething—a*ll my careful plans, dashed by a stupid girl.*

"My son, what is troubling you?" Oberon hissed and seemed to appear from nowhere as he offered a sympathetic smile. "Perhaps I can help you achieve what you desire. Join me for a drink in my chambers and let's discuss our shared ambitions."

Percy hesitated and then nodded. *This may be a bad idea, but I need to talk to somebody.*

Chapter 15

Falling Dream

The sound of rain falling on the thatched roof was loud. "Ezra, are you done yet?"

"Allll…most, there." He said as he dropped his quill beside the inkwell, as he dusted the fresh ink with pounce. I'm glad the widow let us work and sleep up here."

"And she agreed to allow me to use it as my rectory for as long as I want," Caleb said, moving over to admire the penmanship when Ezra stood and straightened his back. "Finally done, I have made a copy for each of us, and another one to give Thaney when I find her again," Ezra said as he looked around the room, carefully rolled up the old scroll, and placed it into the worn leather cylinder. Drying pages were strewn on every flat surface, including the floor.

"In the morning, they will be dry, or maybe the next day," Caleb assured him.

"It depends on when the rain quits. It might be a week before they don't smudge. I'm sure it's morning now, but let's try to get some sleep anyway," Ezra quipped as he tucked the original roll deep into his habit. He bent down stiffly and stretched out across the floor as he emitted a long series of painful groans.

Caleb just grinned as he blew out the candle and

slouched down beside him. After a few minutes, he asked, "Ezra, are you asleep?"

"I'm trying," the reply came in an exhausted voice.

"I want to ask a big favor."

"Yes, I'll do it. Please go to sleep," Ezra grunted.

"Will you stay with me while I begin my ministry to these people?"

"All right, I will stay on until Monday. Now go to sleep," Ezra rolled onto his side with another painful groan.

"It has been a long time since I even attended a church. I don't remember the sacraments; I don't remember the services much at all. I may need you to stay with me for maybe six weeks," Caleb whispered.

"Six weeks!" Ezra sat up, "I need to find Thaney and give her the scroll. I can't wait six weeks; she needs to know that we found it!"

"I know, maybe it won't take six weeks, maybe only three, or maybe you could send her a letter, a coded message to let her know that we found the scroll, but it will take some time to deliver it. I really do need your support to begin serving this parish," Caleb pleaded.

"Let me sleep on it Ezra finally said. We can discuss it tomorrow."

Caleb almost wisecracked. *You mean today.* But quietly lay down with a smile.

———— • ● • ————

At that moment, hot tears flowed into Thaney's pillow. She had tried to hold onto the God-like thoughts and inspirations she had felt in the throne room, but gradually, on the way back to her bedroom, despair had seeped in and diluted her thoughts. Her life and dreams seemed ruined. Distraught thoughts endlessly streamed through her mind. Igraine was dead, Owain had been banished from her life, Caleb and Ezra were gone, and on top of it all, that precious scroll that might give hope and healing to the world would remain lost forever. What reasons were left for living? She thought about cutting her wrists with her mother's dagger, but Percy hadn't returned it yet, and she really didn't want to hurt her father by committing suicide. She was tired and exhausted with an excruciating headache from crying, and finally fell into a restless sleep.

She was running for her life, struggling through brush and briars on a steep hilltop and hearing the ardent shouts of pursuers. There was a thick web of bushes and vines ahead, but she didn't slow, as she pressed her body through the mass of foliage and stepped into thin air. The world spun and blurred as she fell spinning headfirst down the face of a sheer cliff. This is how it ends. Closing her eyes, she felt the rush of air as she fell headlong, and a surge of sadness engulfed her.

"It doesn't end." A quiet voice replied.

Surprised, she looked again and saw Cynde floating next to her, wearing a sweet smile. Thaney was inverted, staring at the wooded ground at the base of the cliff. The air around her was still. "Why am I not falling?" She blurted as her dress fell and covered her eyes.

"Why would you want to?" Cynde replied seriously.

"I don't, I want to live." She said earnestly, as she fought with the folds of fabric.

"You must live, your child needs you, and this world needs him." The woman replied quickly.

A chill swept through her body as she suddenly came awake with her hands wrapped up in bed sheets. What a strange dream. Is it true that I'm going to have a child? Then I have a purpose in this world, but when and how? she wondered. Lying in bed, she prayed earnestly for answers until falling into a dreamless sleep.

———•●•———

"All right, I'll do it, but only for a week or two. I must get the original scroll to Thaney as soon as possible," Ezra replied with a strained expression, as he idly stirred his breakfast around in his bowl. He had struggled to find an answer for Caleb throughout the night.

"Thank you, my brother. I trust that will be enough time. I don't have the courage to take this task on alone."

"You are never alone; the Lord is with you," Ezra glared. "Remember what the master said? **'And he that sent me is with me: the Father hath not left me alone; for I do always those things that please him.' (19)"**

Caleb looked ashamed and simply said, "I'm sorry."

"Never mind, did you make a list of things that need to be done?"

Caleb quickly shoved a beeswax tablet across the table. "This is what I thought we should start with."

Ezra gazed at the scribbles for a few moments until a smile finally creased his face. "A very fine and complete list. Brother Caleb. When these tasks are finished, do you agree that I can leave?"

"Agreed," Caleb replied quickly.

"To work then," Ezra said as he shoved the dish away and stood up.

———•●•———

"Morning, daughter, I hope you rested well." The king said as he bit into a sweet roll.

"I did, Father, except for a dream where a woman said I would give birth to a boy."

"Marvelous, I can expect another prince in my realm then?" King Lot asked with a wide grin as he reached for a sausage.

"If the dream was true, it shall be." As she sat down and grabbed a greasy sausage link herself. *Why didn't I fall? Who will the father be?* As she chewed.

"Good morning, sire and my princess." Percival's white teeth shone as he smiled widely.

The father will definitely not be him. Thaney decided with a pronounced grimace. "Father, may I be excused?"

"But you haven't finished your breakfast!" her father retorted.

"I suddenly lost my appetite," she replied with disdain as she glared at Percy and strode off toward the kitchen.

"You made an enemy for life, my boy," The king said with a grin as Percy sat down.

"I'm sure, that given time, and my repetitious affections, she will learn to love me."

"Obviously, you don't know women," his highness didn't suppress a loud laugh at the man's expense.

"Perhaps you are correct, sire, but she is still young, and my hope is eternal."

"Please stop talking and just shove food into your mouth. Those honey-coated words are making me lose my appetite," the king growled.

"As you wish," and Percival bit into an apple with vengeance. *You obviously don't know me, you old fool.* Percy fumed at the man's laughter. *If I can't possess Thaney, I'll destroy her somehow.*

The kitchen staff scurried out of the way when Thaney walked through, ignoring their stares as she quickly grabbed a small assortment of fruit and dried goat meat on the way back to her room. Once there, she sat near the window and chewed the food slowly as she wondered where her friends were. What was Owain doing? She wanted to beg her father to rescind his decree and let the boy back into the kingdom, but she didn't think he would consider it yet. Maybe in a few months, she could broach the subject with him. The missing scroll was another question. If only she had been able to evade Percy for a few more days, she might have been able to find it. Maybe Ezra and Caleb are still searching for it. Her mind drifted back to the dream the night before. What could that dream mean? Nobody can float in thin air. Why had the lady said: *"You must live, your child needs you, and this world needs him."* *How am I going to have a child? I haven't been with a man. Is Percy planning to rape me? Am I blessed, and the child will be of God!* The idea shocked her at first, but it also filled her with warmth and joy as she remembered the words that came to Joseph in a dream: **"fear not to take unto thee Mary thy wife: for that which is conceived in her is of the Holy Ghost."** (20) "Thank you, God." was all she could think to say as she kneeled on her bedroom floor in prayer.

Chapter 16

Family Talk

A small knock sounded on her door. At that same moment, Thaney stretched her arms and yawned widely. It had taken her quite a while to fall asleep, and Thaney quickly realized that she had overslept. She dressed quickly and heard her father calling her name as she opened her door. "Here, sire." She replied.

"You missed breakfast, young lady, and you looked so distraught yesterday. What can I do for you?"

"I really don't know. I was so happy on my quest with Owain, and now I don't have anything to look forward to. My new friends are gone, and I might never find that old scroll."

"I am sorry, daughter, but it terrified me when you ran off. I sent Percival after you in a fit of rage. I wasn't in my right mind. I don't know what I would have done if I had lost you."

Thaney watched as her father wiped at his eyes. She had never seen him so emotional before, and she immediately wrapped her arms around him. "I'm sorry too, I shouldn't have run away, but I knew that you wouldn't let me search for the scroll since it is a religious artifact."

Her father was silent for a few moments and then spoke

in a faint voice. "You have too much of your mother in you. I don't know how you have adopted her religion."

She couldn't tell him about her grandmother, so she just said, "I listen to my heart."

"Your mother did too, but her God didn't save her! She died, and her God didn't help her!" His eyes reddened and filled with pain as he sobbed.

Thaney didn't know what to say. She just held his hands and tried to pray.

Finally, he said, "That is why I hate your God. He is weak. My gods may not be loving, but they are not weak," he said with a grimace.

"I don't know why my mother passed on. I do know that she is still alive somewhere, and that the one true God is all-powerful, always present, and all-loving. It was all proved to me in my short adventure."

"You know we hardly ever talk like this. Will you tell me all about your quest?" her father smiled.

Thaney recounted everything she could remember about her adventure for the next few hours, and her father listened intently. Trying to understand how his little girl had grown up suddenly into this fearless, independent woman. He understood now how he had destroyed her dreams and friendships, but he couldn't decide how to repair her feelings. "Daughter, I am sorry, what can I do to make amends for my past rash decisions?"

Thaney's brow furrowed as she thought for a moment. "It is simple, I want my friends back. Owain, Caleb, and Ezra are my only true friends."

"I can rescind my decree against young Owain easily enough, but I can't have you running off to Kilpatrick. You are a princess. If you were recognized and captured, you would be ransomed, or maybe even worse," his voice trailed off.

"Could you send word to the monks? They might still be in Kilpatrick searching for the scroll."

"Did Percy see them when he captured you? Does he know what they look like?"

"I think so, we were all together."

"Well, it sounds as though I have another quest for Sir Percival, my dear," smiling, he gave her a gentle hug.

"Thank you, father. Live forever," Thaney whispered as tears of gratitude filled her eyes.

"Daughter, promise me that you will always tell me when I am blinded and ignore your thoughts and desires. I don't know your God, but I do sense your deep devotion. I know your mother is proud of you, wherever she is," he smiled. "Now, let's get some lunch; these family discussions make me hungry."

Thaney's father had actually listened to her and was going to bring her friends back into her life. He hadn't treated her as a petulant child, but as an adult whom he had respect for. She suddenly felt a tremendous connection and wave of love for him that she had never known before.

King Lot was in good spirits also, and they ate and talked throughout the meal. Thaney asked if she could send a note to Owain that he would once again be welcome to visit freely, and the King acquiesced. Finally, he excused himself and said, "I have pressing business, my dearest. Guards have Sir Percival report to me in the throne room."

Thaney smiled as he walked away. Soon, everything would return to normal. She skipped to her room and scribbled a note to Owain, telling him everything her father had said. She sealed it with wax and handed it along with a few coins to one of the couriers in the courtyard.

———•●•———

"Sire, please, I didn't pay attention to the monks. I was focused on Thaney and that whelp of a boy that she traveled with," Percy begged.

"So, are you refusing me?" The king questioned with a

growl.

"No, sire, I will do my best to find them. When must I leave?" Percy replied with downcast eyes.

"Immediately, I know you will succeed, my boy. Don't return without them," he warned.

Thaney was still in the courtyard as Sir Percival stomped out of the castle, calling to the grooms for his horse. He saw Thaney and suppressed an angry countenance, "What were the names of your two friar friends?" he sneered.

"Ezra and Caleb," she replied unsteadily.

"Fine, I hope they're worth it," he spat as he vaulted into the saddle.

"They are. You'd better bring them back safely, or maybe your next bath will be in boiling oil," she felt anger reddened her cheeks as she turned and stomped away.

"Have a nice day, beautiful!" he yelled and rode off.

Chapter 17

The Search For Monks

Percy was seething as he rode westward, fixated on the fact that despite his years of faithful service, he was still only considered to be the king's errand boy. He knew Thaney would never consider marriage to him, and he racked his brain for a way to punish her, even as he plotted on ways to take over the kingdom from Lot.

He trotted into Kilpatrick on the second day and headed directly for the Drunken Chicken. Wrapping the reins over a splintered hitching post, he strode inside and straight over to the skinny barmaid. "Hello, darling. Did you miss me? I've missed you," he cooed.

He noticed she rolled her eyes with a distressed look before announcing with a wide smile. "Why yes, you left without saying goodbye."

"I am truly sorry, my dear. I was under orders from my king to return immediately to the castle."

"A real castle?" she gasped, before restraining herself.

"Yes, a truly beautiful fortress, a couple of days ride to the East. Perhaps you'd allow me to take you there someday? Maybe when I return from my current mission?"

Her voice caught as she asked, "What mission are you on this time?"

"Have you seen two men in friars' habits anywhere in this town? I'm trying to track two monks down."

"No, the old church was destroyed by fire a long time ago. We haven't had any Christians in this town since then."

"Oh, yes, you have. The last time I visited there were two old monks traveling with a young girl and a boy. I have to find them and escort them back to meet a friend of theirs," Percy tried to look sincere.

"They must have been just passing through then. I haven't seen anyone like that. I'm sure I would have remembered Christians," she said as she lowered her eyes and bit her lower lip.

She is lying. Perfect, all I have to do is wait and watch. "Well, I'll ask around for the next few days. Now, how about a mug of your finest ale, darling?" he sat down and made himself comfortable as she hurried away to fill a mug and returned with her eyes downcast. "Do Christians still celebrate Mass on Sundays?" he asked with all the sincerity he could muster.

"I'm sure I wouldn't know," she said in an unsteady voice. "I'm sorry, you'll have to excuse me. I have other customers."

It was a busy night as thirsty patrons filled the tables. Percy watched from a secluded corner throughout the long hours until the last patrons left, and the owner and barmaid began tidying up. Percy eased himself up and wandered outside. It was raining as he slid his hood over his head and waited in the shadows across the street for an hour until he finally saw the girl leave.

Following at a distance, he trailed her to a quiet street lined with a jumble of dwellings and watched as she entered a small home sandwiched between other houses on a narrow street. *Thank you, darling. Now I know where to begin my search,* as he turned and strutted back toward the Drunken Chicken, wearing a wicked smile.

Before sunrise, Percy stood in his room digging

through a large sack in flickering candlelight. He finally dumped the contents across the bed and sorted through the worn and tattered clothing until he was satisfied. *"There, that is an outfit befitting any penniless beggar,"* he smiled.

The morning sun was still low in the sky as Percy approached the girl's house. It was still sprinkling as he stopped next to a small mud puddle and rubbed a few dirty smudges onto his face and clothes. He decided to walk around the block to see if he could find an entrance that led behind the row of houses. He didn't find any gates or doors that weren't locked and continued around three more street corners to find long rows of buildings facing the roadway. *That's odd. There must be a large open space behind those properties, but why?*

A butcher shop was just opening, and he hurried over to the doorway as he pulled his hood low over his face. "What kin I do for ye?" The man asked, as he donned a tattered apron.

"I have a very odd request, sir. I am seeking two of my friends, who may be wearing monks' robes. We were traveling together and got separated when agents of the king pursued us through a forest a few weeks ago. Have you seen anyone like that?" Percy stared at the floor and twisted his hands together in an effort to look humble.

The butcher's eyebrows rose for a moment, then his face froze in a disinterested stare. "Monks, are you daft, man? The king has outlawed Christians on his lands. Go away before I throw you out."

Percy let his shoulders slump, turned, and slowly shuffled toward the door. "I'm sorry I bothered you, sir, but they are my friends."

"Are you going to persist in your search for these criminals?"

Percy hung his head and forced a choked voice. "I need to find them. We were trying to find a safe place to live."

"We are not heartless here. If I hear of those men,

where are you staying?"

Percy gave a pronounced swipe at his dry eyes and sniffed loudly. "Thank you, sir. I am sleeping in the streets for now. I will stop by in a few days." Then he tottered out into the street, wearing a sly smile. *That will pull on those Christian heartstrings.*

"Wait, here this will help with food anyway." The butcher hurried up behind him and pressed a few coins into Percy's hand. "Hey, it looks like the rain is stopping, too, finally!" he smiled.

"Bless you, sir, bless you!" Percy coughed as he was careful to keep his head bowed and out of sight. "I will return soon to check with you. Thank you again." He turned and continued walking slowly down the street, barely able to contain a contemptuous laugh.

Back at the inn, he hurriedly pulled off his damp clothes, dropped them in a pile, dressed, and strode into the serving area still smiling. "Barkeep, what's for breakfast today?"

The man turned around slowly. "Same as every day, porridge and bread. What are ya drinkin?"

"Ale, my friend, that should help me get some sleep this morning."

"Did ye have a late night?" the fat bartender squinted his eyes as he set a mug down in front of Percy.

"Couldn't sleep, took a walk early this morning to relax. After I eat, I'll be taking a long nap. Try to keep the noise down, will you." Percy flipped a gold coin onto the rough table as he tipped the ale to his mouth.

The bartender stared at the coin. "For that much, I'll close the inn for the day."

"No, don't do that, just try to keep it quiet," Percy said as a lecherous smile crossed his face. *Maybe I'll have some sport with that serving wench this evening.*

Chapter 18

The Fox Is Close

It was late afternoon when Ezra carefully touched and then rubbed at a letter on one of the papers. It didn't smudge. *After three days of rain and humidity, it is finally dry.* He gazed at the pages spread around one end of the room, and one-by-one he picked them up in order and carefully checked and stacked them onto three piles. When he was through, he began delicately rolling them up and tying them with strings. "Our copies are finally dry. Now I can give the original to Thaney," as he fingered the small leather cylinder hanging from his neck.

"I can't believe it took so long, but it has been a soggy few days. Mine seem to be drying well with this new ink mixture, although it is a little lighter color," Caleb replied as he thoughtfully continued writing on a makeshift desk in the corner.

Ezra yawned widely as he stacked the rolled-up paper copies of Saint Martin's scroll into a worn leather satchel and hung it on a protruding wooden dowel at a ceiling beam connection. "Mice can't get them there," he announced. "Caleb, are you about finished with your liturgy for Mass tomorrow?"

"Almost, can you read it over?" He pointed to the

carefully arranged parchment sheets that covered the floor in the rest of the room. "Careful, some of them may still be wet."

"Do you think the Mass is a day-long event? What in the world are you writing? A book?"

"I guess I got a little carried away. Maybe I have material for two Masses there," he grinned.

"Or three. I don't have time to read that whole pile. Cut it down by a third and I'll look at it."

"Well, I don't want to run short…"

"Just speak a little slower, give them time to digest the ideas, it isn't a race." Ezra spat.

"All right," Caleb sighed as he began picking the pages off the floor and organizing them to simplify the sermon.

"Is everything else prepared for the service tomorrow?" Ezra asked.

"Yes, John had the members get everything prepared, swept, and wiped clean. I just hope it doesn't rain."

"Then you'd need to have a bunch of smaller services in the larger houses, I guess."

"John said he has done that before, but that it takes him all day," Caleb grumbled and then brightened. "I guess I could use the practice, though."

Ezra laughed as a small knock sounded on a door below, and Mary inquired loudly, "Who's there?"

"It's me, John. Mary, please let me in."

The door creaked for a moment and then slammed shut. "What is it?" the woman asked.

"I need to speak to the brothers. Something happened this morning at my shop"

Ezra was already climbing down the rough ladder rungs. "Brother John, what happened?"

"A beggar came into my shop this morning and I think, inquired about both of you. He said that he was traveling with two monks when agents of the king chased them through a forest, and he got separated."

"It wasn't us. We were with Thaney and Owain when we were separated," as a thought came to him. "What did this man look like?"

"I don't really know, he had a hood over his head and never looked at me straight on. He did have broad shoulders, but he walked stooped over and was dressed in dirty rags."

Ezra fastened his eyes on the butcher. "Do you ever open your shop on the Lord's Day?"

"No, I hang a sign telling customers that it's my one day of rest. The services take up most of the day, and then there is fellowship."

"Yes, I know. That's fine, but I think tomorrow your shop needs to be occupied by your new apprentice. Do you have some clothes and a dirty apron I can borrow?"

"Wait, you can't!" Caleb choked as he clambered down the ladder. "I need you tomorrow to help guide me through the service."

"I'm sure Brother John will be the perfect assistant for you, my friend. He has more experience than I do, and he also knows all of the regular parishioners. If there is anyone new, he can alert you. Meanwhile, I will be defending against any interruptions of your inaugural Mass," he winked as he extended his hand in a mock Roman salute.

Caleb still clutched the ladder with a worried look as John turned toward the back door. "I'll fetch you the clothes now, be back in a few minutes."

"Make sure they aren't too clean," Ezra called out.

"I hope you know what you're doing," Caleb whispered.

"Every word of God is pure: he is a shield unto them that put their trust in him." (21) "I don't know what I'm doing, but I trust he is leading me in the right path. Mary, did your husband own a razor by chance?"

"Yes, he had an old iron razor. It's rusty now, but I'll get it for you."

"Thank you, and maybe a pumice stone if he had one.

The only other thing I will need is a large amount of cobwebs, to staunch the bleeding when I shave my beard. I haven't shaved for years. I'm sure he won't recognize me without this chin fur."

"Who?" Caleb asked.

"The fox, of course."

Chapter 19

Deception

It had been a disappointing night. He hadn't been able to entice the barmaid away from the other customers, although she kept his tankard full of ale until he finally passed out. By the time he woke up, she was gone, and the inn was closed. Percy grimaced as he pulled various cold, damp rags into place. *Why didn't I hang these up to dry? Oh well, this should be the last time I have to wear these rags.* He shivered as he pulled the filthy tunic over his head. *It will be worth it when I find those two friars and take them back to the king whole, or in pieces.* He belted his sword onto his back with the hilt jutting out beneath his armpit before pulling the heavy hooded cape over his shoulders and grabbing a flat iron bar. Once again, it was still dark as he crept through the chilly early morning fog toward the butcher shop. Assuming the shop would be closed for the parishioners to attend Sunday services, he had decided to break into the shop, find a place to hide, and watch for the monks in the area behind the ring of houses. As he approached the building, he was surprised to see the dim flicker of a candle in the window. *No one should be there yet.* Hesitantly, he placed his palm on the door and pushed.

"Good morning, sir! What cut of meat are we looking for today?" came a cheerful voice.

Something was wrong. Before him stood a small man wearing a wide smile and a woolen cap. "I'm sorry, sir, I was looking for the butcher."

"I'm his apprentice, Ethen, how can I help you?" he said as he recognized the man who had captured Thaney and Owain.

"He gave me some money the other day and I…"

"I'm sorry, he doesn't allow me to give anything to beggars, and I don't even have access to the cash box. I could maybe give you a slice of salted fatty pork or maybe a dry chicken neck? I also have an ox tail if you want to make some soup."

Percy felt his eyebrows rise, and a rancid bile suddenly gathered in the back of his throat. He took a moment to swallow. "No need to trouble you, sir," he finally uttered. "I just wanted to see the butcher."

"He had to go help a farmer with a cow this morning. He should be back, maybe mid-morning if you want to come back."

"Doesn't he celebrate Mass today?"

"We are open every day sir, we even try to stay open on most holidays. What is Mass?" the small man held a quizzical look on his face.

"Mass, going to church. I thought he would be closed today."

"Then why would you come to his shop? Wait a minute, are you a thief, or one of those outlaw Christians?" as the man's eyes narrowed and he suddenly grabbed a long iron spit hanging from some wall pegs and pointed it toward Percy.

Percy's eyes darted from the man to the sharp point of the iron rod and back to the man's face that was blood red and seething now.

"Get out now, or I'll run you through and bake you for

lunch!"

Confusion painted his face as Percival stumbled backward out the door.

"And don't come back! We don't need your kind in this village," the man shouted from the open doorway as Percy walked quickly away.

Percy felt the heat of shame on his face, a sensation he hadn't experienced in a long time. *How did I misread the signs? Maybe the girl wasn't a Christian, maybe she hadn't lied, but what now?* Various thoughts plagued him as he slowly walked back to the Drunken Chicken, fuming. Once there, he stripped out of his filthy disguise and fell onto the bed, embraced by depression.

———•●•———

"Ezra looked across the street and nodded at a darkened doorway. In a few seconds, Widow Mary tottered out carrying a basket and meandering from shop to shop, as she followed the beggar down the street."

Ezra slid the locking board into place on the front door with a satisfied smile. *I don't think he will be coming back, but I'd better leave to find Thaney now.* He walked through the shop and out the rear door, which he barricaded too. Then he removed the wool cap, which had covered his tonsure. He felt the cool morning air caress the bare skin atop his head as he walked quickly back to the widow's house.

"You're back already?" Caleb cried as he jumped up from his breakfast and hugged his friend.

"Yes, but not for long, I fear. That beggar was the man who captured Thaney and Owain and took them away. I am going to take the scroll back to her now, before he finds us."

"What about me? I can't stay here. I'll be killed." Caleb's eyes were wide with fright.

"Trust me, God placed you in this community for a reason. You need to shepherd your flock, while I lead Mr.

Fox on a wild goose chase. Agreed?"

Caleb reluctantly shook his head in the affirmative.

"Good, now we wait for Mary to return and tell us where the fox's lair is."

Half an hour later, the front door opened, and Mary shuffled in. "Thank goodness he walked slow; I almost couldn't keep up."

"He didn't see you?"

"Never turned around, but I noticed his sword when he stumbled on a loose cobblestone. It lifted his cloak two feet off his back. Must have been a sword," she repeated.

Caleb shuddered, and Ezra placed a steady hand on his shoulder. "Mary, where did he go?"

"That ramshackled Drunk Chicken inn. The one Amelia works at."

"Amelia?" Ezra asked.

"Yes, she lives three houses down. She hates it, doesn't like the way the patrons treat her, but her mother says she has to have a job." Mary continued.

"Caleb, I think you and I should go and minister to that young lady right now," as he rose and headed out the back door.

"Ezra, I have to begin my service in two hours. I don't have time to chat with anyone," Caleb whined just as Ezra was knocking on the door.

"Who's there?" a girl's voice called.

"My name is Ezra, and I have your new priest, Caleb, with me. We'd like to introduce ourselves before the service today and ask you something about your job."

Boards scraped, and the door opened to reveal a young lady with dark hair and eyes. *Pretty but too thin.* Ezra thought, but then admonished himself. "Excuse us, Amelia, but we would like to know if a stranger is staying at the inn. We have seen a man disguised as a beggar and,"

"Yes, he isn't a beggar, but I saw a pile of wet, filthy clothes in his room when I replaced his candles yesterday.

He is a vile man; he makes my skin crawl," she suddenly wrapped her arms around herself, and her nose wrinkled in revulsion.

"I'm sorry, but I know he is a threat to everyone in this community. I am going to try to supply a false trail for him to follow. Can you tell me where he's from?

She pursed her lips as she concentrated. "He said he was under orders from his king to find two old monks and return them to the castle."

Ezra snorted, "You're only as old as you feel. Did he say where this castle was?"

"Yes, he said it was a couple of days' ride to the East."

"That must be Thaney's castle." Ezra said.

"Castle? She lives in a castle? What is she, a princess?" Caleb laughed.

"Yes," was the reply.

"You never told me that she was a princess!" Caleb wailed in surprise.

"You never asked. Right now, you need to go and get everything ready for Mass this morning. I need to first mislead the fox and then get ready to leave and deliver the scroll and the copy to Thaney at Hailes Castle."

"Do you need me for anything else?" Amelia interjected.

Ezra was silent for a moment until he smiled mischievously. "Would you mind missing a portion of the service this morning and feeding that fox a red herring?"

The girl studied his face for a moment, "Won't it be dangerous?"

"No more dangerous than any other night working in a pub. It may protect your church from being discovered, too."

She pursed her lips as she made her decision, "All right, tell me what to do."

"The same thing you do every workday. Get dressed the same as if you are going to work. If they ask you why you're there on your day off, tell them you were bored. When mister fox shows up, start talking to him. Then tell him you noticed two men in brown robes climb into a wagon headed south for Reidrag. That trip should keep him busy long enough for me to reach the castle and deliver the scroll to Thaney."

"If I hurry, I should be able to hear your friend's first service. I'll let you know how it went," as she ushered them out the door.

Chapter 20

Red Herring

"What are you doing here? This is your day off," the innkeeper said, surprised as he placed a loaf of bread in front of Percy.

"I know, but I'm bored. There's nothing going on today." Amelia replied nonchalantly. "I thought you might need some help."

"If he doesn't, I sure do." Percy quickly answered. "Please, have a seat and share some breakfast with me."

"I don't know, I should be serving,"

The innkeeper cut in quickly with a wide smile, "Amelia, never mind, sit down and entertain this good customer. I will be back with some porridge."

"So, you don't have any obligations on your day off?" Percival cooed.

"No, I usually just clean the house and relax, but today I felt restless, so I decided to take a walk."

"I'm glad you did. Maybe we can find something to do together," as he slid his large hand over her fingers.

"Oh, I almost forgot," she exclaimed, quickly pulling her hand back and grabbing the edge of the table with white knuckles. "Remember, the other day you asked me about two Christian monks?"

Percy's eyes narrowed. "Yes, have you seen them?"

"I'm not certain, but I did see two old men in brown robes climb into a wagon loaded with sacks, and I asked the driver where he was headed as I walked by. He said he was taking a load of grain to Reidrag. They left the day before yesterday and…"

"Where is that?" Percy suddenly blurted.

Amelia sank back with surprise on her face, "I don't know for sure; it's South, maybe five or six days of travel, I think."

"Thank you, my dear," Percy said, as he drew a gold coin from his purse and quickly tossed it at her. "I'd love to stay and chat, but duty calls. I must gather my belongings." He rose and sprinted up the rickety steps to the second floor.

Amelia smiled as she bent and picked the shiny coin up from the dirt floor, stood, and walked over to the innkeeper. Make sure that guy pays you. He's leaving right away."

"Why, what did you do?"

"I did nothing, he just needs to hurry and find some friends of his. I'll see you tomorrow." She stepped out the front door into the sunshine. Walking up the street, she felt victorious for the first time in her life. She had helped herself, but she also helped the church members and maybe the community as a whole. Not many people were in the street, and it didn't take long for her to make the trip back to her neighborhood. She quietly knocked on Mary's door until it opened, and she slipped inside.

"How did it go?" Ezra asked with concern etched on his face.

"He should be well on his way to Reidrag by now," she said politely.

"Wonderful, you have done us a great service. Bless you, young lady."

"It was my pleasure. He didn't even ask me any questions. Now I'm going outside to listen to your friend's church service. Are you going too?"

"I will be happy to accompany you, my dear. After all, now you've provided me some breathing room before my trip."

Together they walked up the hillside toward the group of parishioners who were just standing up to sing a second hymn. They reached the rear of the church ruins just as the hymn was finished, and they sat together on a large flat rock. Quietly, they sat through the rest of the sermon until Caleb began the words that closed the service. "May Almighty God bless you, the Father, and the Son, and the Holy Spirit."

"Amen" rose from the crowd.

"Go and announce the Gospel of the Lord," Caleb cried.

The congregation responded, "Thanks be to God."

Mary and John suddenly stood up and approached the makeshift podium. John raised his hands, and the crowd quieted. "Since this is our first Sunday service with Father Caleb, we need to celebrate finally having a real priest to guide our parish. Let's all welcome him with a surprise potluck banquet today." The crowd cheered.

Ezra leaned back on his rock and smiled. Caleb was a monk, but also the perfect choice of a priest to guide this flock. He watched as Caleb, John, Mary, and Amelia chatted throughout the potluck dinner.

Later that afternoon, Ezra carefully packed his small duffel with food, clothes, and a copy of St. Martin's writings. As he straightened up, Caleb gave him a hug that brought tears to his eyes. "Don't worry, Caleb, I'll probably be back soon."

"I know, but I still worry," the monk said wiping at his own eyes.

"God is my protection. He won't let us down. Look how far we have come in a short time. We found the scroll, we copied it, you have become a priest with a wonderful parish, God is amazing, and neither of us is done serving him yet."

"I know, but I will miss you until you return. Now get going, so you can come back and help me," as Caleb gave him a gentle push toward the door.

"You only need God's help." Ezra admonished.

"But I want yours too, brother."

Ezra nodded, grabbed his walking staff, and stepped through the doorway into the narrow street draped in a few early afternoon shadows. He paused for a moment. ***Deliver me from mine enemies, O my God: defend me from them that rise up against me.*** (22) Then he strode up the road in the afternoon sun.

Chapter 21

New Arrival

Thaney found it hard to sleep anymore. Most nights, she immersed herself in fervent prayers for the protection of her friends, the scroll, and her father. She even repeatedly asked God for Percy to express kindness to others. After hours of meditation, she would finally fall asleep into fitful dreams until sunshine slapped her in the face. Today was different, though. She felt anxious; something was going to happen, but she didn't know what. She finally rolled out of bed in the wee hours and padded around the darkened halls of the castle. *I should be in bed. What is bothering me?* She grabbed some slices of dried apples from the kitchen and nibbled at them as she left the castle and crisscrossed the courtyard under the bewildered eyes of a few sleepy guards. With a loud sigh, she approached the main gate. "I'm going out to visit grandmother's cairn."

"I'm not sure that is wise, miss, since it isn't daylight yet. However, I will accompany you."

"No need, it's right around the corner."

"I will accompany you, miss. Gorgon, you have the gate. Lead on, miss."

"My name is Thaney."

"I know, miss," was his curt answer.

They walked out to a clearing. In the dim light of a fog-shrouded moon, the stack of stones shone in the darkness. The guard stopped at attention as Thaney continued and knelt down before the mound of rocks. *Grandmother, Mother, you both left me with so many questions about your lives, about my life. Grandmother, I thank you for telling me everything you could under Father's severe supervision, but tonight, I really want to know about you, Mother. I want to know who you were. Igraine tried to explain to me what your life was like. I need to know who you were, what you loved, and why you left me. Know that I love you, even though I never really knew you.* She wiped at the stray tears tickling her cheeks, stood up, and walked back to the castle with the guard following closely.

At the gate, the guard said, "Good morning, miss," as he resumed his station.

Thaney continued walking through the castle and wondering about the beautiful mother she could barely remember. As the sun began to rise and the sky lightened, she decided to take the spiral stone steps up through one of the towers and see the view from the top of the walls.

Thaney shivered in a cool morning breeze as she stood atop the castle battlements, staring out at the gloomy landscape. *Percy should have returned by now. Did Ezra and Caleb hide from him? Is he still trying to locate them? Or did Percy just kill them and would return, passing the blame onto others?* She shook her head to clear her thinking as she carefully threaded her way around the fortress walls. Then she stopped, seeing a lone figure standing beside the mound of stones that embraced her mother and grandmother. Ignoring the stairway, she sprinted toward the nearest ladder and scampered directly down to the courtyard, out the main gate, and past the amused stares of the guards. She was out of breath when she passed the last corner of the castle and stared at the man, kneeling now with his head bowed. He hadn't moved. She squared her shoulders and strode toward him.

"Who are ye?" The man hadn't moved, but his booming bass voice stopped Thaney in her tracks.

An alarm rang in her head. *This was a dangerous man.* She swallowed hard before answering loudly. "My father is the king of Hailes Castle. What are you doing here?"

"I'm trying to pay my respects to the lovely ladies interred here. Please leave me alone, I won't remain much longer."

She looked at his tattered brown robe, and it reminded her of Ezra's clothes. "You should not be unescorted on the castle grounds. What is your name?"

She heard a small laugh come from the man as he raised his head, and she saw the white hair surrounding his tonsure. "You may call me Father Lance, princess. Tell me, are you the daughter of Morgan Le Fay?"

"Yes, I am. How do you know of my mother?" The old man remained silent for a few more moments before he slowly struggled to his feet. She noticed he was taller than Percy, and broad-shouldered, too. Slowly, he turned toward her.

"Lancelot?" she heard herself say just before she fell to her knees and retched.

Concern showed in the monk's eyes as he quickly offered his hand to lift her up, "Are you all right?"

She felt her cheeks redden with embarrassment, and quickly, wiped a hand across her mouth, "I think so. It must have been that spiced venison from last night."

A smile began to crawl across the man's lips. "Father Lance, now my child. May I help you up?"

Thaney felt her eyes bulge, "What happened to you?" and then regretted it as she watched ancient sorrows cloud his face as she stretched out her hand.

"One long line of life, love, death, hope, despair, and shame," he added as a wan smile appeared, and he lifted her up. "I had everything in this life that a man could want. Then

I lost it all." Changing the subject, he added, "I remember now that I last saw you on your birthday. I think when you were six years old."

"Somehow, I remember your face too, a year before mother died, I know my uncle was there, too." she mumbled, feeling her own face cloud over.

"Yes, King Arthur, a week before he fell in the battle at Camlann. I made sure I arrived after he had already left. I'm sorry, I didn't mean to…"

"Can you tell me about my mother? I was at her grave earlier this morning, praying to know about her life."

He gave her a quizzical look, "I hadn't planned on coming here, because I know about your father and his hatred of Christians, but then I had an overwhelming impulse to pay my respects to your mother and grandmother, and here I am."

"He does hate Christians, but he is a great admirer of your past deeds. Can you tell me about my mother?" she repeated.

"How much time do you have?" he smiled.

"As long as it takes, now come to the castle with me and meet Father." She paused for a moment. "My prayer to Mother, it came true. You can speak to me for her."

"I will do my utmost, fair princess," as he picked up his well-worn staff and followed her.

Chapter 22

A Monk's Return

Ezra climbed to the top of the hill in the midday sun. He was sweating profusely as he stopped and wiped a soggy sleeve across his face. He had passed Blackness Castle the day before, with the waters of the Firth of Forth behind it. *I should be almost there now. Today, I should see Cynde, if I don't melt first.* He sniffed the pungent air, "Yes, God, I can't stand myself either. I'll make sure to find a stream and bathe first," as he forced himself to continue walking.

———•●•———

Thaney walked quickly to the throne room, ignoring the stares of others as she led the tall monk through the castle. "Father, look who I found, Sir Lancelot!"

The king looked up and bounded off the throne as a small man in dirty black robes left his side and exited the room. "Lancelot, I thought you were dead."

"Not yet, although sometimes I feel like it," he laughed. "By the way, was that Oberon that just left?"

"Yes, it was, he is my royal wizard. Why the disguise?" the king asked, pulling at the man's coarse robe.

"No disguise, sire. Queen Guinevere became a nun, and I became a monk to atone for our many misdeeds in life." Choking on the words, he continued, "I arrived too late to give her Last Rites. I performed the Funeral Mass and the Rite of Committal for her three weeks ago at the abbey in Amesbury. There I heard of the passing of Igraine, and made a pledge to visit her grave," as he wiped a rough sleeve over his eyes.

"My brother, I know how you suffer. You loved Guinevere as I loved my Morgan. She has been lost for more than ten years now, and every day is still filled with agony. I am grateful you came; you are a welcome guest of my kingdom for as long as you like, my friend."

"Can he stay in grandmother's cottage?" Thaney interjected.

"The king furrowed his brow for a moment, "Yes, that would be fine, I suppose."

"Thank you, sire, you are very gracious." Father Lance added as Thaney grabbed his hand and pulled him around.

"I'll show you where it is," she said.

"Make sure you bring him to dinner, Thaney," the king smiled as he turned and walked back toward the throne.

"Your father has mellowed with age," Lancelot said when they stepped outside the walls.

"Oh, he still can breathe fire when he wants to. There, see that roof? That was Igraine's house," she said with a touch of sadness.

"She was such a fine lady. Strong, but caring and protecting others throughout her life, like your mother did."

"Grandmother could never tell me much about mother. She was sworn to secrecy by my father," she answered sadly.

"Well, he didn't make me swear an oath, so I'll tell you everything I know," he smiled. "First, she was the second daughter of Igraine and Gorlois. Her brother was Cador, Duke of Cornwall."

"Second daughter?" Thaney exclaimed, "I have an

aunt?"

"Had, I'm afraid. She was not a nice person, nothing like your mother. She rebelled and became a pagan priestess. Black magic got her what she desired, until she was killed by her own son, Gaheris. She was not a relative you should remember."

"Oh, so mother wasn't anything like that?"

"No, she was beautiful inside and out. She was kind and empathetic with others. She was a healer, but she was a strong woman who stood her ground when she knew she was right."

"But she couldn't heal herself?"

"Patience, little one. I'll get to that. After Gorlois was killed in battle, High King Uther Pendragon took Igraine for his wife, and they had a son, Arthur."

"My uncle." Thaney brightened.

"Yes, a great man whom I was proud to serve, and whom I selfishly destroyed," a ragged sob escaped his throat before he continued. "I didn't mean to, I fell in love with Queen Guinevere, I was young and couldn't help myself."

Thaney looked deep into the man's eyes and saw the pain and shame he felt. She changed the subject, "But what about my mother?"

Lancelot sniffed and continued, "Your mother appointed herself as a spiritual guardian to anyone in pain or sickness, but she especially worked for Arthur's protection and prayed for him continually throughout his life. I used to listen to her and Igraine talk for hours about the history of your family and the miracles and healings of Jesus and the saints who had passed on. Your mother wanted to know everything she could about the one true God, and she worked at it day and night."

"So, she was nothing like her sister?"

"They were complete opposites, although they tolerated each other. Morgan was always caring and compassionate, while Morgause was cold and calculating. I remember, once I saw your mother heal Arthur of canker. She had been watching and warning him about an odd colored spot on his neck that seemed to be growing slowly for several years. One day, she noticed that it had turned black and told him she would pray about it. The next time I saw the King, it was completely gone."

"How?"

"Your mother was a healer; she once told me that she didn't look at the pain or disease of suffering but tried to understand what God saw in a person. I never understood what she was talking about. The gods I knew then were like me, imperfect, prone to fits of anger and violence, but she could see something completely different."

"Like limitless Love?"

"I guess so, several times Arthur was grievously wounded in battle and asked to be taken to her. We would carry him into her castle, and after her treatment, in a week or two, he would ride back to Camelot. I've changed from an imperfect warrior to an imperfect monk, but I still can't see her God clearly," shaking his head sadly. "Anyway, back to my story. Your grandfather, Uther Pendragon, agreed to the marriage of your mother to your father, King Lot. After that, King Uther died mysteriously in a battle with Saxon forces; I think the Saxons might have weakened him with poison. Following Uther's death, your grandmother came here to live."

"And mother studied healing with grandmother?"

"With her, and a handful of other visiting Christians. They used to talk all night about Jesus and his disciples, Saint Martin, Saint Patrick, and a whole host of others who healed and resurrected people. I wish I had listened to those stories, but I was younger then, and their chatter always put me to sleep."

"I love to hear stories of healing. Sometimes my friend Owain and I used to sneak out to listen to a passing monk's sermon. The last one mentioned a scroll that Saint Martin wrote." Lancelot smiled, "You are so much like your mother. She was always searching for the Truth," he laughed. "I went to visit her once because my lower back pain was debilitating. I couldn't ride at a trot. If my horse stumbled, I screamed from the spasms. I knocked on her door, and do you know what she said?" Thaney shook her head. **"Get thee behind me, Satan:"** he clapped his hands. "I didn't know if she was talking to me or what. Later, she told me she was addressing the image of pain that I was displaying. She also told me the rest of that Bible quote, **'thou art an offense unto me: for thou savourest not the things that be of God, but those that be of men.'** (23) She was trying to see the spiritual, untouched vision of me. In those first moments, I did feel better, but in a few days, I awoke with unbearable pain. Every movement brought a cry of anguish to my lips. Your mother said, 'You aren't made of matter, you were born of Spirit, and Spirit cannot feel pain.' **'It is the spirit that quickeneth; the flesh profiteth nothing: the words that I speak unto you, *they* are spirit, and *they* are life.'** (24) **'For if ye live after the flesh, ye shall die: but if ye through the Spirit do mortify the deeds of the body, ye shall live.'** (25) "I still struggle today to understand what she was saying, but in a day or two I could trot again."

"Why did she die?" The monk was silent for a long moment.

"She was a giving person, and if she couldn't help someone, she took it to heart. She devoted most of her life to protecting her little brother. When he died, her fight for life was defeated by dwelling in sorrow, I guess."

"Grandmother told me that all of the Christians prayed for her."

"They did, and she rallied for a long time, but when I visited, I noticed a tinge of sadness that never left her. I think it killed her," he added solemnly.

"Sorrow can kill?"

"Anything can if it separates you from God. That's the way the devil works; sorrow is one of his greatest weapons, unless it promotes repentance and forgiveness and brings you closer to God. Your mother couldn't forgive herself, and neither can I for my mistakes," he added gloomily.

"And forgive us our debts, as we forgive our debtors," (26) she whispered.

"Out of the mouth of babes and sucklings hast thou ordained strength because of thine enemies, that thou mightest still the enemy and the avenger." (27) "Thank you, I will hold that close in my thoughts, little one," as tears formed in the man's eyes.

"Still the devils that persecute you, remember God doesn't persecute, he loves," Thaney said. "We'd better go to dinner now. Father doesn't like to wait."

"All right. What do you think of your father's wizard?"

Thaney felt herself shudder, "I heard you ask about him. He is creepy. I don't like him."

"I've known him for years, but we could never be friends. He learned his craft as Merlin's apprentice, and he can be very dangerous."

"He scares me. He tried to force me to believe in his gods and idols when I was younger."

Lancelot smiled and whispered, **"Regard not them that have familiar spirits, neither seek after wizards, to be defiled by them: I *am* the LORD your God."** (28)

"Grandmother helped me understand that, and I guess he finally gave up trying to convert me after I begged father to have him stop."

"That's good, Merlin and he created quite a bit of havoc around the Round Table, and I know many good people who died because of them."

As they walked back to the castle, she asked. "Why is there so much violence in this world?"

"Because men see themselves as gods, striving for material possessions and power, instead of following the directions of Spirit and living in the kingdom of God. They believe the lies, because they live the lies."

"I guess you're right, we'd better hurry or we'll be late for dinner."

Chapter 23

Owain's Arrival

"Sir Lancelot, please, sit here by me." The king commanded as he and Thaney arrived.

"Thank you, sire, but please just call me Father Lance. I'm too old to be a knight anymore."

"I'm sorry, but you were the greatest knight of the Round Table. What happened to you after Arthur's death by Mordred?"

"The end of an era. It was the end of my life as a knight, but also the end of my periods of rampant madness and thoughts of suicide. I understand now how they were caused by mortal whims and desires. I'm grateful they are behind me."

"So, your life is peaceful now?"

"Yes, since I have finally stopped chasing happiness, riches, and power in this material world. Now, I see glimpses of true happiness, real riches, and the power of God."

Thaney watched as a look of disgust crossed Oberon's face, and he suddenly turned away from the conversation.

"You sound like my dear wife, Morgan," the king replied with wet eyes. "She said the same things throughout our marriage. Then she passed away after Arthur died, I couldn't make her happy," as a wretched sob escaped his throat.

"We make ourselves happy or unhappy; we can't force another person to be happy if they don't want to be. We can only be true friends, supporting and loving each other. I know you gave all of that to Morgan."

King Lot was unable to answer, and he suddenly buried his face in a corner of his robe as a loud wail escaped. Thaney had never seen him cry with abandon. She gently clasped her hand over his.

"Do not mourn, my king," Father Lance whispered. "She still lives, and she still loves you."

A few ragged coughs escaped beneath the cloak before the wretched words, "Why did she leave us then?"

Thaney felt him squeeze her hand hard. "Confusion," the word slipped out.

Her father uncovered his head, and both men stared at her with wide eyes.

"It just came to me," she stammered, thinking, *For where envying and strife is, there is confusion and every evil work.* (29)

"I understand Lance said. I myself have been driven close to death many times by that very thing. It took me a very long time to understand: **'For God is not *the author* of confusion, but of peace, as in all churches of the saints.'** (30) Your mother is still a very loving, caring person, who performed remarkable healings. The very few times I saw her fail in efforts to heal, she was desolate until she prayed and regained her peace."

"I saw that, but I didn't understand," the king said in a whimper. "I tried to force her out of depression."

Lance continued, "You did what you thought was right. You did what works for you in those situations, so don't be sorry. She needed to make herself happy. She had spiritual tools to do that, but she failed because of her personal attachment to her half-brother. I'm sure she just wanted to be with him."

"I'll bet she's miserable now because she wants to be with us," Thaney interjected.

"You are probably right, daughter, but we are suffering too," her father said. "Enough talk, let's eat and discuss happier things."

"Have you heard from Percy?" she asked.

"Not yet, but he won't dare return without your friends," he winked and laughed. "Can you imagine what he would look like doused in boiling oil?"

Thaney and Lance returned polite smiles but kept quietly eating.

"No, I put the fear in him, I did. He will turn over every rock to find them," he chuckled as he picked up a chicken leg and began to gnaw on it.

Thaney saw the questioning look on Lance's face. "I made friends with two monks who were helping me search for Saint Martin's lost scroll. Percy is looking for them."

"Who has seen this mythological scroll?"

"I don't know. He gave it to my great, great-great-grandfather Magnus to protect, and Saint Patrick supposedly had it when he converted the pagans in Hibernia to Christianity. After that, no one knows what happened to it."

"So why were you searching for it in Kilpatrick?" the king thundered.

"That's where Saint Patrick's parents lived. I thought I might find it in the church."

"A wild goose chase," the king muttered.

"Did you know the church was destroyed by fire?" Lance asked.

"Yes, but I thought it might be hidden behind a rock in a wall or beneath a loose flagstone, and it might have escaped the flames." Thaney lied and crossed her fingers.

"Very doubtful," Lance said with a penetrating gaze, as he continued eating.

"Sire, Owain of Rheged has arrived," a guard announced.

"Send him in," Thaney exclaimed before looking sheepishly at her father.

"Yes, send the scoundrel in."

A young man marched into the room. "Greetings, sire, from my father, King Urien of Rheged and I, currently of Yester Castle. Have you and your daughter been well since our last meeting?"

Thaney's mouth fell open. This wasn't the same Owain that she knew. She glanced at Lance and saw his lips tighten before he whispered to them both, "Don't tell him who I am."

"Er, welcome, Owain. Sorry, I apologize for our rash reaction at your last visit," King Lot stood and offered his hand.

Owain half-heartedly shook the king's hand. "Forgotten already, I received a note to visit from Thaney, and here I am. Who is this gentleman?"

"I'm glad you did, ah, this is Father Tuck, a friend of Thaney."

"She makes friends easily. Father Tuck, I feel I've seen you before. Have you ever been to Solway Firth?"

"I don't believe so."

"My mistake, you look so much like a loudmouthed knight who quarreled with my father a few years ago. Thaney, take a walk with me and tell me how you've been since our failed quest?"

Chapter 24

Owain's Confession

Once outside the walls, Owain hissed, "You are very quiet, princess."

Thaney tried to lighten the mood. "I'm glad you came so soon. I had a long talk with father, and he finally seemed to listen to me."

"Where is that old man who caught us," he spat.

"Percy? Father sent him to find Ezra and Caleb and bring them here."

"Why?"

"Because I asked him to, I like my friends to be close to me. Why are you being so belligerent?"

"Your father insulted me and treated me like a peasant. Do you know that I only have to tell my father, and he would lay siege to this kingdom. Especially since Sir Lancelot is hiding here like the coward he is."

"Why? What did he do?" as she felt her voice crack.

"He told my father to mind his own business as they quarreled about Guinevere and Arthur. Lancelot lost his temper and attacked him before our guards subdued and flogged him within an inch of his life. Then they threw him into the waters of the Solway Firth." He laughed, "I don't know why he didn't drown like a rat."

Thaney gasped, "He isn't like that now. He became a monk to atone for his past sins; he told me about my mother."

"I don't care; I still hate him."

"What has happened to you? You were caring and compassionate for others."

"I grew up. When your father threw me out, I got mad and decided to finally act like the Prince of Rheged. Even my uncle at Yester Castle is impressed. You should be, too."

"Well, I'm not. I liked you before, but now you act like a little Percy." Stars swam in her head as she crumpled into the grass. "You hit me," too amazed to cry.

He stood over her with a red face. "Don't you ever say that again, or you can believe that I'll do worse. Better yet, I've learned to do whatever I want," as he bent down and began to snatch at her dress with wild eyes.

"What could a little boy want to do?" a voice thundered behind him.

"Go away, old man, or I'll kill you," Owain yelled as he twisted around and deftly brandished his sword.

Lancelot stood with his hands on his walking stick and laughed. "Be careful, little boy, you might cut yourself."

Thaney watched from the ground as Owain yelled a curse and sprinted forward. He brought the sword up to strike the monk in the ribs, but the wooden staff suddenly parried the sword to the side, just as a huge fist slammed into his jaw.

Lancelot shook his head sadly. "They just don't make princes like they used to," as he looked at the boy's body lying in a heap.

Thaney stood up, "Did you kill him?" Her lips trembled.

"No, but he'll sleep for a good long while," Lancelot replied as he picked up the sword and threw it into a large patch of thorny bushes.

"He acts so differently, he was going to, to..."

"I know." Lancelot stopped her. "Too big for his

britches, just like his father," he laughed. "If I hadn't had six guards hanging on me, I would have spanked his father, too. I really had a bad temper back then."

"How did you survive in the water?"

"It was dark when they threw me in. Luckily, they stripped me out of my clothes and boots before they flogged me, or I would have drowned. It had been raining hard, and there was a slight current. I remember the wounds from that whip really stung in the brackish water and kept me awake. Suddenly, a tree floated by, and I was able to grab a branch and eventually climb up onto the trunk. I stayed there until I recovered enough to swim to land. Just another adventure," he smiled. "What do we do with him?"

"I don't know, he isn't the Owain I knew."

"Let me take him back to the guesthouse. I'll try to talk him out of his delusions and then send him on his way," as he bent and lifted her upright.

"Thank you, tell him goodbye for me," Thaney said softly.

"Good riddance," Lancelot replied as he lifted the boy over his shoulder. "We don't need his childish shenanigans around here."

———— • ● • ————

Lancelot dropped Owain onto a bench and sat down to pray about the situation. He asked God for the right way to protect Thaney, not only for now, but for the future . In a few minutes, he felt he had an answer. **"For whosoever shall do the will of my Father which is in heaven, the same is my brother, and sister, and mother."** (31) *I have to forget that image of a self-righteous teenager and look at this boy the way Jesus would have, in order to heal him. I need to see the good qualities in him, rather than what needs to be beaten out of him.* He felt himself smile. *Let me see courage, humility, honor, selflessness, purity, compassion...*

He noticed the boy began to groan and stir. "Wake up, Owain of Rheged. I was afraid I hit you too hard. Do you like Thaney?" A barely noticeable nod in the affirmative, and a loud moan as he sat up slowly.

"Do you realize how badly you treated her today?" The boy nodded again while eyeing the distance to the door.

"Don't try it, son, I'd hate to break both of your legs, too," he said with an easy smile while he watched Owain deflate. "Now, let's have a man-to-man talk. Thaney told me you were a pretty good guy in the past, but you weren't one today. Why not?"

"I've changed. Her father threw me off his lands, and Sir Percival treated me like scum when he captured us. I shouldn't have been treated like a commoner."

"You aren't a commoner, but you listened to those secret sermons with Thaney. What did Peter say? **'And he said unto them, Ye know how that it is an unlawful thing for a man that is a Jew to keep company, or come unto one of another nation; but God hath shewed me that I should not call any man common or unclean.'** (32) You can't consider anyone common or unclean. They are all God's children."

"I am royalty," with a sneer.

"Men may say you're royal, but in God's eyes, everyone is royal. Peter also said, **'But ye *are* a chosen generation, a royal priesthood, an holy nation, a peculiar people; that ye should shew forth the praises of him who hath called you out of darkness into his marvelous light:'** (33) You aren't greater or lesser than anyone else. You are a child of God just like I am, understand?"

The boy responded with a slight nod. "You don't seem convinced."

"I'm bored; can I leave now?"

Lancelot watched as Owain slowly shifted his weight toward a table with a large pair of shears on top. "Do that, and I promise you will limp the rest of your life."

"You can't tell me what to do," the boy spat as he rushed forward and grabbed the scissors. At the same moment, the wooden staff speared the boy at the base of his head as he collapsed across the table and then fell to the floor.

"Asleep again. What am I going to do with you?" Lancelot asked as he bent down to pick him up again.

"What are you doing?" the boy moaned much later as he woke up. When he suddenly noticed that he couldn't move, he asked: "Why did you tie me up?" Lance watched as he tried to roll side to side on the table, but was unable to move.

Lancelot kept gripping his big hands around Owain's legs, "I'm just trying to decide which tendons I'm going to cut. Do you have a preference, right or left leg?" He felt himself smile as the boy's eyes grew wide with terror.

"Please, I'll do anything. Please!" as the boy tried desperately to kick.

"I don't have a choice, I made you a promise, and I keep my promises. Which one will it be?" as he picked up the shears, snapped them next to Owain's nose a couple times, and watched as tears began to flow, as he slowly dragged them down his body toward his legs.

Uncontrollable screams and jerks against the ropes accompanied the flood of tears until the fight finally went out of Owain, "Pleeease don't, I pray you…"

"Oh, you pray now? What brought about this sudden deliverance from the devil? Are you ready to confess all your sins and be cleansed?"

"Yes, anything. I'll tell you anything. Please."

"I, sir, will take you at your word, but you will lie here, restrained, with me until we come to an understanding about your future and your past. Otherwise, I will finish this job," he said as he slowly pointed the scissors between the boy's eyes.

"What do you want to know?"

"Why did you attack Thaney today? The truth now."

"I guess I wanted to be in charge, have her do whatever I wanted. I'm sorry, I just…"

"See, telling the truth isn't so bad. While you accompanied her on her quest, you also treated her badly once before, didn't you?"

"How did you…"

Lancelot pointed his finger up. "He just told me. He talks if you listen. **'For there is nothing covered, that shall not be revealed; neither hid, that shall not be known.'** (34) You have committed an unpardonable offense."

"I'm sorry, I couldn't help myself."

"You could have easily prevented it, because I know you actually planned how to do it so she wouldn't remember, didn't you?"

Owain nodded, "I'm sorry."

"You're only sorry because you've been caught. If it were up to me, I would kill you right now with no regrets. I've killed many men for less offenses. Yet the Lord forgives as in Jeremiah: **'And I will cleanse them from all their iniquity, whereby they have sinned against me; and I will pardon all their iniquities, whereby they have sinned, and whereby they have transgressed against me.'** (35) He forgives; I do not. She doesn't even know that you were a snake in disguise on her quest. You remind me of a story in the Bible where King David wanted a woman and had her husband slain to get her. Do you know the end of that story?"

Owain shook his head.

"And the LORD sent Nathan unto David. And he came unto him, and said unto him, There were two men in one city; the one rich, and the other poor. The rich *man* had exceeding many flocks and herds: But the poor *man* had nothing, save one little ewe lamb, which he had bought and nourished up: and it grew up together with him, and with his children; it did eat of his own meat, and drank of his own cup, and lay in his bosom, and was unto

him as a daughter. And there came a traveler unto the rich man, and he spared to take of his own flock and of his own herd, to dress for the wayfaring man that was come unto him; but took the poor man's lamb, and dressed it for the man that was come to him. And David's anger was greatly kindled against the man; and he said to Nathan, *As* the LORD liveth, the man that hath done this *thing* shall surely die: And Nathan said to David, Thou *art* the man." (36)

"You are the man. You have taken something that belonged to another; you are guilty. Do you know what it means if she is with child? The laws of these pagans call for a death sentence. You had better pray that you are not the cause of Thaney's death, or I promise you will pay the utmost farthing. Yours will not be a pretty death, understand?" Lance leaned forward until their noses almost touched.

Fear was evident in his eyes as Owain answered, "Yes, sir."

Lancelot grabbed a dagger and deftly cut the ropes. "In addition, if I ever hear that you have tried to contact her without my blessing first, I will look forward to hunting you down, and you really don't want that because I would have to renounce my vows of peace, understand?"

Owain rubbed the back of his head and nodded obediently, "Believe me, I understand," with a strained smile.

"Good, I'm glad we finally agreed," as he offered his hand, and Owain shook it. "Live a good life, my son, and may God bless and guide your future decisions, or else I will see you again," he winked.

Chapter 25

The Scroll Retrieved

"Is he gone?" Thaney asked as Lancelot entered the castle gate.

"He is, and I don't think he'll return anytime soon."

Thaney shook her head in disbelief, "I don't know what could have possessed him to attack me like that. He was always so friendly and supportive," as she led the way into the castle.

"Well, you can't trust boys," Lance hesitated, "I have something to tell you…"

"I can't trust men either. Percy was terrible."

"You can trust some men, young lady. Don't blame us just because we're a little bit slow," a scratchy voice called after them.

"Ezra! You came back." Thaney spun around, smiling and rushed to embrace the elderly monk in a hug.

"Brother Lance, meet Brother Ezra. He went with me on my quest to Kilpatrick. Where is Caleb?"

Ezra's smile showed a lack of teeth as he shook Lancelot's hand. "He is now Father Caleb, priest of Kilpatrick church."

"Oh my, he is so shy, I can't imagine him in a pulpit."

"He couldn't either, but he's doing a wonderful job,"

he said, looking around cautiously. "Is there somewhere we three can talk?"

"Grandmother's house," Thaney whispered as she turned on her heels and headed back out the gate.

Lancelot closed the door of the cottage as Thaney asked, "Did you find it?"

Ezra grinned as he reached into his robe and drew out the lanyard attached to a battered leather cylinder. "We did, and I even brought you another copy," he said as he patted his satchel and handed the cylinder to Thaney.

Her hands shook as she scraped sealing wax away with her fingernails and twisted the fitted wooden plug out. Turning it over, a small scroll slid out.

"What is that?" Lancelot asked.

"Saint Martin's Scroll," Ezra whispered as Thaney slowly unrolled the ancient paper across the table.

"It has been lost for a century, and now it's found," she said through happy tears.

"Don't get it wet," Ezra laughed.

The door squeaked open as a young voice asked, "What are you doing in here?"

"Nothing, just talking," Thaney replied as she quickly rolled up the paper onto the spool.

"Is that a treasure map?" Gawain asked.

"No son, just a bunch of words. Do you want to find treasure?" Lancelot interjected.

"Thaney said I could help search for it if she found a map."

"I don't have a map, but I've heard stories that the Holy Grail is hidden not far from here. One of the greatest treasures in the world," he spread his arms wide and continued. "The story is that Joseph of Arimathæa hid the cup that Christ drank from in the last supper near Glastonbury, south of here. You can search for it when you get older, and if you find it, you'll be the richest man in the world."

The boy's brow furrowed, "Can't I search now? Who was Christ?"

Lancelot wrapped an arm around the boy's shoulder and led him toward the door. "I will tell you all about him, so you know where to search when you come of age. You'll have to be a fearless knight for the quest, though."

"I'm going to be a knight, Father says so," Gawain exclaimed as they walked outside.

"I like your new friar friend," Ezra exclaimed. "He looks familiar. Where is he from?"

A giggle escaped Thaney's throat before she answered. "Why, have you ever seen Sir Lancelot of the Round Table before?"

Ezra's eyes flew open. "He's a monk now?"

"Yes, he's been telling me about my mother and her life of prayerful healing. No one was ever allowed to tell me much before, including Grandmother."

"Goodness. I've never met one of King Arthur's knights before," a wide grin spread across his face.

"I don't think you should mention his life as a warrior, too many bad memories. He's a soldier of Christ now. Try to lift his thoughts above his raucous past."

"All right, I will try. Here, let me give you an extra copy of Martin's scroll," as he pulled the pages out of his satchel.

Before he could hand them to her, she enveloped him in a hug, "Thank you so much for being my friend." She noticed his eyes were moist as he pulled away.

"Believe me, it's my pleasure," he stammered as he handed her the papers.She hesitated for a moment, and he asked, "What's wrong?"

"This is the first time the knowledge of the scroll has been shared outside of our family. I hope it blossoms and helps to heal this world." She hugged the papers to her chest. "I'm going to hide these right now before father sees me with them and asks too many questions. Wait for Lancelot and meet me at the entrance to the castle in about an hour. There is a sundial behind this house." As she looped the cord with the scroll over her neck and hurried out the door.

When she neared the main gate, she saw a rider approaching slowly with his shoulders slumped and head held low. Raising her hand to shield her eyes, she barely recognized Percy. He looked exhausted and somewhat frail. "Hello, Percival, I trust you had a pleasant journey?"

The man didn't raise his head and just glowered at her as he rode past.

I guess he got up on the wrong side of the saddle this morning. She felt herself smile. *This was going to be a wonderful day.*

Chapter 26

Percy's Reprieve

Thaney entered the first tower and ran up the spiral stone steps to the wall walk and along the battlements to an upper entrance close to her bedroom in the keep. Just before she went inside, she looked down and saw a circled group of guards roughly pull Percy off his horse and shove him into the great hall. For a moment, she felt pity for the man until she remembered how brutal he could be. Continuing to her room, she pulled the loose stone from the wall and placed the paper copy of the scroll in with her other treasures. Then, feeling a sense of obligation, she ran down to the throne room. Walking in, she saw Percy kneeling, head down before her father.

"So, you have failed in your quest to find the monks. What do you suggest your punishment should be, Sir Percival?"

Thaney shouted, "Father, it is all right. The one monk has arrived at our castle, and the other is doing well in Kilpatrick." All faces turned toward her in surprise. "It's true, I'll bring him to lunch with Lancelot," she added.

The king looked disgusted and spat at Percy, "Stay out of my sight until I call for you, understand?"

Percy nodded his head, arose, and quickly slunk out of

the hall. As the king turned back to his daughter, "When did this other friar show up?"

"This morning, after Owain left. I'm going to the main gate to meet Lancelot and Brother Ezra now."

"Bring them straight to me, I want to see what your elusive monk friend looks like."

"Yes, your majesty," she turned her head and rolled her eyes just as Gawain wandered in and asked King Lot what the Holy Grail was. She quickly hurried out the nearest exit toward the main gate.

"I suppose I should thank you," a low growl emanated next to her.

"Why, Percy, shouldn't you be hiding from the king?" She forced a look of concern on her face as his coal-black eyes bored through her.

"Yes, because of your friends. Somehow, they eluded me in Kilpatrick, but you know that, don't you?" he hissed.

"As a matter of fact, I do not. I haven't had a chance to find out how you missed them in that town, but I certainly will ask. Now, please excuse me, I have things to do," as she stepped into the courtyard on her way to the main gate, a grin slipped to her lips. She saw Lancelot and Ezra standing just inside the wall and waved to them. Suddenly, she felt ill, knelt behind a nearby barrel, and threw up again. *That's odd, why am I throwing up?*

"Are you all right?" Ezra's scratchy voice asked scant moments later, as Lancelot grasped her arm and gently lifted her to her feet.

She saw Percy staring at her as she wiped her mouth. "Yes, I think so…"

Lancelot looked at her with concern etched on his face, "I need to tell you something."

She didn't like the look he gave her, and quickly decided she didn't want to hear it, "Dear Lancelot, not now, Father wants to meet you both immediately. Follow me." Then she turned on her heels and led them both back into the castle.

King Lot's face was red as they approached him, "Who told Gawain stories of this Holy Grail?" he thundered.

"I did, sire, the boy wanted a treasure to seek, and that one is supposedly buried on this island," Lancelot spoke. "I just tried to give him something to think about."

"Well, I guess I understand. That boy can be a pest at times. I just wish it wasn't a holy relic."

"I understand, sire. If he asks again, I'll tell him to search for Excalibur instead."

The king emitted a bellowing laugh, "Now that is a prize worth chasing. I wouldn't mind searching for that myself if I were a few years younger. So, this must be Brother Ezra that you told me about. How are you, sir?"

Thaney watched as the old monk hesitated before stepping forward and bowing to the king, "I am well, also humbled and honored to be received by your majesty."

"Daughter, I must say you have done well picking your friends, even though they are monks," he winked. "Tonight we shall dine, celebrate, and share our stories. I will see you all at dusk." He turned and walked away, leaving a warm feeling in Thaney's chest.

"That went well," Ezra's toothless grin spread across his lips.

Thaney gave the old man another hug, "I can't believe he was so gracious, he looked really happy, I'll meet both of you in the dining hall at dusk," she said. *Maybe things will be better now.* Glancing at Lancelot, she noticed worry in his eyes.

———— • ● • ————

As King Lot walked back toward his bedroom, a page ran up to him. "Sire, Sir Percival asked me to deliver this to you. Do you have a response for him, your majesty?"

That scoundrel better not ruin my good mood. He tore

open the wax seal and stared at the words as his shoulders slumped. "Tell him to meet me in my bedroom."

"Your bedroom, sire?"

"That is what I said, go," he said the words evenly, although he was seething inside as he continued down the long corridor.

Minutes later, a small knock on his door, "Come in, Percy."

"Sire, I apologize, but I thought you should be aware of the possible situation. It could have been just a sick stomach in the courtyard, but I also noticed a slight swelling in her belly from when I saw her last."

The king sat heavily on his bed. *I had hoped she was just gaining a good appetite. If it were true, the laws of his fathers demanded a verdict of death for his only daughter.* He suddenly felt very old. "Tell her to come and see me here," he whispered.

Chapter 27

Suspicion

A fist pounded on her door as she was getting ready for dinner. "What do you want?" she hollered.

"It's not what I want, it's what your father wants. He wants you to go see him immediately in his chambers," Percy's voice cooed.

"Why? I'll see him at dinner."

"I don't think that will be soon enough. He is expecting you now." The voice trailed off as it retreated down the hallway.

Worried, Thaney flung the door open and ran toward her father's room. His door was cracked open, and she ran in. Thaney suddenly stopped and stared at the man sitting on the bed. She had never seen him look so distraught, "What's the matter?" she heard herself say.

He stared at her with reddened eyes. "Are you with child?" he managed to say.

"No, I have never known a man. None has ever touched me. Why would you ask me that?"

"Percy saw you get sick in the courtyard, and he noticed your belly looks fuller. He said it could be morning sickness."

"But how could I be pregnant? I have never been with

a man. I swear that I am not lying, Father."

He gently took her hands in his. "Thank you, daughter, I will take you at your word. Give me a few minutes, and I'll meet you and your friends in the dining hall."

Thaney pulled away reluctantly. *Father loves me; how could he believe such a thing? It couldn't be true. I can't be pregnant; Gabriel didn't visit me like he did with Mary.* **"And the angel said unto her, Fear not, Mary: for thou hast found favour with God. And, behold, thou shalt conceive in thy womb, and bring forth a son, and shalt call his name JESUS. And he shall reign over the house of Jacob for ever; and of his kingdom there shall be no end. Then said Mary unto the angel, How shall this be, seeing I know not a man? And the angel answered and said unto her, The Holy Ghost shall come upon thee, and the power of the Highest shall overshadow thee: therefore also that holy thing which shall be born of thee shall be called the Son of God."** (37) She took her time walking to the dining hall, pondering. *Could I be pregnant with a child of God?*

"What's wrong?" Lancelot asked as soon as he saw her.

"Father thinks I might be pregnant, but I can't be," she heard her voice die.

"Here, Thaney, sit down," Ezra said, patting a spot on a bench.

She sat down, just as Lancelot said, "There is a chance you are. That's what I've been wanting to tell you. That worthless knave, Owain, confessed that he abused you before I sent him away, but I was hoping it wasn't true."

"How? He never touched me; I would have known, wouldn't I?"

"He didn't tell me how, but he did confess."

Looking at him with tears in her eyes, "Do you know what it means if I am?"

Pain shone in his eyes, and she didn't need an answer.

Malice resonated in his voice as he slammed a large fist into his palm, "I should have killed him."

"If he did this, if I am pregnant, I should hate Owain, but all I feel is pity for him being so weak. Why did God allow this to happen? I'm good." She covered her eyes with her hands and began to sob.

Ezra wrapped a skinny arm around her shoulders. "You are good, and this didn't happen by chance. God has a purpose for you, I know it."

Thaney dropped her hands, and sarcasm took over, "How? I know the penalty is death. What purpose is served by that?"

Ezra squeezed her shoulders harder. "God knows you are innocent. It says in the Bible; **'For the LORD *is* our judge, the LORD *is* our lawgiver, the LORD *is* our king; he will save us.'** (38)"

"I'm asking how? I know my father, although he loves me, he must follow the laws of his pagan fathers who decreed that I will be cast headlong from a high mountain."

Lancelot leaned in close, "Do not worry, princess, **'Fear not: for they that *be* with us *are* more than they that *be* with them.'** (39) I know God will protect you."

The king entered the hall, followed by Percy and Gawain. "Be seated, gentlemen. This is Sir Percival. I have brought him along so that Ezra can tell him how he eluded him in Kilpatrick."

"You, the butcher's apprentice?" Percy interrupted.

"Good evening, sir, would you like a slice of salted fatty pork?" A toothless smile appeared.

Percival reached for the hilt of his sword, but Lancelot grabbed his wrist. "A fine joke he played on you. Laugh it off," he said with a menacing tone.

"And who do you think you are?" Percy questioned as he strained to wiggle his arm free.

"Brother Lance, at your service," as he stepped back and bowed, never diverting his eyes.

The king stepped between the two men. "Yes, he has become a harmless monk now, but don't you recognize him, Percy? This is the famous Sir Lancelot of the Round Table."

Percy's eyes grew wide, as he nodded and rubbed the pain from his wrist. He addressed Ezra, "So, the church is hidden behind those houses, as I surmised."

"Only rocks and ruins now, but I trust someday it will be rebuilt," Ezra answered proudly.

"You were so close, Percy, but these Christians are clever. Now let's eat," and the king sat down as he pulled a small roast hog closer to himself.

Thaney was grateful that most of the conversations stopped as the others ate. Although after he was full, the king asked Lancelot and Ezra a series of endless questions about their lives and adventures. Gawain listened intently to all the stories. She sat quietly, lost in her own prayer, repeating the words of Jesus at the Garden of Gethsemane in an endless refrain: **"Father, if thou be willing, remove this cup from me: nevertheless not my will, but thine, be done."** (40)

Chapter 28

Pregnant?

Thaney didn't sleep well. She had taken the pages of the scroll out of her hiding place and read through them for several hours before deciding to try to sleep. One section of Martin's writings really interested her, and she read it over and over, trying to memorize it: ***"With God realized as each individual's only father/mother, mortals would see God as their one true relative, the only creator. If you perceive everything and everyone as spiritual ideas, discrimination disappears. There is no gender, age, race, or human history to hate; all becomes Love. When material history is seen to be a lie – all anger, resentment, fear must pass into the nothingness that spawned them. Reality then appears as harmony, health, and purity untouched by the lie of an existence separate from God."***

Lying awake in bed, she also kept thinking about her dream of floating in the air, and hoping that it would come true if she were pregnant.

In the morning, she pushed depression away and slid out of bed. Dressing quickly, she walked to the Widow's Cottage just before daybreak. Stopping some distance away, she paused and retched.

"Morning, young lady." Lancelot's voice sounded

from some nearby bushes.

"Morning," she said with wide eyes. "I had hoped to keep my sickness a secret."

"It is safe with me, fair maiden, and Ezra is off picking berries somewhere."

"Thank you," as a wide yawn escaped.

The man looked at her with a knowing expression. "I'm sorry for your struggle. I wish I could do more than just pray for you."

"That might not be the will of God. I'm sure Saul thought he was doing the will of the Lord when he persecuted Christians. Then he met the one true God on the way to Damascus, was blinded, and his life changed forever. He learned what the Love of God was."

"Yes, and I'm sure Ananias's life changed forever when he was charged by the Lord to restore Saul's sight before he became Paul. **'And Ananias went his way, and entered into the house; and putting his hands on him said, Brother Saul, the Lord,** *even* **Jesus, that appeared unto thee in the way as thou camest, hath sent me, that thou mightest receive thy sight, and be filled with the Holy Ghost.'** (41)

Thaney said, "I'm trying to have that much faith, but I'm scared."

"Don't just have faith, have understanding. Know that God will save and defend you, because he loves you and created you perfect in his own spiritual image. You reflect infinity. Spiritual reality can't be harmed or touched by matter."

"But my father, my family…"

Lancelot cut her off, "Don't you know that God is your Father and all souls in the world are your family? Jesus turned away from this world when he prayed. **'Thy kingdom come. Thy will be done in earth, as** *it is* **in heaven.'** (42) He saw the real Kingdom and mankind in the image of Spirit and Harmony."

"You, who have fought and killed others in mortal battles, see this now?"

"I'm a slow learner and somewhat stubborn," he chuckled. "My life has been blessed after I learned a few simple truths that my obsession with mortal life obscured for decades. I only wish I had learned them sooner," he confessed.

"So, you're saying that I really live in Spirit, and this world that I can touch is an illusion?"

The monk continued; **"So God created man in his *own* image, in the image of God created he him; male and female created he them."** (43) **"And God saw every thing that he had made, and, behold, *it was* very good."** (44) "The first chapter of Genesis is the spiritual record of creation that Jesus saw, but what happens in the second chapter?"

"I don't know," she admitted.

"It says, **'But there went up a mist from the earth, and watered the whole face of the ground.'** (45) What does a dense mist do?"

"Obscures your view of what is real."

"Correct, and then the record continues, but it has changed from the spiritual, perfect record of creation, into a material and limited viewpoint. **'And the LORD God formed man *of* the dust of the ground, and breathed into his nostrils the breath of life; and man became a living soul.'** (46) Why would God create man a second time? The first one was perfect."

"So, are we living a lie?" she gasped.

"Unless you can see God's Kingdom on earth as well as in heaven, you are definitely living a lie. Jesus and his followers understood the real record of creation, saw the perfection, and brought healing to those suffering. I know your mother caught glimpses of the real world too when she healed and protected others."

"Thank you, Brother Lance. I'll hold on to the image

of God's Kingdom throughout this trial of mine."

He laughed, "Bless you, my child, I love hearing that."

"I think it gave me the support I need to talk to my father."

"Now?"

"Yes, I need to finish it. I need to be honest with him now that I know what happened."

"But you might lose the baby, then no one will know." Lancelot pleaded.

"I would know, and that wouldn't be honest or honorable. I'll see you later," she turned and walked away.

"Do you want me to go with you?" he called out.

She just shook her head and kept walking toward the castle.

Chapter 29

The Confession

Thaney searched through the hallways until she found the king talking with his personal guards. "Father, I need to speak to you privately."

Lines creased his forehead. "Excuse us." The guards filed out, and Thaney bolted the door. "Must be serious," he grumbled.

"It is, I found out what happened to me. You're going to have to kill me."

His jaw went slack for a moment. "What? You told me that you never were with a man!"

"I did not lie; I never loved a man or gave my affections to one. However, if I am pregnant, It is either going to be a virgin birth like Christ Jesus, or I was apparently drugged at some point. I have no recollection of any experience with a man."

"No one can be born of that God; he doesn't exist, those Christians filled your head with fairy tales," he shouted. "I'll have them flogged. When did this happen? Who was the blighter? Was it that puny Owain?" I'll have him beheaded; he thundered as he hit a table with his fist.

"I've told you, I don't know, and I'm not going to guess and let you kill an innocent man. I came here to tell you the truth, and I've done that. Pass sentence on me or leave me alone." She spun and reached to unbolt the door.

"Stop, wait a minute. Let's discuss this calmly," he took a deep breath. "I believe you; you're like your mother. She never lied to me either. So, you don't know who did this to you?"

"No," she spat.

"Could it have been Percy?"

Thaney paused for a moment in surprise. *I wish I could say yes, but that would be a lie.* "No."

King Lot vigorously rubbed his hands across his temples. "Why do these things happen? You are my daughter, and I will always love you. All right; you have been honest with me. It is in my power to delay the sentence until the pregnancy is undeniable. I will wait to see if your stomach grows in the next months. I will wait as long as I can and then I must decide on your fate, my darling." He took a strip of leather off a peg in the wall and wrapped it around her belly. Then he took his dagger and sliced a line where the end came to. "There, now we will have proof either way."

Thaney felt as though she was living under the Sword of Damocles as the days rolled by. Her belly did get fuller, and she tried to hide it under larger clothes. Nearly eight months later, Thaney was sitting at the Widow's Cottage when someone knocked on the door. A solemn Lancelot opened it, and the king, Oberon the pagan wizard, and Percy entered.

"Show time," Percy said, but quieted after he received a severe look from the king.

King Lot sighed, pulled the leather strap from a pouch and slowly wrapped it around his daughter's waist. Frowning, he stepped away. "I'm afraid it is the news we feared. She is larger."

Oberon cackled, "We knew that months ago. You have delayed judgement on the princess long enough.

"Change the law; it needs to be changed when the girl has done no wrong." Ezra cried out.

"He cannot change the laws of our fathers," Oberon spoke up with a dark smile.

"He could renounce your false gods, become a Christian, and save his innocent daughter's life."

Oberon hissed with an evil smile, "He vowed on his life to follow our gods and laws when he became king. I crowned him. He knows his life is forfeit if he breaks that covenant."

The king stood silently for a few moments, "I agree it should not punish the innocent, but the law was not written that way. It punishes the acts, not the unintended consequences," the king continued with a weak voice. "I have no alternative other than to pass the traditional sentence."

"I understand, I am ready. Don't worry, Father. God will protect me." Thaney said with quiet determination. ***"Deliver me from mine enemies, O my God: defend me from them that rise up against me."*** (47)

"You will be led to the highest mountain in this region and thrown from that crest to lie at its base, broken and dead," tears streamed down the man's face as he continued, "Do you understand?" as his legs gave way, Lancelot helped him stand.

"That's the mountain called Traprain Law. Have you seen it? Percy leered.

Thaney ignored Percy and smiled, "Father, it's all right, it's God's will. He will protect me."

"That I want to see," Percy said gleefully.

"The sentence will be carried out in one week's time, I'm sorry, it is our ancestor's law," the king whimpered and wiped at his eyes as Lancelot helped him sit down on a nearby bench.

"Until that time, you will be held in the castle's dungeon. Maybe we can have some fun," Percy added with a wicked leer.

Lancelot lunged toward Percy, but the king was closer; he sprang to his feet and delivered a crushing blow to the man's jaw that produced a loud crack. Sir Percival collapsed in a heap as several of his teeth rattled across the floor. Oberon frowned.

"He shouldn't have said that. She's still my daughter, and she isn't going to be imprisoned," the king wheezed.

"Sire, I'm impressed, you certainly improved that cockroach's smile." Lancelot grinned.

"I'm sure I broke his jaw, too. I've wanted to do that for a long time. He's such a blowhard. Would you mind dragging him down to my dungeon? I need to decide on his punishment."

"My distinct pleasure, sire."

Ezra jumped up and bent down to grab one of the man's arms. "Let me help take out the trash."

As they dragged Percy out the door, Thaney put her hand on her father's shoulder and felt him tremble. "It will be all right, Father, I promise.

"How could it be all right? I am about to lose you, the living image of your mother." Tears flew from his eyes as choking sobs filled his throat.

"You will still have Gawain. He'll make you proud," she said with a forced smile. "Do you want me to walk you back to the castle?"

The king took a few deep breaths to compose himself. "No, Oberon come along," he walked toward the door and turned with a pained expression. "I hope to see you at dinner this evening."

"Of course, Father," she watched them walk away until Oberon glanced back, and she quickly closed and bolted the door. Stumbling over to her grandmother's bed, she collapsed, crying.

Knuckles rapped on the door sometime later, and she pulled herself upright. "Thaney, open the door," Lancelot called.

"I'm coming." Her head ached as she walked to the door and released the iron bolt."

Lancelot's concern was etched in his face, "I'm sorry, I thought your father would have stayed with you until we returned."

"He will see us at dinner," she replied quietly.

Ezra took her hand and led her back to bed, "Rest awhile, my child. I will watch, and Lancelot will protect us."

"For the LORD *is* our defense; and the Holy One of Israel *is* our king." (48) Lance said.

Chapter 30

A Gang Stopped

"Is that you, Oberon?" Percy mumbled painfully as he clung to the rust-covered bars of his cell.

"It is."

"Please help me."

"What would you have me do? I can't fix your stupidity." Oberon laughed. "You don't care what others think. You deserved what you received."

As Percy clenched his jaw in anger, pain surged. "Gaawwhh!"

Oberon walked up to the bars and sneered at him. "My advice is to rest, practice appearing humble and contrite, and only eat thin soup until your jaw mends," he chuckled. "Then you can plan your revenge, my friend," his scratchy voice echoed as he turned and walked through a doorway to his lair.

———•●•———

Thaney led the two monks into the dining area. Her father was already seated with his red-rimmed eyes filled with sorrow. "Evening Thaney, please sit by me," he announced.

When she sat down, Gawain hurried over and grabbed her arm. "I don't want you to leave."

"What?"

"Father said you are leaving us," as tears welled up in his eyes.

She glanced at her father, who averted his eyes. "Don't worry, I'm not leaving yet, and you need to concentrate on becoming a strong, fearless knight. Here, sit by me."

Oberon walked into the room, followed by a large group of chattering locals who stared and pointed at Thaney.

"Wizard, what is the meaning of this mockery?" the king stood and thundered. "I want these people cleared from the castle."

Oberon ignored him as he calmly turned and addressed the crowd. "Take your seats now. Dinner will be served soon."

King Lot turned purple with rage, but Oberon raised a hand to stop him. "These are our friends and followers who must be allowed to visit as guests of the castle after you declare a sentence of death. This week of celebration was also written into our fathers' laws; did you forget your majesty?"

Thaney could tell that her father had forgotten as he glared at the gathering of pagans with his fists clenched. Finally, he took a long breath and sat down. "I'm sorry," he whispered to her.

Thaney nibbled at some bread and a few vegetables. Conversation was impossible as the raucous visitors emitted waves of gaiety that echoed off the stone walls. She knew she was the focus of the crowd's derision. After enduring the humiliation for nearly an hour, she asked to be excused. Lancelot and Ezra accompanied her back to her room.

"Will you be all right?" Lance asked as she started to close the door.

"Yes, I'm going to read Martin's scroll again until I

can sleep. Thank you for your support. I'll see you both in the morning."

———•●•———

As they reached the end of the hallway, Lancelot turned to Ezra, "You go back to the cottage. I'm going to stay here for a while."

"Trouble?" Ezra asked.

"Only if they try to harm her," he grinned as he leaned his staff against the wall and sat down. The single torch that had been providing light for the passageway burned out before he finally fell asleep. Suddenly, he woke up, noticing sounds of muffled laughter and a faint glow growing brighter at the entrance of a spiral staircase nearby. Words drifted up to his ears as he grasped his only weapon and pulled his cape's hood down over his face. He heard low voices, "She's going to die anyway; we might as well have some fun with her, right, boys?" Holding his staff horizontally, he squatted before the arched doorway. As the torch came into view, he exploded forward. The two men leading the group were caught in their bellies by his staff and thrown into the air by the thrust of his attack. They hovered there for a split second before crashing down on the men following them. The torch extinguished as it smashed against the stone wall. Screams of agony and pain mingled with the sounds of bodies rolling down the steep stone steps.

Lancelot felt himself smile in the darkness. *I will need to do serious penance for this.* He heard shouts and the sounds of men running in armor. Quickly feeling his way down the dark passage, he found Thaney's door and knocked loudly. "Thaney, it's Lancelot, let me in." In a few moments, the door rattled and opened.

—————•●•—————

"What happened?" she asked as he rushed past her.

"Close the door, I escorted some of your visitors away," as he ran over and rolled beneath her bed to hide.

Thaney did as she was told and crawled back into her bed, just as someone pounded loudly on the door.

"Thaney, are you all right?" her father's voice cried.

"Yes, I'm in bed. Is everything good?"

"Can you open your door?"

"Just a minute," she said, trying to sound sleepy as she removed the locking board again.

King Lot strode in wearing his night clothes. "Did you hear or see anything? Apparently, a group of Oberon's visitors was creeping up the tower stairway and tripped or fell over each other. I think some of them might have died, and the others must be injured," as he looked around the room and then out the small window.

"Oh no," she brought a hand over her mouth. "I didn't hear anything."

"All right, but I am going to station a guard outside your door."

"Really, Father? Let me just bar it shut again. No one will get in. If they try, I'll scream, and the guards will come running."

King Lot thought for a moment. "My brave little princess," he said proudly. "All right, but lock it as soon as I leave."

"I will, Father. Good night."

"I hope so," he replied.

Thaney slid the board back into place, crawled into bed and whispered. "Lance, you'd better wait a while before you leave." In a few moments, she heard him snore.

Chapter 31

Oberon's Partner

"Thaney," the whisper came.

She shook herself away from a dream and stared into the darkened room. "Yes."

A large shadow moved away from the window. "I think things have settled down now. I'd better make my exit before morning. Can you please check the hallway for stray eyes?" Lance uttered.

"Of course." She swung her legs out of bed and pattered over to the door. She lifted the locking board out of its braces and quietly set it on the floor. Then she pulled the heavy door open enough to stick her head out. The passage looked empty. "Let me check the stairwell," she said as she crept over to the archway and peered down into the darkness, before retracing her steps to her room. "I didn't see anyone."

"Good, I hope to see you at breakfast. Make sure you bar your door," he said as he silently glided past her.

As he approached the stairwell, he heard a thin, scratchy voice, "I think she's a little young for you, isn't she, Sir Lancelot?"

He stopped in his tracks, seething. "I understand that all kinds of vermin crawl through these old castles at night. Good to hear from you, Oberon. Step out where I can see you."

"No, my friend, you might do something hasty. No, I

don't want what happened to my friends to happen to me, but who knows, it might happen to you sometime." A laugh crackled and echoed off the walls as it receded in the darkness.

Lancelot strained to hear anything in the silence that followed. *I should have expected that. That little wizard is cunning; I'll have to be more careful.* He soundlessly moved down the staircase until his left sandal slipped and he fell down onto a wet step. He was angry with himself. *Of course, there is blood still on the steps. I hope no one heard me.* Just then, a faint cackle came from below, and he cursed silently.

Stepping more carefully, he continued down to the first floor. It was a moonless night with heavy fog, and he easily evaded the guards wandering about the courtyard. He crept close to the horse stalls and found a water trough for the horses beside the wall. Reluctantly, he took off his robe and slowly swirled the lower part around to wash the blood out. Pulling it out, he tried to wring it out the best that he could before laying it across the broad back of a warm horse to dry a bit. Then he found the pile of grass hay and burrowed into it for a few more hours of fitful rest.

A rooster crowed at first light and woke him up. He retrieved his coarse robe and slipped it on, trying to ignore the dampness. *What a night.* He waited, hidden behind a straw cart, until the guards opened up the main gate for a cart delivering vegetables and grains for the kitchen. He quickly slipped outside the walls as it rumbled past. Making his way to the cottage, he rapped on the door, "Ezra, let me in."

Ezra quickly opened the door. "Where have you been? I was worried all night." As Lance brushed past, he asked, "Why is your robe wet?"

"A long story, my friend. Let me have an hour or so of sleep, and I'll tell you about it."

—•●•—

"Who's there?" Percy mumbled painfully as he raised his head from the splintered wooden bench that served as his bed.

"Percival, my friend, would you like to do me a favor?" the voice hissed.

"Yes, anything," he answered, holding the side of his jaw with tears in his eyes.

Percy heard a key rattle in the lock, and the door swung open. Oberon was holding a large flagon as he stepped into the cell. "Here, drink this. It will make you feel better and stronger soon. Is there anything else you need?"

"Blankets, it is freezing down here. How do you stand it?"

"I have become used to the chill, but I will see to it my friend. For now, keep drinking my elixir, and you will soon grow stronger."

"And the pain?"

"It should diminish as soon as you empty this mug. I'll bring another one as soon as you do."

It looked to Percy like the dark wizard was trying to conjure a warm smile onto his wrinkled face, but the wicked glint in his eyes betrayed his lips. He hesitated for a moment, and then he put his mouth to the vessel and drank a few painful sips. "Ahh, that's awful."

"It is very bitter at first, but the taste will grow on you, and it will end your pain."

"Why are you helping me?" Percy rasped.

"I have always known you are a brother spirit. We have the same dreams and aspirations for this kingdom. I know you want to be king, and I want to help you," Oberon whispered.

"Why?'

"Because together, we can defeat the surrounding kingdoms, plunder this country, and live out our wildest dreams. Everything that I tried to convince King Lot to do, but his stupid bride swayed him from my grand plans, and made him desire peace with his neighbors," he spat.

"So, you poisoned her?"

The wizard's eyes opened in surprise and narrowed again with a warning hiss, "You will be wise to never mention that speculation again."

Percy almost grinned, but thought better of it, "Your secret is safe with me. I swear to protect my benefactor. How did you know that I want to be king?"

"I read your thoughts. I watched you in the king's presence. You don't even try to disguise your pride and envy. I see your desires and want to help you achieve them. Drink up, my boy, together we will be successful."

His tongue felt a bit numb, and his jaw didn't hurt as much as he raised the cup again. "I'll drink to that."

Chapter 32

Christian Lies

"Good day, Princess," Ezra bowed as he approached the table.

"Hello, my friend. Where is Father Lance?"

"He told me he had trouble sleeping last night," the monk winked. "So, he is catching a few extra winks this morning. I'm sure he'll be up in a few hours. I heard there was a ruckus last night. Did you hear it?"

"No, but Father woke me up and told me about it."

"Where is the king?"

"I'm afraid he decided to sleep late too."

"Did you get much out of reading the scroll last night?" he whispered.

"I got stuck on the first paragraph and read it over and over. Martin wrote, **'For prayer to work, you must look at the spiritual evidence hidden beneath layers of human thought and emotion and strive to understand God's perspective. Every one of my life's questions has been answered through a broadened spiritual understanding.'** The rest of the night, I prayed to see God's perspective."

Ezra nodded, "We are deceived by the material images that surround us. Before that, mankind was blinded by the mist that obscured the true view of God and his ideas. That mist in the second chapter of Genesis continues to hide God's Kingdom from the eyes of this world, and leaves the false impression that people were formed from dust. God is not dust. He is not material. Jesus said, **'God *is* a Spirit: and they that worship him must worship *him* in spirit and in truth.'** (49) He saw the true world of the first chapter of Genesis, where God made everything good, a world of Spirit, not of matter."

A scratchy voice yelled, "Lies, more Christian lies.

This Jesus of yours was a man like any other. He was killed, and a multitude of lies sprouted that he became alive again. Your church is built on lies."

Ezra spun around to face Oberon, who had snuck up behind them. Thaney watched as the little monk appeared ready to strike the wizard. "How many have you healed with your vile incantations? How many people have you resurrected from the dead, wizard? Saint Patrick resurrected scores of men and women, some who had been dead for decades."

Oberon spread his hands as though he were giving a blessing. "Deceit propounded atop more fairy tales. You are victims, my friends. I am truly sorry you accepted that false record of existence. If you want to know the truth of the ages, come and visit me in my sanctum sometime. By the way, princess, I hid in the stairwell and watched Lance leave your room last night after he hurt those innocent villagers. Oh, and I hope you two enjoy your breakfast," as he glided off.

Ezra sat back and sucked in a long breath. "He wouldn't know the Truth if it bit him," Ezra said sourly.

"He makes my skin crawl, the way he sneaks up behind people," she said with an involuntary shudder. "I thought you were going to hit him."

"I would enjoy that, but it's a sin. Thank goodness Lance still breaks a commandment once in a while," a grin spread across his face.

"One of the guards told me three people died, and the others all had broken bones. Did Lance do that to them?"

Ezra took a deep breath and lowered his voice, "Yes, he heard them planning to attack you and took matters into his own hands. That is one monk who still has a bit of the devil in him, and a penchant for protecting the innocent," he added.

"He shouldn't have done that since my life is forfeit anyway. Those poor people," she shook her head sadly.

"Ruffians, murderers, and would-be rapists. Don't feel

sorry for them. Remember, they created that situation. Father Lance prevented a greater atrocity."

"Why did they want to attack me?"

Ezra shook his head sadly, "Some people are taught to destroy and pillage rather than build and share good. That in itself is a crime."

—•●•—

"Oberon. I would speak with you," the king pounded on the door.

"He isn't in there," Percy called out.

"Where is he?" the king demanded.

"I saw him leave. Hard for me to tell, I'm locked in this cage."

"As you should be for threatening my daughter."

"I know, sire, my emotions overtook me when I learned that she was to be killed. I wanted to be close to her. I didn't mean it as an insult to either one of you. Sometimes stupid words just fall from my mouth, and I do apologize to both of you." He bowed his head.

"You seem to be doing quite well after my sock on your jaw. I didn't think you would be speaking so well, so soon."

"Well, sire, truthfully, it still hurts. You gave me quite a jolt, but I do heal quickly. If only I can get rid of this lisp from my missing teeth," he touched his jaw gingerly.

The king laughed, "I'm sorry, my boy, but words can hurt, and I lashed out in fury."

I'm glad you don't know what I'm thinking, or you'd really be mad. Please, sire, the fault was all mine. You protected her honor. Let's leave it at that.

"Have you heard anything about the disturbance last night?"

"No, sire, you are the first person who has spoken to me since I was incarcerated. Was anyone hurt?"

"No one important, just some villagers who fell down the tower steps. Oberon hasn't spoken with you?" The king looked past him, where a flagon was sitting on the floor.

"Oh, I called out to him because I was thirsty. He was kind enough to bring me some water, but he never spoke a word."

"Tell him I wish to see him when he returns," the king said as he turned to leave.

"Please tell Thaney I am sorry for what I said."

"I will," as he hurried up the stairs.

Percy turned back to his bunk and picked up the mug. As he tipped it to his lips, he thought, *I cannot wait to see you locked behind these rusty bars, my king.*

Chapter 33

Ezra Hatches A Plan

That afternoon, Thaney and Ezra walked around the castle and the surrounding landscape calling out, "Lance, where are you?" Finally, next to some bushes by a stream, they heard a response.

"Here I am. What do you need?"

"We needed to know where you were and if you're all right," Thaney replied.

"I need time to fast and pray after last night's ordeal. I should be flogging myself for penance, but I'm building up to that."

"No, don't you dare hurt yourself. You had to do it to protect me, and besides, God doesn't want you to suffer."

"Are you sure about that?"

Thaney hesitated for a moment, **"For we ourselves also were sometimes foolish, disobedient, deceived, serving divers lusts and pleasures, living in malice and envy, hateful, and hating one another. But after that, the kindness and love of God our Saviour toward man appeared,"** (50) God loves you, Lancelot, and Ezra and I love you for protecting me. That is not a sin.

"Maybe not," he replied softly.

"Certainly not," Ezra cried. "You are a protector of the downtrodden. I look at you and see the image of Gabriel, the angel."

Lance brightened at that comment, "Really?"

"Who else could embody that image other than a man like you, who knows war but would rather spread peace? Let's go back to the cottage and discuss it."

"All right," Lance agreed.

They had just returned and sat down when a loud knock sounded on the door. "Thaney, are you in there?" her father's voice rumbled.

"Yes, Father, come in."

The king strolled in, followed closely by Gawain. "Thaney, whenever you are here, I want you to keep this door locked, understand?"

She nodded her head.

"I have posted guards around the perimeter of this cottage, and from now on, I've informed the castle cooks that you will take your meals here until..." his face clouded up. "Until later on," he finally said.

"Why?" she asked.

"I don't want a repeat of last night," he swallowed hard, thinking about it.

"Will Oberon be dining with us tonight?" Lance asked as Gawain pulled on his sleeve for attention.

"Yes, I planned on it. Why do you ask?"

"Because he controls that group of zealots that were going to attack the princess. I don't think we can talk freely around him."

The king brought a hand up to his bearded chin as he considered the words. "He is my trusted advisor, but he does seem to be pleased watching our agony in this foul situation. Perhaps you are correct. I will ban him from the cottage."

"No, sire, that would make us all sitting targets for his dark arts and fanatical followers. We need to give him a distraction to think about. Something that seems important to preserve his safety or power," as he turned and tickled the boy until he squealed.

"His reputation," Thaney said, and then looked

embarrassed.

"Brilliant," Ezra chimed in. "We can dribble a bit of gossip in their pagan ears about him being a fraud that will get back to Oberon. With his pride, it will drive him crazy.

Lance spoke up, "But where can we say the information is coming from? We can't tell them it's a real person, or they might hurt them."

"Are the injured pagans still in the castle?" Ezra asked.

"Yes," the king snorted.

Ezra smiled, "I heard that an old monk lived in a thistle patch west of here. If they search, they might find him at his hovel."

"Your home?" Thaney asked.

"I'm never going back there. I'm going to spread a few rumors with those injured pagans before I leave. I'll tell them I heard the wizard used them and conjured a spell to make them want to attack Thaney, which I think he may have. Oberon will be out beating the bushes to find me, while I travel to visit Father Servanus at his monastery in Culross."

"You are rather devious for a monk," the king smiled. "I believe that might work and give us three or four days of peace. Leave at once, we will be indebted to you."

Lance stopped playing with Gawain for a few moments and whispered something in Ezra's ear. "Really? Thank you." He replied.

"You won't be with me…" Thaney suddenly sobbed.

Ezra folded his arms around her and, through a flood of tears choked, "I'm not a coward, but I can't stay. I need to lead the wizard away from you. God will be with you, and I'll be praying every step of the way for your protection, princess."

"Here, take the scroll and protect it," she reached up to grab it, but he stopped her.

"No," he said. "Whatever happens, you keep that close. Those ideas will protect you. God is everywhere. Remember Eutychus?"

She wiped her eyes and stammered, **"And there sat in a window a certain young man named Eutychus, being fallen into a deep sleep: and as Paul was long preaching, he sunk down with sleep, and fell down from the third loft, and was taken up dead. And Paul went down, and fell on him, and embracing *him* said, Trouble not yourselves; for his life is in him. And they brought the young man alive, and were not a little comforted."** (51)

"You hold on to those words. Our Life is always with God and him alone," as he turned and hurried out the door.

The king sat down next to his daughter and wrapped an arm around her, "I pray your friend is right."

"You pray?" Lancelot's eyes sprang open.

"I do," was all he said as Thaney lay her head on her father's shoulder as a knock sounded on the door, "Food your majesty," a voice called out.

Chapter 34

Oberon's Pursuit

"What?" Percy heard the scream from the wizard's quarters and walked over to his cell door. A jumble of words was flowing at once, but nothing he could understand. The door opened, and several pagans limped away up the stairway.

"Oberon, what happened?" The wizard was seething as he stepped out.

"One of the condemned girl's friends, that little monk, spread lies about me last night," he spat. "I need to find him."

"Let me out, I'll help you search for him."

The man twisted his head slightly, "Yes, that will be a good reason to ask the king for your freedom," as he began to quickly climb the steps.

***

"Father, can I visit my room with you today?" Thaney asked as she ate a muffin.

"I hate to have you exposed to those ruffians, but I imagine you would be safe with me as an escort."

"I would like to volunteer also," Lance said as he lifted a grail of ale to his lips.

The king fastened his eyes on Lancelot, "I don't think that would be a good idea. I have a theory about what happened to those pagans the other night, and it includes you."

"Lancelot suddenly choked and coughed. "Drank too fast," he said sheepishly as someone rapped on the door.

"Enter," the king announced as he rose and placed a hand on his sword.

Oberon shuffled in, "Sire, the small monk Ezra has spread lies about me. I need to find and punish him."

"Is he in the castle?"

"I doubt it, but some of the villagers think they know where he lives.

"Do you need guards?"

"No, your majesty, but I do have a request. Can I take Percival with me? He knows the area where the monk's dwelling is."

"I didn't plan to release him until his hair turned white."

"Please, sire, he would be a great help to me. Besides, he is not fully healed, and a trip on horseback would punish him more than simply sitting in a cell," he grinned wickedly.

"All right, have him let out, but he is your responsibility."

Oberon smiled and bowed, "Thank you, your majesty. I will leave at once," he turned, sneered at Lance, and shuffled out the door.

"I believe it should be safe for you to visit your room this afternoon," the king smiled.

— • ● • —

A key rattled in the lock as Percy woke up.

Oberon swung the door open as the rusty hinges protested, "Wake up, we have work to do. How is your jaw?"

"It feels fine if I don't move it too much. The king released me?" he asked, surprised.

"Yes, you are to help me pursue and punish Ezra the monk. Bend down," the wizard said as he produced a scarf from inside his robe and proceeded to wrap and tie it around

Percy's head. "There, that should hold you together for now. Let's go."

"Can I have a bath first? I can't stand myself."

Oberon picked up a heavy bundle and thrust it into Percy's arms. "No time, but that reminds me. Try to ride downwind of me," he snickered as he led the way up to the courtyard.

They walked to where the stalls were and found a stable boy. "I need two horses saddled at once."

It didn't take long before the young man cinched the saddle on the second horse and led them both over, "Here, sir, need anything else?"

Percy looked into the young eyes that showed a trace of fear. Oberon laughed, "No son, that's all we needed," as he mounted the first horse. "Percy, tie that bundle on and let's go."

Oberon pushed his horse into a trot as he passed the gate, and Percy tried to match his speed. "Snop, swoo down," he tried to scream as each hoof pounded pain into his jaw.

"Sorry, Percy, we aren't going to let the horses walk, but a gallop should give you less pain," as he kicked his heels into the horse's flanks and leaped ahead.

The smoother gait lowered the pain to a tolerable level, and Percy tried to relax a bit. *At least I'm free, but why are we chasing a monk?*

Oberon suddenly yelled, "Ezra spread rumors that I bewitched some of my followers to attack the princess. Several of them were killed, and the rest had broken bones and other injuries courtesy of Lancelot. I can't have my followers believing that I'm working against them and controlling them with my magic. We have to find that monk and take him back to confess."

Percival just nodded as they rode on through the countryside.

"What did you need from here?" the king asked as they stood outside her door.

"I have hidden some things that are from Mother and Ezra, and I want to disperse them to you, Gawain, and Father Lance so they will be preserved." Her father's eyes began to water. "I won't be long," as she slipped through the door.

Removing the loose stone, she took the items out and spread them across her bed. a purse filled with coins, a lock of hair tied with a pink ribbon, a small scroll with the Lord's prayer written in longhand, an ornate silver dagger, the scrap of cloth from Cynde, and the pages that Ezra copied of Martin's scroll. The first three items she folded into a handkerchief for her father, she shoved the dagger into her bodice for Gawain, then she rolled the papers together for Lancelot and tied a ribbon around them. The faded scrap of cloth she gently shoved into her bodice for luck. Looking around her room, she let out a long sigh as tears threatened. She would miss it, but it was going to be wonderful to see her mother and grandmother again. She took a deep breath and pulled the door open. "Here, these are for you, Father."

He took the folded cloth gingerly. She had never seen a look of fear in him before. "These were your mother's?" he said slowly.

"All except some of the coins," she replied as she placed a hand on his shoulder. "Let's go back to the cottage."

He nodded silently and led the way.

Gawain and Lance were wrestling on the floor when they walked in.

"Hey, you two, stop that," she said. "I have something for both of you."

Gawain scrambled to his feet, while Lancelot rolled onto his knees and struggled to get up. "Thanks for rescuing me," he laughed.

"Gawain, I have a very special present for you that belonged to our mother," she dug into her bodice and pulled out the silver dagger. "Never play with this; it is very sharp."

"Wow, Father look," as he cradled the knife and rushed over to show it to the king.

"This is for you, Father Lance," she handed the roll of parchment to him as she looked at her father. "Open yours," she commanded.

He looked like he was going to cry as he carefully unwound the knotted fabric. When he stopped and tenderly lifted the lock of golden hair, the dam burst. The purse, the tiny scroll, and tears fell to the floor as he clutched the ribbon-wrapped tuft to his lips.

Thaney was silent as she knelt and retrieved the fallen items. Lance turned away, and Gawain played with the dagger. "Are you all right?" she asked, knowing that concern was etched on her face.

A faint nod was her answer as the man continued to agonize for a few minutes before he could regain his composure. "I will be. I just miss her so much," he said as he reached out for the two other items. "Her purse and what's this?" he said, fumbling to open the rolled paper.

"The Lord's prayer, Father, written by mother's own hand."

He dropped his hands and looked deep into her eyes, "I wish I could believe in your God, but I don't understand why she died. I don't think she understood. I guess I'll never know."

Lance was reading the sheets of parchment and glanced up at the king. "I swear I will try to find the reason King Lot or die trying."

"Thank you, but even my wizard couldn't tell me why. I fear I shall never know."

Lance spoke up, **"For there is nothing covered, that shall not be revealed; neither hid, that shall not be**

known." (52)

"Who said that?" the king asked.

"Jesus told a crowd that."

"I wish I could believe his words," the king muttered.

Thaney watched Lancelot's eyes sparkle, "You can believe mine; I keep most of my promises he said with a sly smile."

Chapter 35

One Day Left

Thaney rolled over as morning sunlight assaulted her eyes—*one more day to live.* The thought plagued her again as it had throughout the night. "No, God is my life. I won't succumb. **'Father, if thou be willing, remove this cup from me: nevertheless not my will, but thine, be done.'** (53)
I will follow in our master's footsteps, and place my trust in you, Father," after thinking a few moments, she added, "Father/Mother God who is Love and Life." Reluctantly, she crawled out of bed and dressed. That feeling of unease washed over her, and she ran to the nearest window to retch, surprising one of the guards standing by some bushes nearby. "Sorry," she said as she ducked back inside.

"Princess, are you up?" Lancelot asked through the door.

"I suppose so," as she forced herself to glide into the room. "Beautiful day, I pray it isn't my last one," as she pirouetted in front of him.

He looked glum with a knowing smile, "I did all night, too."

"So, what should we do to celebrate life today?"

"We shouldn't waste our time sleeping, although I feel like it," he grinned.

"Maybe father will have a suggestion," then she added,

"Do you have any idea how to find out why mother died?"

"I know a place I want to search."

"Where?"

"The wizard's lair."

She felt herself smile, "We can do that today, while Oberon is looking for Ezra."

"Now wait just a minute."

"I'll be the lookout while you search. It'll be fun."

Lance pulled in a deep breath, "Yes, it might be fun at that."

The king and Gawain arrived for breakfast but didn't leave. Hours stretched on until Thaney announced that she was going to take a nap. The king said he understood, but it was another half hour before he finally left.

"This situation is killing your father."

"Not to mention me," she quipped.

"You know what I mean. You need to change into other clothes. Are there any work clothes here?

"Let me check the servant's room." She came back in a few minutes. "She was kind enough to leave an outfit."

"Perfect. Are you ready to go?"

"I follow you, commander," as she gave him a Roman salute.

Lancelot rolled his eyes and slipped out the door, "She needs to talk with her father," he said, pointing over his shoulder. The guard just nodded as they walked past.

They reached the main gate and walked in behind an oxcart as it rolled toward the kitchen. "Down." Lance said and pointed, "Behind those barrels."

Thaney peeked out and saw Gawain run down the steps chasing a little girl. They ran into an open storage area. Lance smiled. "Don't say it, I know what you're thinking."

"Come on, but be careful," he whispered as they crept closer to the main edifice. "This is much easier at night. See that small door to the right? That's a corridor that connects to the dungeon stairway." They waited until another cart rumbled past them and walked beside it until they reached the door and entered a dark and dingy hallway. "Be careful, there may be slick spots on the floor, and some of the rocks are sharp.

She nodded and then realized that he couldn't see her anyway in the low light. She followed the sound of his footsteps, feeling her way along the damp, cold walls. Several times, she got too close and collided with him, but he stayed silent. They heard a door open somewhere and footsteps coming toward them. Lance reached back and grabbed her arm, pulling her several steps forward and then, off to the side. It was an alcove; she stretched out her hand and felt a splintered wooden door.

They waited silently until the footsteps passed by, then Lance lifted an iron latch and swung it open. A torch burned below, faintly illuminating steps that led down. "Come on," he whispered as he started descending. She hesitated. "Come on, this was your idea," he chided, and she reluctantly followed him down.

"It smells awful," as she held her nose.

"Oh, the gentle fragrance of stale air, sweat, and human waste. A very rare odor, fill your lungs and enjoy it."

"I'm about to throw up, and not from morning sickness."

"You'll get used to it," as he walked past the rusted bars of the cells toward another door.

Not likely. "Where should I stand?"

"Once I open this door, I'll leave it open a crack and you can watch for visitors," he said as he twisted a bent copper rod in the lock. She heard a snap, and the door swung open. "Come on." They stepped into a large room. The shelves that covered the walls and reached the ceiling were filled with strange objects. A large table sat in the middle of the room with an unlit oil lamp in the center sitting down between tall stacks of dust-covered books. Lance carried the oil lamp over to the torch on the dungeon wall and carefully lit it. Watch the door, he whispered as he returned and set the oil lamp back down in the center of the table.

Thaney crossed over to the door. The oil lamp's flame was blazing now, as she glanced at the shelf beside her. A mummified human head stared at her with empty eyes. "AAAAH!" she yelled and staggered back.

Lancelot was at her side in an instant, wrapping his arms around her. In a calm, easy voice, he said, "We are supposed to be quiet, aren't we?" She nodded her head. "All right now. Don't look at anything in this room, just watch the crack in the door." She nodded again, and he released her.

She could hear him opening and closing books. It seemed like it was taking him forever to find any evidence against the wizard. Finally, he blew out the oil lamp. "Let's go."

He followed her out the doorway and relocked the door with the copper rod. Then he brushed past her with a subtle, "Follow," command. The afternoon shadows had grown longer when he pushed the door to the courtyard open. A minstrel was playing on the main staircase, and all the people were watching him. "Perfect," Lance whispered as he led her unseen out the main gate. Lightning flashed, and a downpour began just as they reached the cottage.

"Did you find anything?" she asked as she shook her wet hair, and thunder sounded.

"I think so, but my French is a bit rusty. I need to find someone to translate for me." He dug beneath his robe and held up a small book with the title: Plantes et Eléments et leurs Poisons Dérivés.

"Plants and Elements and their Derivative Poisons," she announced.

"You are a girl of many talents. Where did you learn French?" he said, surprised.

"The maid for Grandma was from a French family. She taught me enough to talk and write notes to her. It was like a game."

"All I could read was Plants and Poisons," he laughed.

"You think my mother was poisoned?"

"I don't know, but with Oberon, there is a distinct possibility. I'll ask your father some questions when I see him, maybe she and the dark wizard didn't get along. Let's go back to the cottage."

———•●•———

Hours later, two rider's horses slogged through ankle-deep mud as they approached the gate. "Halt." A guard on the wall yelled through sheets of rain as he peered down at the duo.

"I am Oberon, and this is Sir Percival. Are you planning to stop us, so we drown atop our horses?"

"No, sir, of course not. Open the gate quickly," he shouted, and with some grunts and rattles, the heavy door swung open.

They rode over to the stalls and slid off their mounts. "See, I told you that you didn't need a bath when we left. Now even your clothes are clean."

"Yes, my saddle rash is clean too," as Percy grimaced and tugged at the seat of his pants. "We didn't find a trace of that monk."

Oberon's face darkened. "No, and I can't understand why. Where could he be hiding? He hadn't been at that hovel in the thicket for several months. Oh well, I'll take care of my righteous task tomorrow, then we shall search for him again. I hope tomorrow's spectacle of violent death fills our Christian populace with shame and fear," as he turned and sloshed his way over to the nearest door. Percy followed, walking bow-legged and wincing at every step. Once they were in the dungeon, Percy watched Oberon stop and scowl as he stared at the door to his chamber. "Wait," he commanded. Taking a torch from the wall, he knelt beside the lower hinge of his door and felt the small crumbles of wax that had fallen beside it. "Someone has violated my sanctuary," he snarled.

"How do you know?"

"When I leave, I always seal the crack above this hinge with candle wax. Someone has opened it," as he fumbled to remove a cord holding a large key from his neck and opened the lock. "It will take me a while to see if anything is disturbed or missing. Go get us some food and hurry back."

"Yes, sir," Percy said as he waddled painfully away. *First, I've got to find some dry pants.*

Chapter 36

Wolfsbane

"Find anything?" Lance called out.

"This book is filled with all kinds of poisons that sicken or kill in various doses. Poor Mother probably suffered for years before dying if Oberon did kill her," Thaney said as a tear rolled down her cheek.

"We need proof before I avenge her," the monk said sadly. "This book is incriminating, but without notes on how it was administered and by whom, it isn't conclusive."

"There is no extra writing in it, but there was a string placed in this chapter on Wolfsbane. It says that it is a weapon against werewolves and causes people to be excited, sick, and vulnerable to dying. It paralyzes nerves and, if enough is administered, it stops the heart. I remember Mother seemed frantic and desperate at times."

"Sounds like the symptoms fit. He could have administered small doses over the years, so it seemed like a malignant sickness. I wonder..."

"What are you thinking?" she asked.

"Oberon is filled with selfish pride. Could he have confessed his former misdeeds to his new acolyte?"

"Percy? Maybe, I guess."

"He will be my next target. I promise that I will discover if your mother was murdered and bring the perpetrator to justice," he vowed as he stood up.

"Thank you, but I had hoped to be alive to see it," she said as she felt tears begin to flow.

"I pray you will be, princess," as she felt his strong hands lift and guide her to the bedroom. He set her on the bed and walked to the door. He paused and turned, "Never give up on God, Thaney. **'I will say of the LORD, *He is* my refuge and my fortress: my God; in him will I trust. Surely he shall deliver thee from the snare of the fowler, *and* from the noisome pestilence. He shall cover thee with his feathers, and under his wings shalt thou trust: his truth *shall be thy* shield and buckler. Thou shalt not be afraid for the terror by night; *nor* for the arrow *that* flieth by day;'** (54) He will protect you and yours," as he pointed to her stomach. "He turned this sin-filled, violent man into a sinning, somewhat less violent man of God," he grinned, and she couldn't help but smile. He paused. By the way, how is Wolfsbane spelled in French?

"Uh, Tue-loup, why?"

"What does that translate as?"

"Wolf-killer."

"Very appropriate, I'll see you tomorrow," as he left her room.

She was awake most of the night, tossing and turning, and praying that her premonition of falling from the cliff and suddenly floating was going to come true. She declared her innocence over and over as she fought shame and the fear of death. She had fallen into a deep sleep when a knock came on her door.

"Thaney, are you up?" her father's voice called softly.

"Hello, not yet."

"Can I come in?"

"Yes," as she gathered the blankets over her.

The door opened slowly, and her father crept forward. "I didn't see you yesterday. I spent most of the day in bed, too sick with sorrow to move."

"Don't worry, Father, God is in control, and I can never

be separated from Life, because He is Life."

"Lance asked me questions about Oberon and your mother when I came in. I know the wizard hated her religion as much as I did, but I don't think he would have dared to kill her.

"I hope not, but I know Lancelot won't rest until he finds out for sure."

Her father shook his head sadly, "I just want you to know how sorry I am. I know you don't deserve this fate, but I am constrained by tradition."

"Is Gawain here?"

"No, I have a nurse woman tending to him. I don't want him to witness…"

Suddenly, she was mad as her hands formed into fists, "Stop it, I have forgiven you. I am ready to face and conquer whatever the future holds for me and this child in my belly. Let me get dressed, and let's get this over with."

His eyes opened in surprise. He nodded silently, rose, and left the room.

She heard the voice of Oberon begin talking to Lance and her father as she finished dressing. As she strode into the living area, the conversation stopped. "Is breakfast here yet?"

"I didn't think you'd be hungry," her father said.

"Why not? You don't expect me to get tossed off a mountain on an empty stomach, do you? I'm going to the kitchen," she announced as she walked past them into the sunshine and into a group of pagans that stood with open mouths outside the cottage. "Out of my way, I'm hungry," she commanded as she strode forward.

Lance, her father, and a guard suddenly brushed past her and created a pathway through the crowd as she marched forward toward the castle.

"Are you done?" her father finally asked as he stared at several empty platters.

"Yes, I feel much better now," she said as she patted

her mouth with a napkin. "I'm ready to go."

"Finally," Oberon announced with indignation. The king quickly shot him a glare that silenced him.

The king stood slowly and marched out the door toward the great hall. Lancelot stood up and offered his arm to her. As they entered the hall, palace guards pushed the crowd of onlookers back.

"My subjects. You are aware of my sad obligation to our forefathers. To uphold their laws that were conceived without regard to extenuating circumstances, but only facts and punishments. Today, my only daughter will allow herself to submit to one of those laws. She was found to be pregnant, but cannot verify who or how this calamity occurred. I say now as a father that she tells the truth, although I cannot change the law nor the verdict," he paused for a moment before continuing. "She will be transported to the top of the mountain called Traprain Law and cast off the precipice to find death waiting below for her body." He turned and asked solemnly, "Do you, the accused, have anything to say?"

Chapter 37

The Fall

She saw Oberon looking gleeful beside Percy. "Yes, I do," as she watched the wizard's wide smile fade to a sneer. "I am honored to give myself to this punishment. Not because I'm guilty, but to help take away this world's guilt. The Egyptian pharaoh's words were false when he uttered the statement; **"Now therefore forgive, I pray thee, my sin only this once, and entreat the LORD your God, that he may take away from me this death only."** (55) Those words ring true in my heart and soul. You people have faith in a multitude of false gods. Oberon has lied to you," a loud chatter came from the crowd, and she raised her voice. "There is one God of whom all things are possible. **'For *there is* one God, and one mediator between God and men, the man Christ Jesus;'** (56) God of Jesus, deliver me from death. Keep me from harm under the shadow of your wings. I promise to deliver this child that I carry as a gift to You, and to this world," she stepped back and smiled as her father looked dumbfounded, and the wizard looked furious. She mustered a wide smile and looked upward, **"Father, forgive them; for they know not what they do."** (57)

"Look at her, she doesn't even know who her father is anymore," Oberon yelled, and the sounds of derision rose in the crowd.

"You're the one who doesn't know the one true

father," Lancelot snarled.

"Enough," the king cried, and motioned them out the doorway.

A group of guards quickly encircled her and Lance as they made their way out of the great hall. The crowd became enraged after hearing her comments, and several attackers came close to breaching the wall of escorting soldiers. They walked across the courtyard where Thaney crawled into a waiting oxcart with the king, Lance, Oberon, and Percy. A driver on the ground waved a switch in the air, and the animal plodded toward the castle gate. Guards ringed the cart and violently cleared a path through the protesters. Once outside the castle walls, the driver urged the animal into a trot, and the horde of people followed more respectably. Although, once in a while, a villager would yell or scream when they were beaten by a soldier. Less than an hour later, the road began to climb upward toward the crest of the mound.

Lancelot raised his voice, "Let me out. I want to run to the base of the cliff at the other end of the hill." He winked at her as he clambered out of the cart and began to lope through the tall grasses.

Now she was left alone, surrounded by a crowd of unbelievers as the cart jostled and bumped up the hill. She retreated into the stillness of prayer, striving to feel at one with the Love that is God.

"We're here," her father said softly as the cart came to a jerky stop. She opened her eyes and looked at the view. It was beautiful with the blue ocean twinkling in the distance. Several guards assisted in her climb out of the cart.

The wizard announced loudly, "Beautiful, isn't it?. Take a closer look. It's over seven hundred feet straight down.

She walked over toward the cliff top as the villagers crowded around her. A gentle breeze was blowing. A row of shaggy bushes stood like a fence along the edge. She held onto the jagged bark of one as she peered cautiously over the edge. Far below, she saw a tiny figure in a brown robe, kneeling in prayer. *Thank you for your thoughts, Lancelot.*

Oberon puffed up his chest, "Let this be a lesson to all who disbelieve in our gods. Our gods are powerful, and if you refuse them, you will be severely dealt with."

"Your gods don't exist," Thaney spat.

"Let's get this done," Oberon snarled as he grabbed her wrist and pulled her a few feet away from the edge. "Percy, help me."

She didn't struggle as Percival took hold of her other wrist. She thought he mouthed, "I'm sorry." Glancing over her shoulder, she saw her father holding onto the cart for support as tears flowed from his eyes.

"Now." Oberon cried, and she was suddenly pulled and flung forward by the two men, bursting through the bushes and falling. *This is like my dream. I wonder if the lady is here?* As gravity pulled her down, she toppled end over end as her garments swirled in and out of her vision. The airflow increased, and her eyes blurred and watered as the rock-studded ground below rushed into view. She thought of the phrase in Psalms, ***"They shall bear thee up in their hands, lest thou dash thy foot against a stone."*** (58) A strong wind increased her discomfort, and she closed her eyes tightly against the blast as it suddenly increased.

The cart and its procession of villagers arrived at the base of the cliff nearly an hour afterward. The king raised his fist, stopping the procession when he saw Father Lance smiling and sitting next to a jumble of white fabric that began to stir. When Thaney stood up, half of the villagers fled in terror. She helped Lance stand up and walked slowly toward the cart. Her father stood with white knuckles, holding onto the wooden stanchion while Oberon and Percy silently huddled in the rear.

"Hello, Father, your grandson and I are fine," she said as she patted her belly. "Can Lance and I get a ride home?"

Speechless, the king just nodded.

The villagers who remained watched in awe as Thaney and Lance climbed aboard. King Lot nodded again, and the driver urged the animal in a wide circle, turning the cart around. Oberon and Percy's faces were painted with a mixture of fear and confusion.

"How?" her father finally mouthed.

"God," was the short answer she gave. When his brow furrowed, she continued, "I was falling, until a strong wind hit the bottom of the cliff and pushed upward. It blew hard enough to slow my descent, and I landed softly on the rocks. Then it dwindled and stopped."

Her father looked horrified and relieved at the same time. "What in the world could have caused that?" he wondered out loud.

"The breath of God, protecting the innocent," Lance smirked, glaring at a red-faced wizard and a white-faced Percy.

"Amazing," was the last word of the king until they arrived back at the castle.

Chapter 38

Spreading Lies

The door leading to the dungeon slammed shut behind them as they descended the steps. "What trickery was that?" Percy demanded.

"I don't know, let me think," Oberon hissed, as his hand slid down the rock wall to steady his steps. "I've never seen or heard anything like it." He was quiet until he reached his doorway. "But that isn't our problem at the moment. Lancelot said she was innocent. We have to make the people believe that it was a trick, that she is sorceress and a worker of evil like her mother was. We have to destroy her now, or the people may start to believe in her God."

"What can we do?"

"You go up and spread the word that she is a witch, working to trick and deceive the villagers and peasants. Tell them she survived the fall by practicing the dark magic she learned from her mother. Say, perhaps she transformed herself into a Raven to survive the fall? Paint her as a corrupter of men, tell the women that she is a vicious siren who will use her dark powers to draw all men to her, destroying the love in their lives."

"And you?"

"After you spread those tidbits of information, I will come up and preach my 'truth' to them. My words will be to protect them and to keep her from summoning demons, evils, and plagues to punish them for throwing her from the summit of Traprain Law. We must destroy her quickly, my friend, or she will destroy us."

———•●•———

"It is inconceivable. I can't understand why you weren't killed," the king shook his head in disbelief as they sat down in the cottage.

"My fall slowed as a great wind engulfed me near the base of the mountain. It was like a dream I had where I stepped through bushes into space, falling end over end. But in my dream, I stopped falling and just hung in the air."

"That gust of wind blew me over, too. I lay there on my back, watching you float down like a feather. It was beautiful," Lancelot added.

"It's the power of prayer. Like Jesus said, **'And Jesus came and spake unto them, saying, All power is given unto me in heaven and in earth, and, lo, I am with you always, even unto the end of the world.'** (59) Christ is still with us. Prayer saved me from the fall. The power of God is still here to heal and save from the ills of this world and will be until this world is eventually transformed from concepts of matter into spiritual understanding."

The king stared at her blankly. "Your words are confusing and meaningless to me. I'm just grateful that your life was spared."

"I wasn't worried about death, but I am grateful that God used me as a testament to his power for your subjects to see."

"I hope they do see, but I imagine that your experience is being twisted and lied about to deceive them." Lance said, "Oberon will never accept a defeat of that magnitude. He was certain you would be killed."

"Why does he hate my daughter?"

"Because she knows the Truth about God and

mankind. He wields power only because his followers believe the lies he tells them. If they ever understand what she knows, he will be powerless." Lance said seriously. "Your wizard will not give up unless he is dead."

The king shook his head, "She was sentenced to death, but lived through it. The people must see that she is innocent."

Lance stared with sad eyes, "I wish that were true, but I fear Thaney will face another challenge invented by Oberon."

"I will stand up to him. I can't possibly take a chance on losing my daughter and grandson a second time," the king's voice shook as he held her hand.

"It won't be just the wizard father; I also feel your subjects will demand another death sentence for me at his vehement urgings. Be courageous. God will sustain me through whatever challenge I face and deliver me to my perfect place. I'm sure of it."

"You have that same spark of Life that your mother had, but she still died. Somehow, I feel your words are true, but please be vigilant. I'm going to find Gawain and bring him here so we can enjoy the rest of the day as a family."

Thaney saw him wipe a tear from his eye as he rose and left the cottage. "What's our plan?" she asked Lance.

"It seems you will have family time, while I try to find Percival and begin to befriend him."

"You're going to be his friend?"

Lancelot shook his head, "No, but I have to see if he knows that your mother was poisoned. If I can get him to talk, Oberon's wizardry will end abruptly." His mirthless smile made Thaney shudder. "I made you a promise and I intend to keep it."

"Where will you go when this is all over?"

"After you are safe, and Oberon is defeated. I'd like to travel north and stop by the abbey at Culrose to see Bishop Servanus, and Ezra if he's still there."

They stopped talking as the door opened, and Gawain ran and jumped into his sister's arms. Where were you today? I looked for you," he said.

"Really? I should have been easy to find," she smiled, but added a serious note. "If you ever have trouble finding me, know that I am fine and still love you," as she gave him an enormous bear hug until he squirmed free.

"Father is having dinner brought here. Are you hungry?"

Thaney nodded her head as Lancelot slipped by them. "I just remembered an appointment, I'm sorry, but I'll have to miss dinner tonight."

Gawain frowned as he watched the man leave, "I like him, but he never has time to play with me."

"You'd better wash your hands before father gets here," she said, changing the subject. "Then we can play until the food arrives."

The door suddenly opened, and Oberon stood there wearing a wicked smile as she felt a cold chill run up her spine.

Chapter 39

Lancelot Attacked

"Congratulations, princess," the voice hissed as a cold chill passed through her.

She saw the wizard take a step in. Instinctively, she moved in front of Gawain. "Get out of here, I didn't invite you in.

"There are no closed doors to me. I am the number two man in this castle, remember? Besides, I just came by to compliment you on your miraculous survival today," he paused. "How did you do it?"

"I did nothing, **'Let every soul be subject unto the higher powers. For there is no power but of God: the powers that be are ordained of God.'** (60) God saved me.

The wizard took a dirty finger and swirled it in his ear, "I must have missed something. There are so many gods in this world. Which one saved you?"

"Jesus said, **"The first of all the commandments *is,* Hear, O Israel; The Lord our God is one Lord:"** (61) There is only one God, yours don't exist.

A low snarl grew in the man's throat as hatred boiled in his eyes.

"Oberon, what are you doing here? I told you to stay away. Get out and leave Thaney alone," the king thundered as he entered.

Surprised, the wizard quickly turned and left the room,

"As you wish, sire," he spat.

"What did he mean you survived today? Did he try to hurt you?" Gawain's voice quivered.

"No, we just played a game this morning, and I won. Now, what do you want to play until we eat, young man?"

———•●•———

Lancelot crept through the late afternoon shadows of the wall toward a crowd of villagers milling around a few food vendors in the courtyard, while pulling his hood lower over his face. He blended into the crowd by wearing clothes he borrowed from a few bushes where the local washerwomen had laid them to dry in the sun earlier that afternoon. *It's not stealing, I'm going to return them.*

"What are you smiling about?" an obnoxious peasant snarled.

"I smell food," he nodded at the man and took a step forward as a foot darted into his path. He barely avoided tripping over it and forced himself to laugh out loud. "You'll have to be quicker than that, sir. Excuse me, I'm hungry," as he glided past. *No, I'd better not rip his throat out. Might cause a scene.* He felt a smile cross his lips and took a deep breath to calm himself as he pressed deeper into the crowd. He saw Percy talking to several women and edged closer.

"She's a witch. You've heard the stories about her mother. She has bewitched and used men for her own personal whims; that's why she became pregnant," he waited for the women's loud chatter to quiet before continuing. "The daughter has followed in her mother's dark footsteps. Nobody could have survived a fall from Traprain Law, other than a witch," he ended loudly, while the women began to babble excitedly among themselves.

Lancelot hunched over, moved closer, and whispered. "You may be correct, my friend. I have seen and heard things pass between her and her father. Skeletons of the family closet, I fear."

"Really?"

"Aye, you and I should get together and talk sometime. When might you be free?" Lance continued.

"Get away from him." Oberon's voice cut through the noise of the crowd. "Leave us alone, minion of that she devil. Look here, all you people, here is a Christian trying to worm his way into your kind hearts. Trying to create sympathy for a witch who wants nothing but to destroy you all."

Percy opened his mouth, "But he was going to tell me…"

"Silence, Percival. You began to fall under his ghastly spell until I arrived in time to break it. Villagers, protect yourselves. Remember this man who killed and wounded a group of you in the tower? Throw this servant of Satan out of the castle, kill him," the wizard yelled as shouting from the crowd began.

Lancelot felt his skin crawl as he searched for a way to escape the blind wrath of Oberon's followers. There was a loaded hay wagon parked behind the wizard that reached up almost to the wall's walkway. He sprinted forward, hitting the wizard in his chest and driving the smaller man into the ground with his heels. Then he scrambled up the rough wooden rails of the wagon. Several hands grabbed at his ankles, but he kicked them away and rolled over the top rail onto the soft pile of grass. He glanced back and saw Percy lifting the wizard to his feet as he hurriedly waded knee-deep to the other side of the wagon. Balancing on the top rail, he leaped up and grabbed the rock walkway beside the battlements. His sandals clawed for purchase on the rough rock until his elbows were on the walkway and he was able to swing one leg up onto it. In one strained effort, he rolled onto the walkway and stood up.

"Get him, kill him, you fools," Oberon's weak screams rose in the air as Percy steadied the wounded man.

He'll still feel my heels tomorrow. Looking around, he

saw villagers climbing up ladders to the curtain wall walkway and beginning to run toward him. Looking out between two merlons, he saw a forty-foot drop to the hard ground. A large oak tree stood about thirty feet down the wall with branches reaching within ten feet of the battlements. He sprinted forward, jumped atop a crenel, and launched himself toward the top of the tree.

Branches snapped and cracked around him as he fell through a cloud of leaves. Larger branches began to batter him as he fell deeper into its grasp, and he reached out in desperation. His thigh hit a large limb as his right arm hooked over a large branch, and he stopped falling. Suddenly, a rock hit the trunk next to him, and he scrambled across branches to the side of the tree away from the wall. The villagers were screaming curses as a few more rocks were thrown, but at least none of them were crazy enough to try to jump off the wall. *I'm the only one who is that stupid.* He worked his way down to lower branches, dropped to the ground, and ran toward the cover of a nearby thicket.

It was dark before Lance thought it safe to return to the cottage. He watched the guards making their rounds for an hour before he stepped out into the moonlight.

"Halt, who be ye?" The nearest guard called as he pointed his spear.

"I am Father Lance, returning to my quarters at the cottage. Is the king inside?"

"He is. Follow me and I'll announce you."

Lance watched as the other guards began to converge toward them. Alarms rang in his head as he quickly turned and sprinted back toward the woods. "Stop him," the guard with the spear yelled as a dark image appeared before him. It was a giant of a man with a huge broadsword that shone in the pale moonlight.

"Have we met before?" Lancelot said as he slowed to a stop next to a young oak tree. He noticed all the other guards paused too, waiting to watch the spectacle.

"No, I fear we will never again. My master Oberon said kill you," a gravelly voice announced before the man lifted the sword and crashed through low brush edging the woods.

Lancelot stood rooted next to the tree until the giant was footsteps away. "Kill me if you can, varlet." He darted to the side just as the sword cut into the tree, and he felt a shallow slash wound cross his back. *Powerful swing, he must have driven that blade halfway through the trunk.* He thought as he fled into the night.

Hours later, he sat beside a small creek and washed the wound. *I'm getting a bit slow, I guess, but at least it's only a scratch. What happened to Thaney and the king? They might have been taken prisoners.* He felt too tired to form a plan after his run through the forest, so he lay down on his belly in a bed of soft pine needles and fell asleep.

The sun was high in the sky when he awoke, and a grumble from his stomach reminded him that he had missed dinner the night before. His back was a bit sore as he lifted himself onto his knees and stood up. He first cupped his hands and drank from the stream for a few minutes before he decided to follow it. A quarter mile further, he found a large group of blackthorn bushes loaded with purple/black sloe. Then he prayed and gave thanks before wading in to eat. **"Praise ye the LORD. O give thanks unto the LORD; for *he is* good: for his mercy *endureth* for ever."** (62)

Carefully, he threaded his way around the masses of dark spine-covered branches, eating the clusters of berries. His mouth protested as tannins in the unripe fruit dried it out and made it feel like sandpaper, but he persisted until he ate his fill. Then he returned to the stream and drank until the puckering sensation lessened. *Now God, what can I, one man, do to protect Thaney from Oberon and a castle full of guards? First, I have to find the castle again. Where am I?* He walked for hours, trying to find some landmark that he recognized.

"Halt," a voice called, and Lance stopped mid-step as

he slowly raised both hands.

"Who are ye?"

"I am Brother Lance, a monk who is lost," straining to see where the man was, but the forest and bushes were too thick.

"You're not wearing a monk's robes."

"No, I'm not, I fell into a creek and borrowed these until mine dry, but then I got lost."

"Your words do not ring true."

"You're right, but I am a monk, and I did borrow these yesterday to walk unobserved around Hailes Castle."

"Why?"

"Because the wizard there is trying to overthrow King Lot and murder his daughter. Can you tell me where I am, please?"

In a few moments, the voice responded. "All right, drop your hands," as a peasant armed with a crude bow and arrow stood up from behind a bush and stepped forward. "You seek Hailes Castle?"

"Yes, sir," Lance bowed, which brought a look of surprise from the man.

"I'm sorry, no one has ever bowed to me before."

"I bow in gratitude, sir. I need to hurry and help save my friends."

"Yes, well, you're going the wrong way. Hailes Castle is several hours away in that direction," he pointed westward.

Lance looked up and saw that the sun had passed its zenith several hours before, "Thank you, sir, I apologize for interrupting your hunting."

"Don't tell anyone? The king would have my neck."

"My lips are sealed, sir. Good luck and thanks for the directions," Lance said as he totted away.

Chapter 40

Oberon's Vendetta

"Rise and shine, you two. Today is the day of retribution for your crimes," the wizard's voice hissed through the darkness with a note of glee.

"What crimes?" Thaney heard herself say.

Percy emerged from the wizard's lair and lit a torch on the other side of the room. Thaney saw Oberon standing outside of her cell.

"For you, my dear, the crimes of witchcraft and dark magic. For your father, let's say, condoning your actions in the black arts. Turning a blind eye to your evil endeavors against his subjects."

"What are you going to do to him?"

"Nothing. I will keep him confined in these luxurious accommodations until he either acquiesces to my demands or expires."

"He is the king."

"And so, he shall remain as king, but I will make all the decisions from now on. We had a very animated discussion last night after your friend Lancelot tried to infiltrate the locals. Luckily, I arrived in time to drive him away," Oberon coughed and clutched at his ribs.

"What's wrong?" she asked.

"Nothing that won't heal in time. As I was saying, the villagers voted last night after Lancelot ran away. Some of them were in favor of considering you innocent. Others were convinced you were evil."

"I know who convinced them."

"In the end, it was determined by a fair vote that you escaped death at Traprain Law by witchcraft. Thus, it is my sad responsibility to pursue the sentence of death on you and your unborn child," he produced a devious smile.

"I can see it breaks your black heart, magician. Step over here, we'll see who dies." Thaney heard her father yell from the next cell.

"Only thin crusts of bread and a little water for the king Percy, until he comes to his senses."

Thaney saw Percy nod his head. "So, when am I to be killed?" she said defiantly.

"Now," he smiled again as a group of peasants began filing down the steps. "These loyal subjects of mine will escort you to the courtyard. Should I bind your wrists?"

"I don't think so, I see no possible escape for me. How am I going to be killed?" her voice wavered just a bit.

"I thought about that for a long while until an inspiration struck me. I didn't want you killed in this kingdom, because there might be some backlash or lame heroics by unbelievers in our midst, so I told a little white lie." He held two fingers up with a space between them and laughed. "I announced that I would be merciful and allow you to live. That you would be transferred to the custody of Tantallon Castle, where your black magic could never harm us." He clapped his hands together. "But it gets even better. Instead, you and your illegitimate child will take a short sea voyage to the afterlife. Load her into the wagon," he commanded as he twisted the key to open her cell.

Men flooded into her cell and lifted her to their shoulders as she screamed and fought them. She heard her father yell, "Take your hands off her," as the bars of his cell rattled. She glanced at Percy and saw him staring and looking ashamed as the men followed the wizard and carried her up the narrow stairway. The wooden door burst open into the courtyard, and she closed her eyes against the bright sun rays. She heard a crowd of people laughing and yelling as garbage was thrown, and hot tears slid from her eyelids. She screamed, "Don't' believe him, he's a charlatan. His magic lies in delusion. Do you want real magic and miracles in your lives? Then follow in the footsteps of Christ Jesus. God is Love, and he loves all of you."

Oberon's scratchy voice sounded, "Now, one, two, three…," as she was thrown into a wagon with a slight covering of straw. She landed hard on her hip and let a cry erupt from her throat as the villagers cheered, and the wagon lurched forward.

Several men scrambled on and finally helped Oberon climb in with great difficulty. "Leaving Percy behind?" she sneered.

"He is too sentimental at times. He might recall good times with you and cause issues. This way, all my problems are left behind me."

"Until you return," she smirked.

His eyes grew wild as he slapped her hard across the face, "At least you won't be around to see it," he hissed.

"Did you poison my mother?" She stared at him and saw a flicker of panic.

"How did… No, of course I didn't." She saw him bite his lower lip. He turned his back to her as he told the driver to hurry.

She lay down in the thin straw covering the rough boards of the wagon bed as it rattled and bounced. *I know the truth now, my mother didn't want to leave either God. She didn't know that she was being poisoned. Please protect me and my child from the evil one that claimed her. There is no evil in you, Lord, and you are everywhere. Let me know that there is no power that can oppose you. Let me see Oberon as you created him, in your image of perfect Spirit.* In a little while, she fell asleep.

"We are here. Wake up," the scratchy voice assaulted her ears. "I don't understand how you slept all the way."

"Better than listening to you," she smiled as she rubbed sleep from her eyes. "I listened to God."

He glared at her, "Get out."

She climbed over the rail and jumped out gracefully, somewhat surprised that her hip felt fine. A strong sea breeze mussed her hair as she looked at waves breaking on a rocky shore below. "Where are we?"

"The Firth of Forth, an inlet of the North Sea." The other men had to help the wizard down as he reluctantly emitted painful sounds and held onto his ribs. "Are you going to tell me what happened? Why are you in pain?"

"Lancelot knocked me down and stomped on me if you must know. With any luck, my men have tracked him down and killed him by now."

"I doubt that, knowing Father Lance the way I do. Tiny people like you should stay out of his way."

"Take her to the coracles and bring that coil of hemp rope," he sputtered.

They led her down a narrow path winding between boulders toward the sounds of the sea. They followed a sandy path where the rocks became moist as they drew closer to breaking waves. Thaney realized that the tide had recently gone out. She saw several strange hide-covered objects resting atop larger flat rocks that had remained dry. A small strip of pebble beach separated the sea from scattered boulders perched in the shallow water, where the sea spray erupted in a fine mist each time a wave hit.

"Beathan and Eanraig, climb up and pass those three coracles down," Oberon commanded as the men quickly climbed up and carried the lightweight vessels over to the boulder's edge, handing them to the others who carried them to the water.

"Those are boats?"

"Inventions of our ingenious forefathers. A few woven

willow branches and some animal hides can provide a seaworthy boat. Or should I say barely seaworthy," he chuckled. "Tie this one behind the other two."

"Done, master," one of the men grunted after a few minutes as the little boats bobbed in knee-deep water.

"Para and Sachairi, you two take oars and paddle out to the middle of the Firth and then untie yourselves from the princess."

"But I can't swim," one of the men said with fear in his eyes.

"Then don't capsize," the wizard spat, but then added with disgust, "Who else can swim?"

A scrawny peasant raised his hand. "All right, Tormod, take his place."

After the two men were seated and paddling offshore, Oberon continued, "Beathan and Eanraig, place the princess in her royal barge," as he bowed to her.

Before they could move, she walked past them into the frigid surf and clambered inside the last coracle. There was barely enough room for her to lie down in a fetal position, but she wanted to stay low to prevent capsizing.

"Have a pleasant voyage, princess. Feel that strong westerly wind? That should blow you out to the North Sea in no time. Those ocean waves will swamp your tiny coracle, and you will drown where no one will ever find you," the wizard waved and cackled as the rope pulled taut with a jolt, and they headed out to sea.

Her child suddenly gave a strong kick, and she gently rubbed her belly as the craft rolled with the breaking waves. *Never mind, baby, we are leaving our old life behind, but we are traveling with God, and he will provide our protection.* The up and down motion of breaking waves was making her sick, but as the two men paddled away from shore, the swells became more gentle. She started to compose a low, sweet lullaby to her baby.

"As *I wait to hold you close, I made a wish up to a star*

God will protect both of us, and keep us safe from harm.

No matter what the danger, we travel free from fear
God's is always greater, than evil, dark and drear
For our Lord is always guiding, on a safe course, far or near
Toward our destination, Christ's harmony is here."

"I'm tired," she heard one of the men say as he quit paddling.

"Oberon said we had to go halfway across the firth."

"I'm done; otherwise, I won't have enough strength left to make it back to shore, and look, the sky is darkening in the west. If it storms, we'll both die out here."

"All right, let's untie our ropes and we'll leave her here."

Thaney heard the splashes as the men untied the ropes and threw them into the water.

"Have a nice voyage, missy," one called as she heard them paddle away. She felt a gust of wind on her face as the little coracle rode the swells.

"Just the three of us now, little one, you, me, and God.

Chapter 41

Lancelot's Return

Lancelot crept closer to the castle grounds in gathering darkness. There were no lights showing in the Widow's Cottage, and he didn't see any guards posted either. *I hope I don't run into that killer giant.* He sprinted across the open meadow to the front door and slipped in. He felt his way through the parlor until he came to the rear wall and touched his well-worn staff. *At least I have a weapon now, but they must have moved Thaney back to the castle.* Next, he found his habit and slipped it on. He paused and thought for a moment before putting on the peasant's coat again. With a sigh, he exited the cottage and walked toward the dark walls of the castle.

He could hear sounds of a celebration drifting out as he crouched in bushes near the front gate. *Surely, they hadn't killed her already.* He felt muscles tighten throughout his body as he heard plodding hoofbeats approaching. It was a wagon drawn by one horse, loaded with a few men. As it drew closer, he tucked his staff into his waistband. *Now, I hope I'm as good as I once was.* As the front wheels rolled by, he flung himself forward, rolling prone beneath it and quickly grabbed the slide bar before he swung one leg over the reach beam. He hung there as the wagon bumped and rolled through the gateway, greeted by welcoming shouts. *Thank goodness it's dark.*

The wagon finally rolled to a stop next to the stable. He waited breathlessly as the occupants exited. Finally, several of them helped a smaller man down among cries of pain and curses. He recognized Oberon's agonized voice. *Maybe my fancy footwork did some good last night for him, but where is Thaney? Am I too late?*

The group moved away from the wagon toward a bonfire on the other side of the courtyard, and Lancelot eased himself down on the ground and rolled away from the crowd. *I've got to find the king, if he's alive.* He crawled alongside the wall to the nearest entry door for the keep and eased it open.

In the darkened hallway, he heard a voice. "About time you showed up, grab a basket of food, and follow me. It's great, ain't it? We have the run of the castle now. Oberon said we can eat what we want and take what we need. Didn't Para tell you to help me?"

"Uh, yes. I just have trouble believing we can do whatever we want. Where is the king?"

"On a trip, he should be back in a few days, but until then, we have the run of the castle. Hurry up, Para and the others just returned and will be hungry.

"I'll be right along, but I need to see the castellan first. He owes me money for the vegetables I brought him last week.

There was a pause, "All right, but please hurry."

"I will," he said as he brushed past the woman and headed toward the main hall. He opened the door to a raucous party going on. A minstrel sang and plucked at a homemade instrument as a crowd of peasants cavorted around the benches and tables. He closed the door quickly. *Where can the king be? His quarters or the dungeon?* A shiver ran up his spine as he hurried through the corridors to the only stairway leading down to the base of the castle. He stopped at the door and eased it open. No noises were coming from below, but there was a dim flickering light from a wall torch as he crept down the rough stone steps. When he reached the bottom, he walked to the cells clustered along the wall. In the third cell, he saw a man's dim form huddled on a wooden bench. "Pssst, sire, King Lot, is that you?"

The form moved slightly and coughed. "Sire, it's Lancelot," he whispered as the man's head popped up.

"Lancelot? Oberon gave orders to have you killed."

"And yet, here I am. Where are the keys for the cells?"

The king stood up and steadied himself by hanging onto the rusty bars. "In Oberon's quarters, but Percy is guarding them."

"I've missed him. This should be fun," Lance winked. "Be back in a minute or two," he grinned as he walked up to the heavy wood door and knocked. "Oberon sent some wine and food down for ya," he said in a high-pitched voice.

"It's about time, I'm starving," a slurred voice responded as a key rattled in the lock.

Lance didn't wait; he burst through the door, and the man flew across the room, hitting his head on a heavy oak support beam. He lay moaning and holding his head on the stone floor.

"Good day, Sir Percival. I need to have a word with you, but first let me release the king," as he grabbed the ring of keys from the door and headed back to the cells.

Percy somehow staggered to the door, "It wasn't my fault. He threatened to kill me if I didn't help him," he pleaded.

Lance unlocked the cell and helped the king walk over to the steps, "Oberon is in the courtyard, and peasants are everywhere in the castle. Can you sneak up to your quarters and stay there until I call for you?" The king nodded his head as Lancelot took his filthy jacket off, "Here, wear this so you blend in."

"Thank you, Sir Lancelot. That title is not undeserved," as he pulled on the coat, gritted his teeth, and headed up the stairs.

Lance looked up toward Oberon's doorway, where Percy still clung to the door frame. "Percy, we have a few things to talk about." The man's shoulders fell as he shrank back into the room.

When he entered, Lance stopped and locked the door, pocketing the heavy key ring.

"I swear he forced me," the words quivered in the air.

"Just relax, I'm not here to punish you. Hey, do you have any more wine here?" Lance asked, smiling. *You are one drink away from passing out. Just where I want you.*

Chapter 42

A Drink With Percy

"One bottle left," Percy slurred, moved to a nearby shelf, returned, and set the bottle on the table with shaky hands.

"What should we drink to?" Lance asked as he tapped around the seal with a small hammer until the wax was exposed, pulled the wax stopper out, and hoisted the bottle in the air. "And flagons?"

Percy pulled two dusty tankards down and handed them to Lance. "To the king?" he murmured.

"To the king." Lance raised his vessel, and they both drank. "I'm glad you made that toast, Percy, because there are some terrible rumors being spread that the wizard killed the queen gradually with poison. Did he ever discuss that with you?"

Percy looked ready to bawl as he nodded almost imperceptibly.

"It was wolfsbane, wasn't it?"

"I don't know, he didn't tell me what he used, just that it was poison. He'll kill me for telling you." He clenched his lips tight.

"Don't worry about Oberon," Lance said with a relaxed smile. "After tonight, his wicked reign is over. Refill?" He poured more into Percy's flagon.

"How will you defeat him? He has powers. The villagers will do whatever he asks. He made my jaw feel better." Percy's eyes were wide.

"Did he bring back the teeth that you lost?

Percy shook his head sadly.

"I'm a man of God. I give you my word that I'll be gentle, very gentle with the wizard," as he rose, unlocked the door, and extinguished the only torch illuminating the dungeon. "Do you want to watch?"

Percival's head shook back and forth, and he spilled some of his wine.

"I need to find something now. Stay here and wait for me." He closed the door and locked it.

"You don't trust me?" Percy whimpered.

"Of course I do, I locked that door in case the wizard comes back before I find what I need. Just relax, I'll try to hurry.

Then he lit a candle as he began to search through the aisles of shelves and he read countless dusty bottle labels. Finally, he smiled and slipped one into his robe.

"I found what I wanted, Percy. If you don't want to watch the festivities, go and stay in Thaney's room until I call for you. Here, take this bottle with you and be careful walking up those steps in the dark. I don't want you to fall and break it, or you," he said as he unlocked the door and stepped into the dungeon.

"What's in it?"

"A gift for someone. Hurry and be very careful."

"Thank you, thanks," Percy said as he hurried away.

Lance shook his head. For some reason, he couldn't hate Percy the way he wanted to. *He's like a lost puppy. I hope it's because he's had a change of heart.* Then he returned to the doorway and closed it just enough that a sliver of light escaped and barely illuminated the dungeon. Sitting down, he waited for the fun to begin.

Chapter 43

Thirst Slaked

Thaney awoke with a start; it was raining gently, although a strong wind was blowing and making large waves. *The waves must have lulled me to sleep.* She rubbed her eyes and stared at the water surrounding her in the twilight beneath dark clouds. She couldn't see any land, began to panic, and almost stood up. *No, if I do that, this boat might tip, and we'll drown.* So, she sat quietly and considered the situation. Her throat was dry, and she was thirsty after so many hours exposed in the boat. She stared down at the small puddles around the woven willows that rippled and glittered in the dim light. Thaney ripped off part of her undergarment and soaked up one of them. Raising it above her mouth, she squeezed and drank the dribble of water. She paused to say, "Thank you, God," before continuing to slake her thirst.

The light rain continued as she forced herself to lie down, relax, and repeat the Lord's prayer over and over. Although her clothes were wet, she once again fell into a deep sleep.

She was standing next to a clear, rippling stream. Her mother was sitting on the opposite bank, smiling at her. *"Momma, come get me."*

"Not this time, Thaney, you'll have to do it yourself."

"But the water is deep, I'll get wet. Come and get me," she held her arms out.

"I can't, honey. You need to be a big girl and walk upstream. There is a bridge there, cross it, and I'll be waiting here for you."

"Maybe I can walk on the water like Jesus did."

"No," her mother commanded. "You're not ready for that. Do as I say and be patient. I will always be here waiting for you."

The light was bright, shining high in the sky when she opened her eyes. A soft breeze was blowing from the East, which was odd, and she could see land in the distance to the North and South.

Dear God, thank you. I will be patient. "You be patient too, little one," as she rubbed her stomach and settled herself into an uncomfortable fetal position, and eventually fell asleep once again.

Something awakened her. Her eyes fluttered open in the near darkness when she felt a hard bump. The little coracle hit something. *Oh no, if it punctures the hides, we'll drown.* She struggled to get her knees under her, while being careful not to tip the boat too far. Then she noticed something else, she could hear waves breaking. "Baby, I think we are near land."

Spews of white foam were erupting on either side of her like dancing ghosts where the waves were hitting large boulders, but ahead, she could only see darkness. The East wind had increased in force and was driving her forward. The bottom of the boat was being pummeled by rocks as it rode through the low points of the swells. When it stopped with a final grinding sound, Thaney stepped out into frigid knee-deep water and struggled toward the shore. *We made it, little one. Thank you, Lord.*

The moon peeked out from behind high clouds as she walked up a sandy beach. There was a faint smell of smoke in the air, and she followed her nose to the remains of a cooking fire. Thaney pulled some small sticks from a dead tree branch and stirred the ashes with the largest one. A small red coal rolled out of the black pile of soot, and she carefully laid smaller sticks over it. Smoke began to waft up, and a flame licked the sticks a few moments later. She forced herself to continue dragging over more dead branches until the fire was blazing. Finally warm, she lay down to rest in a nearby bed of grass. She was puzzled. *How in the world did we survive? God is good.* Exhaustion overtook her, and she fell asleep.

She awoke when her water broke. Dawn was breaking, and she shivered in the cool air as she hurried to stoke the fire in between painful pauses for her contractions. The flames rose high as she lay down once again and screamed, pulling handfuls of tough spiky grass out of the sandy ground as the birth process continued.

Thaney suddenly saw several men with thick beards and tattered clothing materialize out of the fog-shrouded shoreline. Fear seized her. They stood in a semi-circle, watching her suffer.

One of them smiled and held up his hands, "I help."

She shook her head no for a moment until pain seized her again. Thaney watched through squinted eyes as the man knelt between her legs. She was too weak to argue.

"I help my sheep, I help you," he smiled.

Her trial continued as she pushed again and again. She was hungry and exhausted. She felt ready to pass out as she struggled to breathe. *Did Mother feel like this when I was born?* One last scream and push. Finally, she heard her baby cry.

She watched as the man wiped as much blood off the child as he could before wrapping it in portions of cloth torn from Thaney's clothes. Then he gently placed it in her arms, as tears sprouted from her eyes.

"You welcome," he said. "Fine baby boy."

"Who are you?" she asked.

"Emok, shepherd," he added.

"Where are we?" she asked.

"Culross, we take you to bishop,"

Culross? Maybe Ezra is still there. "When?"

"As soon as you can walk," he grinned. One of the other men handed her some hard bread and an animal skin flask of water.

"That yours?" Emok asked, pointing at the coracle bobbing at the shore.

"It's yours now for helping me," she smiled.

He nodded gratefully, walked over, and pulled the craft onto the sand. "This ours now," he proudly told the others.

"You'll have to make a paddle," she saw that he didn't understand. She moved her arm, sweeping sand with it.

"Oh, yes. We will make one," Emok said. "First, we take you to bishop."

Chapter 43

Thaney's Arrival

Saint Servanus awoke in the early morning and felt something wonderful was happening. He began singing a hymn, to the astonishment of a few clerics who crowded into his cell. "I heard the invisible angels singing praises of sweetness, and I had to join them in song. Something momentous has happened, my brothers. It shall be revealed to us soon."

"Could it be Thaney's child?" Ezra excitedly cried from the back of the group.

"Possibly, let's all earnestly pray for the answer to be delivered to us," as Servanus motioned them out, got down on his knees, and prayed until it was time to teach his morning class. It was nearly noon before Servanus heard a clamoring down the hallway, and he excused himself from the classroom with a stern admonition that all the boys stay seated.

"Abbot, these shepherds found a woman and child on the beach," a priest yelled.

"It's Thaney, your eminence. She had her baby," Ezra cried, running forward and showing him a child wrapped in rags torn from the woman's clothing.

"A blessed child is born," Servanus said reverently. "What is his name?"

"Mungo," Thaney replied quietly.

"Meaning, my dear one?"

"He is to me," Thaney replied.

"A very appropriate name, given the trials that you must have endured. Give them the cell at the end of the hallway. It is the largest, and bring her food and water. Give the shepherds plenty of food and drink in return for their charity in delivering this precious gift to us. I have to return to my class now, but I'll check on you soon," he waved at Thaney, who smiled weakly, and hugged and thanked Emok, before being led away by Ezra. Servanus turned and walked back to his class, smiling. *I know why the angels sang this morning.*

• ● •

Thaney stretched out on the hard wooden bench that served as a cot. She didn't care about the hard bed after being confined in a fetal position for more than a day. She looked at the child resting in the crook of her arm. *Father would love him.* She wondered if Lancelot ever found evidence against Oberon, and then decided it didn't really matter. That part of her life was over now.

Ezra's grinning face appeared at the door. "Thaney, I'm glad you made it here. I hoped and prayed that you would, but I didn't think it would be by a voyage in a coracle."

"Neither did Oberon," she laughed. "I thought you'd be back in Kilpatrick by now, helping Caleb with his flock."

"I keep thinking about it, but something made me wait. I guess it was you," he smiled. "Caleb and I keep in touch through letters, though. He's doing very well without me."

"Good to hear," she said weakly.

"Do you need anything?"

She wrinkled her nose, "I think he needs to be changed, do you offer that service?"

"Anything for a princess," he made an attempt to bow.

"Sadly, a princess no longer."

"We are all princes and princesses in God's Kingdom. You are still royalty, and look, I'm the royal baby changer," he laughed as he lifted the little tyke from his mother and wrinkled his own nose. "I'll be back as soon as I air him out," as he hurried out of the room.

A small knock sounded a few minutes later. Looking up, she recognized the bishop. "Sir, I am extremely grateful for your hospitality."

"Please, call me Servanus, my dear. Ezra has given me some knowledge of your efforts to find the Scroll of Saint Martin and your challenges since then. Can you tell me what happened after he left you?"

"She recounted the stories of being thrown from Traprain Law and then being set adrift in the ocean. "This morning, I made landfall, started to give birth to Mungo, and then the shepherds found me, helped and fed me, then brought me here."

Servanus was quiet for a few moments as tears flowed from his eyes. "Bless you, child," he finally said. "God has been protecting you and your son for some great purpose. You must stay here with us for as long as you want to. Consider yourself our treasured guest, Princess Thaney."

She felt herself smile, "Just Thaney, please. What can I do to help?"

"Take care of your child. I have a feeling that he will be very important to our humble order, but I have no idea why yet. I heard the angels sing when you arrived on our shore though."

"God and his angels have certainly been watching over me, and now my baby. I feel now that I have finally found a safe refuge in this world."

"You have, and we are blessed to have you here." The bishop smiled.

"Mother, here he is, all fresh and clean." Ezra brushed past Servanus and handed Mungo into his mother's arms.

"Thank you, Ezra, I should have done it myself."

"Nonsense, that's what friends do for each other. Call on me anytime. I love washing diapers."

"Call on any of us at any time, Thaney. As I said, you are our treasured guests. We are here to serve God and our fellow man."

"I do have one request, if you hear about Lancelot…"

Servanus walked over and placed a gentle hand on her shoulder, "We will let you know as soon as we hear anything."

"I could go back to Lothian and see what happened," Ezra spoke up.

"Not yet," as he put a restraining hand on the monk's shoulder. Let us be patient as we wait for God's perfection to work. I'm sure we will have word about Lancelot soon enough." Servanus replied.

Chapter 44

Oberon's Surprise

"Percy! Why did you let the torches go out?" a shrill voice cried in the darkness.

"What will you do to him?" a low voice grumbled.

Lancelot sighed with resignation. Oberon was bringing his pet giant with him, and he only had his wooden staff to battle that huge sword. *At least he won't have as much room to swing it in here.*

"Wait here, I'll get a torch from my quarters," the wizard's voice drifted down.

Lancelot forced himself to relax as soft steps drew closer. "Percy, are you drunk? Didn't you hear me?" Oberon thundered as he threw open the door and marched in. He stopped and turned when the door shut quietly. "You," he spat.

"Yes, dear wizard, it is I," as Lancelot turned the key and locked the door.

"Gro," was all that escaped Oberon's yell as the knobby end of the staff smashed into his mouth. Lancelot raised a finger to his lips.

"What you say?" the big man asked. Lance just pointed at the end of his staff.

"Nothing, no nothing, go on up to the courtyard. I'll meet you there later," the wizard said.

"All right, I go, but you bring my gold with you."

Lancelot waited until he heard the door close at the top of the steps. "How much did you pay him to kill me?"

Oberon ignored the question. "Get out of here, this is my abode. Where is Percy and the king?"

"First, where is Thaney?"

"She is safe. I passed sentence on her and banished her to Tantallon Castle. We drove her there this morning."

"You didn't kill her like you did her mother?"

"No, I mean I didn't kill her mother either," he stuttered.

"Now you are lying to me again. What did Jesus say about liars? **'Ye are of *your* father the devil, and the lusts of your father ye will do. He was a murderer from the beginning, and abode not in the truth, because there is no truth in him. When he speaketh a lie, he speaketh of his own: for he is a liar, and the father of it.'** (63) Have you ever understood Truth?"

Oberon's wicked smile answered the question as he suddenly threw two handfuls of dust toward the monk, that ignited in a brilliant flash of light and heat. Blinded for a few moments, he heard a cackling laugh receding behind the dusty shelves. *No telling what tricks he has hidden, but I've got to finish this for Thaney's mother,* as he ran forward and reached the end of a row of shelves. Lance glanced out before pulling back. A bolt from a crossbow slammed into a bookcase and stuck inches from his head. "You'll have to do better than that, little man," as he pulled the sharpened bolt from the wood.

"Leave now, or you'll die in this castle," the magician cursed from the darkened bowels of the room. Lance could hear him moving away. Then he heard some squeaking sounds, followed by a door slamming. *He must have another exit somewhere.* He picked up the crossbow and wandered between the shelves until he reached a rock wall. Feeling his way in the darkness, he stumbled into a ladder. Placing his foot on the lower rung, it squeaked. He fed the bolt onto the weapon and climbed upward to a trap door, slowly raising it with his staff. Nothing happened, but he recognized the kitchen pantry and clambered out.

———•●•———

"Grok, come here." Oberon wheezed breathlessly as he ran into the courtyard.

"You got my money?" the large man replied.

"I'll pay you, but Lancelot is in the castle. Would you please kill him first?"

The giant nodded and lumbered past him into the main hall, just as Lance entered from the kitchen. "Wizard said you die," Grok raised the huge sword as Lancelot quickly sprinted up the stone steps to the second level.

"Running won't help. I catch you," Grok yelled. Oberon felt himself smile when he saw Lancelot flee up the stairs.

———•●•———

A wooden balustrade beside a walkway overlooked the main floor about fifteen feet below. Several hallways snaked through the living areas of the castle from the balcony, and Lance darted into the third one.

"Come and fight me," Grok called as he reached the top of the steps. He bent down to enter the first hall.

"He ran into the third hallway," the wizard yelled from below. Grok looked up and lumbered forward.

The giant paused a few moments to stretch before he finally moved to the third entrance. He was just bending down to enter when a loud screech filled the air. A large table shot out of the hall and caught Grok in the waist, shoving him backward. He tried to swing at Lancelot, but the table was too long, and the sword didn't reach him. The balustrade shattered as Grok slid into it and fell, along with the table.

———•●•———

Lancelot took a breath and surveyed the room below. The people were silent. Grok lay below him on his back, a pool of blood spreading across the rock floor beneath his head—the smashed table off to one side. Oberon stared at him from in front of the crowd. "What is going to kill you?" he sputtered.

"Kindness," Lance smiled. He shrugged and stepped off the balcony, his staff held in one hand, and the crossbow clenched in the other. The crowd shouted as he fell. His feet and knees drove into Grok's soft belly and absorbed most of the shock. He rolled off to one side and jumped up, ignoring a burning pain in his groin.

"Kill him," Oberon called over his shoulder.

Lance took a step forward, and the crowd stepped back, just before they began running out the doorway.

The wizard hesitated for a moment before he turned to escape. Lance lifted the crossbow and shot from the waist. The bolt punctured Oberon's right buttock, as he howled in pain and dropped to his knees. He fell to one side, trying to pull the shaft out.

"Don't run off, wizard, we haven't finished our chat." Several heads peered through the open doorway. "Close that door and leave us alone, unless you want to be next," Lance commanded, and the door slammed shut.

"You're a devil," the little man said as he writhed in agony.

"No, sir, but I believe that you are in league with him." Lance grabbed the bolt and yanked it out with a tinge of satisfaction as Oberon shrieked in pain. Lancelot loosened the sash around his waist and pulled it free, slowly wrapping it around the wizard's throat. "Are you ready to tell me the truth now?"

Lance noticed Gawain looking at him from the kitchen doorway. "Gawain, run up to your father's bedroom and have him come down. Bring Percy from Thaney's room too. Hurry."

Gawain stared for a moment at Grok's lifeless form and then darted across the room and up the stairway.

Lancelot looked into Oberon's hate-filled eyes. "I will tell you nothing," as he spat on his captor.

Lance chuckled as he wiped the spittle from his face with a dirty sleeve. "Now, don't be like that, I thought we were friends." He spun the magician around, grabbed the wounded flesh, and squeezed hard.

"Aaaaaaaah, curse you."

"I've been cursed before; they haven't stuck yet," as he squeezed again.

Oberon grimaced and spurted, "Please, let's make a deal, what do you want?"

"I've got everything I want right here," he patted the man's shoulder.

"Do you want money? Do you want power? I can give you anything," the wizard whimpered, let me go.

"You sound just like your father when he tried to tempt Jesus, **'Again, the devil taketh him up into an exceeding high mountain, and sheweth him all the kingdoms of the world, and the glory of them; And saith unto him, All these things will I give thee, if thou wilt fall down and worship me. Then saith Jesus unto him, Get thee hence, Satan: for it is written, Thou shalt worship the Lord thy God, and him only shalt thou serve.'** (64) The only thing I want is Thaney, give her to me." Lance tightened the cord around the man's throat and watched lines of sweat running down the man's face as it turned blue.

"I can't," he choked.

Lance leaned in and almost touched noses with the little man, "Why?" he snarled as he noticed the man's shoulders sag in defeat.

"I, I don't know where she is," his eyes closed tightly.

Lancelot lost his temper and violently shook the wizard, "Why, did you sell her for a slave?"

"No, we released her on the Firth of Fourth in a coracle."

"A coracle? You set her adrift?"

The wizard nodded slowly, "I had to get rid of her. She had too much influence over the king."

"Who you imprisoned and probably would have killed?"

"All he needed to do was what I told him. None of this needed to happen."

"I believe it did, but only because you're a vile narcissist who doesn't care spit about other people. I believe now is a good time for you to atone for your sins," he whispered, "especially if we can't find Thaney."

"My gods, strike this worthless knave down," Oberon yelled loudly.

"Sorry, your gods must have taken the day off. Mine is around every day of the week, though. Do you want to confess your sins to Him and me?"

Oberon shook his head and grimaced, "No, just kill me."

Lance smiled, "Now, what fun would that be?"

Chapter 45

A Gift

"You shouldn't be out of bed," Servanus said when he found Thaney sitting on a boulder and staring at the waves breaking on the rocks the next morning.

"I couldn't sleep and wanted to walk around after being trapped in that tiny boat. Ezra is watching Mungo for me. Look at the waves crashing and the strong winds. Is it usually like this?"

"I have never known it to be different, except on the day you arrived. An East wind is nearly unheard of here, especially a gentle one driving rolling waves. God spared you and your child for a reason," he choked as a tear rolled down his cheek.

"I know he did, but I don't know why. I don't have a gift of healing like my mother, maybe Mungo will."

"I've heard wonderful stories about your mother. Don't ever limit yourself or God's grace. Healing comes when you forget this life, the claims of sin, sickness, and death. Try to become one with your Creator. You are His spiritual child, you know?"

"He cares more for me than my earthly father."

"He cares more than any mortal can. Never forget that He Loves all of his creation, because He created it all perfect. You have to learn to love His creation like He Loves his creation to be able to heal, **'for God is love.'** (65) You need to see the world as spiritual and perfect. Ignore the material images you were raised to believe."

"I'll try."

"Good, now let's walk back. I haven't yet seen your son this morning, and now I find myself looking forward to that each morning."

"Where are you from?"

Servanus chuckled, "I was born in Canaan and I also am the son of a king."

"A prince?"

"Yes, but my life took a different path. I grew up in Alexandria, and decided to give my life to Christ."

"Have you healed many souls with prayer?"

"I don't usually talk about it, but I have been blessed to help quite a few. I even resurrected two who had passed on."

"Really? How?"

"It was when I was first in this country a woman's two sons died in Tillicoultry. I prayed to understand how they must continue to express the qualities of young men, since life is infinite because God is infinite. In a while, they stirred, and I returned them to their mother. I told you the process I used; now you have to put in the effort to find what works with your prayers," he smiled.

"I will strive for the Mind of Christ to guide me."

"Let's get out of this cutting wind now and get something to eat. I'm sure you're famished after your ordeal. Tell me more about your life as we walk."

Thaney suddenly stopped, "How much do you know about Saint Martin of Tours?"

"Not much, I had a few discussions about him during my time in Rome, but it was just a general discussion. Ezra showed me the copy that he made of Martin's scroll. Some remarkable revelations concerning Spirit, I must say. How did you know where to recover it?"

"I have something to show you when we reach the

monastery," she said and forged ahead.

———•◉•———

When they reached the heavy wooden door, she waited while Father Servanus grunted and swung it open against the wind. "Thank you," as she stepped inside and they both walked to her room.

"He's still sleeping, he's such a good boy," Ezra whispered when they entered.

"Thank you for watching him. I felt restless and needed a walk."

"No problem, I will watch him anytime you want me to," Ezra said as he left.

"Father Servanus, I want to give a gift to your order for the protection and care you are providing to Mungo and me."

"My dear, that is not necessary."

She held up her hand to stop him. "I want to," as she dug in her bodice to retrieve the scrap of cloth. "This was my great-great-great-grandmother's needlework. It had a riddle on it that told me the location of the scroll. I thought you would like to display it."

"My dear, this is a precious relic of Christianity. We are honored."

"It is barely legible now, but you can see some of the letters. It used to read: 'The greatest gift lies beneath the soul's shower.' It meant the baptismal fount in the Kilpatrick church."

"Oh my, thank you, my child. We will treasure this gift forever, which is also, how long we will treasure you as our guest. Are you hungry?"

"Yes, I think I am," as a strong yawn escaped her throat. "Sorry."

"No excuse necessary. You need more rest, I will send up some food right away," as he turned.

"Wait, I have more to show you," as she lifted the

leather thong from her neck.

"Is that the scroll?"

"The very original one, penned by Martin himself. Ezra left an added message off the copies he made, and I want you to see it," as she broke the wax seal and slid the roll out.

The bishop drew closer as she carefully unrolled it on the table. "When St. Patrick borrowed it for his return to Hibernia, he wrote a final message. Look here, she pointed at the end of the paper."

Servanus squinted at the scrawled words.

"Remarkable."

"Ezra didn't include it since it was an addition, but I think it's beautiful. I wanted you to see it because of the wonderful stories about him awakening those who had passed away, sometimes decades later."

"With your permission, I would like to have copies made of this scroll with his comments. I can have one of my scribes do it now," he said, reaching down.

"Wait, don't misunderstand. I trust you and your scribes. My one condition is that they copy the words in my presence. The scroll must not be removed from me."

"Understood, Princess," he said with a grateful smile. "I will return with a scribe and have vittles sent here right away," as he turned and sauntered off down the hallway.

Mungo was asleep. Thaney crawled next to him and had almost fallen asleep, too.

"Thaney, are you awake?" she heard Ezra's voice whisper.

She stretched and muttered, "Yes."

"Here is a platter of food that Serf ordered me to bring you," as he set down a large tray covered with a cloth.

"Serf?" she asked as she reached for a biscuit sticking out of one corner.

"Yes, that's a nickname Father Servanus uses. Can you tell me how my friend Lancelot is?"

"I wish that I could, but I don't know. I haven't seen him for three nights now. He was going to ask Percy if the wizard poisoned my mother. I didn't see him after that," she frowned.

"Oh my, I pray he survived."

"Yes, so do I, Ezra," as she nibbled on the hard biscuit.

"Do you want me to send a letter to your father to let him know you're safe?"

"No, Oberon may still be alive and holding him captive. I don't want him to know I survived his plot. All we can do is pray for him and Lancelot's protection until someone brings us word."

"Do you think I should return to Kilpatrick to help Caleb?"

"I'm sure Caleb would like that, but what will Mungo do without his Uncle Ezra?"

Ezra looked deep in thought for a few moments, "I'll send Caleb a dispatch explaining your trials, tribulations, and my new obligations," he threw a glance at the baby and smiled. "Maybe he can use it in his homilies. I'm sure he won't mind if you visit him in a few years when Mungo is older."

She clasped his hand, "I'd like that. What else did you bring us to eat?"

"Some porridge and sliced apples. I hope you enjoy it."

"Sit and eat with us, here, take some bread. What do you do here at the monastery?"

"Oh, this and that, I mainly help in the scriptorium. I showed them my copy of Saint Martin's scroll, and I've been copying manuscripts since then. I enjoy it."

"I'm glad you found something to do while you've been waiting. I can't believe that my little vessel ended up so close to Culross.

"Do you think it was God's will?"

"What else could it have been?"

"You're right, nothing else could have protected and

guided you here. It was a miracle that you survived Oberon's attempts to kill you."

"He killed my mother," the words slipped out.

Ezra's eyes flew open. "Oh no, how?"

"Poison, I asked him if he killed her, he said no, but I could tell he was lying."

"That's terrible, I'm so sorry."

"At least I know now, I pray every night that Lancelot has succeeded in confronting Oberon and ending his reign of terror. Father must be beside himself if he is still imprisoned."

"I pray he shows up soon to tell us."

"I pray that someone will. I fear for Gawain, too. Who is taking care of him?"

"The same one who has protected you through your trials," Ezra patted her hand. "God is the only one who can truly take care of any of us."

"But Gawain and Father don't know God."

Ezra smiled, "They don't have to, because God knows them."

Chapter 46

Oberon's Confession

"Lancelot, you caught him," the king said with a vicious smile as he bounded down the steps.

Lance looked up as the king, Percy, and Gawain descended. Looking back at Oberon's ashen white face, he said, "We have our audience now."

"Should I send Gawain away?" the king asked, holding onto the boy's shoulders and staring at Grok's body.

"No, I think he should hear this man's confession so that he will be wise when he has to deal with the treachery of others," he grinned as he tightened the cord around Oberon's neck until the wizard's eyes bulged. "Percy, please hand me that bottle."

"No, I'll tell everything, don't touch me," he was shivering now as he stared at the flask.

"Did you kill Queen Morgan Le Fay with poison?" The man nodded. "Why?"

"I hated her. She had the king wrapped around her finger. She was always doing good, protecting, and healing people. She was my rival. I thought if she was gone, the king would listen to me," he sneered.

"How did you murder her?" Lance bent and tightened the cord again.

"With wolfsbane, a little bit at a time from that bottle, so she thought it was just chronic sickness after King Arthur died. The king blamed her God and her friends," he gasped.

"The king lunged forward, but Lance blocked the blow that might have killed the murderer and set the bottle on the floor next to the wizard. "Wait, sire, he has much more to tell us. Where is Thaney?"

"I set her adrift in the Firth of Forth in a coracle."

"Why, she'll die out there, she'll be swept into the North Sea," the king thundered and tried to attack again.

Lance picked the wizard up and spun around to keep himself between Oberon and the king, "Stop, there is more to learn," he commanded over his shoulder. "Why did you want to kill the princess?"

There was a pause as Gawain clenched his fists, ran forward, and head-butted Oberon in the groin. "You bring my sister back," he said as he backed away crying, and the king knelt and hugged him.

Lancelot stifled a laugh as he turned the wizard to face him and shook his shoulders, "Why?"

Oberon groaned in pain, "She was just like her mother was. Trying to heal and help others. The king listened to her more as she grew older, and I waited for an opportunity to dispose of her, so he would only listen to me."

"So, even though you punished her and she survived the trial, which proved her innocence, you continued to persecute her and fill everyone's ears with lies so you would be justified in murdering her by setting her adrift in the sea. Why have you done these things?"

Oberon hung limply in Lance's grasp. "To usurp the king, to gain power and control over the neighboring kingdoms. It would have worked if you had just died," he spat in Lancelot's face once more.

Lancelot opened his hands, and the man fell to the floor in a heap, moaning.

"Let me kill him now," the king pleaded.

"Sire, that would be a mistake. He's poisoned many of the people against you, and that's dangerous. Let me pray for a few moments for the proper solution. The monk walked to the outside wall and stayed silent for a few minutes. Then he turned, walked to the main door, and opened it to let the people in.

"What are you doing? Are you crazy?" the king sputtered.

Lancelot raised his hand to silence him. "Good people of Lothian, I want you to see what's left of the man who has deceived you and murdered your queen with poison from that bottle," he pointed to Oberon, who was whimpering. A murmur spread through the onlookers as they filed in.

"Let's kill him now," the king said as half the room filled with faces.

"No," Lance yelled. "I have killed many men in my former life as a knight of the Round Table, and unfortunately, a few in my new life as a 'peaceful' monk. Some deserved it, and some did not, but I regret contributing to all their deaths. Ours is not to judge; that was a hard lesson for me. All judgment belongs to God. We need to express more kindness and gratitude for others in our lives."

"You won't kill me?" Oberon looked shocked as tears filled his eyes.

"Love doesn't kill."

"But he killed my wife and probably my daughter, and you just killed that giant," the king shook with anger as Gawain hugged his waist.

"Grok would not stop until he killed me, so I regretfully had to finish him first. Oberon will be judged, but not by me. His reign of terror and selfish greed is over, and he knows it. His lies will deceive you and your subjects no more, your highness, and your hands will be clean, sire," Lance shouted over the increasing crowd noise as he watched the wizard quickly snatch the bottle and tip it to his lips until it was empty.

After a few moments, Lancelot spoke again, "With your leave, sire, I will take him to the dungeon until he passes."

"The king's eyes were wide, "How did you know?"

Lancelot ignored him as he bent and picked the wizard up. "Percy, come along and open the doors for me."

The man was already holding his stomach. "I, my face feels numb, but it tingles in my mouth, and it feels like something is crawling around on me." He was sweating profusely by the time they reached the cells in the dungeon. Percy held a cell door open, and Lancelot laid him down gently on one of the wooden beds. "Why are you so nice?" he asked before a pain in his abdomen doubled him up.

Lancelot grasped his hand. "I try to see you as God made you, not the terrible things you've done. I hope you know that He and I both Love the real you, made in His spiritual image. Not the lies and evil that have infected your mortal life."

"I don't understand," the wizard said before he retched and began gasping for breath. "I can't breathe," he wheezed.

"Hold onto my hand, I won't leave you," Lancelot said as he wiped sweat from the man's brow. "I pray the Lord's grace will touch you here or hereafter." In a few minutes, Oberon's hand relaxed, and he was still.

Chapter 47

The Search Begins

"Is he?" Percy asked.

"Yes, his personal reign of terror is over, although it continues to plague us. We must know if Thaney survived his last horrific act?"

"We have no way of knowing," Percy admitted, "I'm sorry, I should have..."

"Don't say it." Lance hissed. "We all needed to do better. At least you have an excuse of being under his spell, I have none. I should have returned sooner, and she might be alive."

"After being a witness to the Divine intervention at Traprain Law, I believe she is still protected by your God. I never talked to her mother, except to make fun of her beliefs." Percy suddenly fell to his knees, sobbing. "Please tell me about God."

Lance laid a large hand on the penitent man's shoulder. "Brother Percy, I believe you are correct. God's Love is still Thaney's protection in all ways and conditions. Thank you for reminding me, and where should I begin? **'God *is* a Spirit: and they that worship him must worship *him* in spirit and in truth.'** (66) It says in John: **'Beloved, believe not every spirit, but try the spirits whether they are of God: because many false prophets are gone out into the world.'** (67) You have to know that God's ideas have no taint of earth; they are pure."

"I have always followed false ideas; I've always looked for pleasure in matter."

"But you are growing, my son. Now you are seeing the Truth that this world hid from you before. Again, it says in John; **'We are of God: he that knoweth God heareth us; he that is not of God heareth not us. Hereby know we the spirit of truth, and the spirit of error.'** (68) You can see the difference, correct?"

His eyes and lips were shut tight, but Lance saw Percy's slight nod as he continued, **" for love is of God; and every one that loveth is born of God, and knoweth God. He that loveth not knoweth not God; for God is love. In this was manifested the love of God toward us, because that God sent his only begotten Son into the world, that we might live through him. Beloved, if God so loved us, we ought also to love one another."** (69)

"Can I see God?" Percy asked with his eyes still closed. **"No man hath seen God at any time. If we love one another, God dwelleth in us, and his love is perfected in us."** (70)

———•●•———

"Father, are you all right?" Gawain asked softly.

King Lot stirred and looked up from his throne, "I'm sorry, son. Everything is a shambles. I don't know what to do," as he settled his face back into his hands.

"You are the king, be a king," the boy responded.

The fingers of his hands moved, and he looked out from between them. "With that clarity, you are going to be a great knight and king, my son," he dropped his hands and stood up. "You are absolutely correct. I live to guide and protect my subjects. Castellan, where are you?"

A stout man hurried in from a nearby room, "Here, your majesty."

"We need to forge ahead. Send two guards to the dungeon to retrieve the body of Oberon for burial in an unmarked grave. He should be dead by now. Tell them to have Lancelot report to the throne room," with a grin, he added, "Please."

The man's wide eyes registered his surprise, "Yes, sire, immediately, thank you," he added before marching off.

Gawain stood with his mouth open.

"What? I'm going to follow Lancelot's example and be more courteous and grateful for everyone and everything. I feel better already. I just pray that Thaney is well and happy. The sun is coming up now, let's have breakfast."

Gawain's mouth twisted into a smile.

———•●•———

"Thank you," Percy replied. "You make it sound simple and real."

"It is reality. It's seeing the kingdom of God here and now, rather than what the masses see. It's Love enthroned and limitless life. **'Ye adulterers and adulteresses, know ye not that the friendship of the world is enmity with God? whosoever therefore will be a friend of the world is the enemy of God.'** (71) We stand apart from them and embrace spiritual views of God and man in His image."

"Lancelot," the castellan called.

"I'm here."

"The king asked that you report to the throne room. Is the wizard dead?"

"He is for now," he winked at Percy, "You may take him, he's in the first cell."

The castellan looked puzzled but motioned to the guards to follow him as Lance arose. "Can't keep the king waiting. We'll add to this conversation later," and he left Percival in deep contemplation.

He took the stone steps two at a time and only paused

for a moment to look down as they hauled Oberon's body from the cell. Lance sighed and headed up the corridor.

"There you are, Lance. Sit with us and share our bounty the king said. I want to talk to you about a permanent position in my kingdom. Don't stand there with your mouth open, sit down, er please," Gawain grinned.

Lancelot shuffled forward and sat down, grabbing a bowl of porridge. He stuffed a handful into his mouth before responding, "Sire, I am grateful beyond all bounds for your offer, but I must decline at this time."

"But I need you, I am just starting to embrace this Christianity in my kingdom, you have to remain here," he demanded.

"Your majesty, I pledge, on my honor, to return to you if the Lord allows it, but I must leave and search for Thaney. I made a promise, and I will keep it. I need to tell her Oberon is dead, if I can find her," as he dug another handful of porridge out.

The king looked deflated. "You wouldn't be Sir Lancelot unless you honored that decision. Go with my blessings, but if you see a wayward monk on the road, send him to me. Hopefully, he can teach me in your stead. Where will you start?"

"The coast, I'll work my way West and then follow the North coast. I'll stop at Culross to see Ezra at the monastery there. As soon as I have news, I'll contact you. I'll be leaving after I finish my breakfast."

The king shook his head, "I need to get used to saying this. Go with God's protection, my friend," as he picked up an apple and took a sad bite.

Chapter 48

Lance's Search Ends

A small knock sounded on Thaney's door. "Come in."

Father Servanus stepped into the room with a wide smile. "My goodness, he is growing fast. You're a stout little man, aren't you?" he walked over to the bed and stuck a finger into the baby's hand.

The baby returned a toothless grin.

"He likes you."

"Not more than I like him," he responded. "In only a month, he looks almost twice as big as he was."

"I thought men of the cloth were not supposed to exaggerate."

"Well, not in most cases, but your baby is special."

"I think so," as she played with his toes. "Have you heard any news from Lothian?"

Servanus shook his head slowly, "Nothing yet, but your kingdom isn't exactly next door. With winter approaching, I don't want to send any of my monks away from the monastery if I don't have to."

"I understand. I just pray to hear something, anything, soon."

"I'm sure you will, my dear, be patient. I have to teach my first class now, but I'll see you later," he paused. "I had a dream last night, it was midday and angels were singing. Perhaps it portends that good things are coming."

Father Lance shivered in the morning chill as he struggled through deep sand next to the water. *I should be close now, maybe I'll make it to Culross by noon. A month now, and I've found no trace of her. I hope Ezra is still waiting here; maybe the brothers have heard about Thaney.* The beach ended, and he climbed up a jumbled pile of large rocks to follow the coastline, always scanning for any trace of a dead body. In the distance, he could see buildings. "Culross." He followed the coast for the rest of the morning until the buildings were directly off to his left, and he headed toward them.

A few monks were involved in various tasks around the main building, and he nodded greetings to them as he approached the main doorway where an older man sat. "Good day, sir. Can you tell me where to find the bishop?"

"He is teaching now. Come back later."

"Have you seen a monk named Ezra?"

"You know Ezra?"

"And he knows me. Could you tell him Brother Lance is here."

The old man reluctantly struggled to his feet. "Follow me." He opened one of the large doors and walked inside. The man hobbled through several corridors and up a set of stairs to a long hallway lined with doorways. "These are our cells, Ezra should be in the third one on this side," he muttered and left.

"Ezra," Lance called softly.

The door burst open. "Lancelot, I can't believe it, you're here." He threw his arms out to hug him and then went suddenly silent. "What's wrong?"

"Oberon put Thaney adrift in a…"

"She's here, she's safe, she's a mother," he winked. "Come on, I'll take you to her," as Ezra squeezed past him and headed down the hall. "Come on," he fanned a hand.

Lance took a few halting steps and then ran after the little man as he felt a smile spread across his lips for the first time in his journey. Tears streamed from his eyes as he wiped them away to peer into a doorway Ezra had stopped at.

"You have a visitor, princess."

Thaney looked up, ran across the room, and jumped up on Lance, wrapping her arms around his neck as he dropped his staff and squeezed her waist.

"My goodness, I think you're glad to see me," he wheezed.

"Why are you crying?"

"Sun was bright outside, oh, and by the way, I'm so relieved and filled with joy to find you alive." He raised a hand and swiped at his tears. "Little mother, can I see him?"

"One more hug first," as she pressed herself against him before dropping to the ground. She turned and walked back to the bed. "I named him Mungo."

"He is a dear little man," as tears fell from his eyes, and he raised a hand to hide them. "I've been so worried that I would never find you, or if I did…" his voice trailed off in sobs as he dropped to his knees in prayer. "Thank you, God." Thaney knelt beside him and wrapped him in a gentle embrace.

"Thank you, God," Ezra echoed outside the door.

Lance wiped a dirty sleeve across his face and turned to look at Thaney. "I need to return and tell your father and little brother that you survived and are well."

"Right away?"

"Princess, they are as worried about you as I was, but they couldn't leave to search the coastline with me."

"You searched the entire coast from Lothian?" Tears obscured his vision, and he just nodded his head.

"What happened to Oberon?" Her voice shook.

Lance wiped his eyes again and composed himself.

"The poor man committed suicide after confessing his crimes in public. He drank a bottle of Wolfsbane."

"You got him to confess?"

"It just took a little encouragement, and no place to run," he added.

"And Percy?"

"Percival has gained a great sense of humility and a desire to know God. "It was an amazing transformation."

"Hard for me to believe," she pursed her lips.

"Oh, it is true. By the way, would Father Servanus have a monk willing to make his residence in Lothian? The king wants religious instruction, too."

Thaney's mouth dropped open as Ezra clapped his hands and said, "Praise the Lord, I'll ask Serf at once," as he disappeared from the doorway.

Tears swelled in her eyes as she asked, "Seriously?"

"Yes, my dear. Your father is well on his way to becoming a Christian. The dark clouds have finally lifted from Lothian." They knelt beside each other in silent prayers until Ezra returned.

"Brother Lance, I'd like you to meet Father Servanus," Ezra announced.

Lancelot stood and helped Thaney up as he extended his free hand. "Pleasure to meet you again, sir. do you remember me?"

Servanus took it and shook it heartily. "I certainly do, and you have made me very proud for introducing you to the one true God. Ezra has told me so many stories about you, but I never let on that I knew you already. You will have to tell me about some more of your adventures with King Arthur and Camelot sometime, but above all, thank you for everything you've done for this young lady and her precious child."

"You knew each other before?" Ezra questioned.

"Long story, Ezra. No thanks required, your excellency. If Ezra told you much about my latest adventures, you know I have much more to atone for."

"Well, I think God has forgiven you, or else he wouldn't have given you such a strenuous and holy quest, my son. Come, let us all eat and discuss which of my monks would be most able to spread God's word in Lothian."

Thaney spoke up, "What about Mungo? I can't leave him alone."

"I will take care of the little one, princess," Ezra said with a toothless grin as he pointed at the baby. "See, he's smiling. He has my smile," and they all laughed.

"I hope your teeth come in soon, my friend," Lance joked.

"I'm sure they will, I'm in my second childhood now."

The three of them turned and walked down the hallway. Thaney reached out and took Lance's hand in hers.

"How long did it take for you to journey here?" Servanus asked.

"Nearly a month, but I did it the hard way, walking every step along the coast."

"I'll say you did. A horse shouldn't take a week. I'll see if any can be borrowed from our local farmers for your journey."

"I believe you have one available here. Didn't Ezra arrive on a horse?"

"Yes, you are correct, I forgot about that one."

"How did you get a horse for Ezra?" Thaney asked in an accusing tone.

"I borrowed one, so Ezra could outdistance Oberon in his search to kill him," Lance replied apologetically.

"A monk who's a horse thief?" Servanus's eyebrows raised.

"I'm not a thief, you see, I plan on taking him back," he smiled.

"I wish you weren't traveling back to Lothian at this time of year; the weather can be hostile," Servanus said.

"I know, I've traveled most everywhere on this island,

in all types of weather. I kept several pages busy polishing my rusty armor for years on end, but that was another life. Now I carry very little that corrodes."

"The armor of God never corrodes but only gets brighter with use." Servanus smiled as he opened the door to the dining hall. "Let us eat."

Chapter 49

Trip To Lothian

"How much further?"

"At least three more days. Why do you keep asking?" Lance replied as the two monks rode down a dusty cart path skirting the coast.

"I don't know what else to do, I'm bored. Tell me another story."

"Father Ewan, I'm not bored, but I am praying, try that. Rehearse how you are going to teach the citizens of Lothian, and especially their king."

"And when they bring you unto the synagogues, and *unto* magistrates, and powers, take ye no thought how or what thing ye shall answer, or what ye shall say: For the Holy Ghost shall teach you in the same hour what ye ought to say." (72)

"Touché," Lance replied. "I've told you enough of my stories to give you nightmares for years. Tell me a story or two from Jesus's times."

"Do you know the story of Balaam?"

"No."

"Balaam went for a trip on his donkey, but the donkey went off the path into a field, and Balaam smacked him with a stick, then the donkey squeezed his foot against a rock wall, and Balaam hit him again."

"All right, what happened?"

"Balaam didn't know that the donkey was trying to avoid an angel with a flaming sword. **'And the angel of the LORD went further, and stood in a narrow place, where *was* no way to turn either to the right hand or to the left. And when the ass saw the angel of the LORD, she fell down under Balaam: and Balaam's anger was kindled, and he smote the ass with a staff. And the LORD opened the mouth of the ass, and she said unto Balaam, What have I done unto thee, that thou hast smitten me these three times? And Balaam said unto the ass, Because thou hast mocked me: I would there were a sword in mine hand, for now would I kill thee. And the ass said unto Balaam, *Am* not I thine ass, upon which thou hast ridden ever since *I was* thine unto this day? Was I ever wont to do so unto thee? And he said, Nay. Then the LORD opened the eyes of Balaam, and he saw the angel of the LORD standing in the way, and his sword drawn in his hand: and he bowed down his head, and fell flat on his face. And the angel of the LORD said unto him, Wherefore hast thou smitten thine ass these three times? Behold, I went out to withstand thee, because *thy* way is perverse before me:' (73)"**

"The donkey talked?"

"That's the story."

"That's ridiculous. How could a donkey talk?"

"How could the Red Sea be parted? How could the dead be raised, the dumb speak, the blind see, the disabled walk? What story do you want next?"

"Let me think about this one for a while," and they rode on in silence.

"It's a story about pride, only seeing what you want, not what is the right thing to do." Lance finally said.

"Go to the head of the class," Ewan said, "How much further?"

Lance groaned and rode on in silence.

On the sixth day, they rode out of a forest and could

see a castle in the distance. Lance pointed, "There, that is Hailes Castle."

"Will we reach it today?"

"Yes, and now you never need to ask again how far it is."

Elam was silent for a moment, 'How far does the kingdom extend?"

Lancelot raised an arm to knock him off the horse until Elam suddenly laughed, and Lance just shook his head and growled.

Twilight was beginning to caress the earth as they rode up to the main gate. Lance nodded at the guards, who moved aside and let them plod through the opening. They rode over to the stable area and dismounted. Lance handed the reins to a stable boy and arched his back. "Come on, Elam, time to meet your students," as he marched across the courtyard, followed by stares and sounds of welcome from the inhabitants.

"Looks like you're quite popular."

"I don't think I'm popular, but I did make a big impression the last time I was here," Lance said as he climbed the steps to the double doorway. He pulled one open, "After you."

"Sir Lancelot. You've returned, is Thaney with you?" Despair coated the king's voice.

"She is alive and you are a grandfather now."

"Sir Lancelot?" Elam whispered with wide eyes.

"Did you bring her back?" the king clapped his hands.

"No, sire, your grandson is a newborn, too young to travel, but I found her well and healthy at the Culross monastery."

"How did she survive?"

"Well, your majesty, she plummeted from the top of a mountain, and then she rode across the wild waters of the Firth of Forth. She has God's protection."

"Thank goodness, I've been so worried. Who is this

with you?" He rose from the throne and stepped down.

"Allow me to introduce Father Elam. Bishop Servanus is allowing him to leave Culross indefinitely to minister and teach in your kingdom."

"So, once again, you will not stay with us?" the king frowned.

"I will for a few days, but I want to return to protect Thaney and Mungo for as long as they need me."

"I understand. So be it. Let me send for Gawain. I want to begin our lessons immediately."

"Will Percy join us?"

"If you insist," the king muttered. "Call Percival and Gawain here, please," he shouted to a nearby guard who started up a stairway toward the repaired balcony.

"Your carpenters did a fine job; did they repair the table too?"

A smile etched the corners of the king's mouth, "No, it was beyond repair, like Grok was. You never told me how you knew Oberon would kill himself?"

"Because I didn't know. I only knew that I should open the door and tell the people what he did. That was all God told me."

"Marvelous," the king turned to Elam. "Can you teach me to listen for God's commands?"

"I will try. It is like when Elijah heard the word of the Lord, **'Go forth, and stand upon the mount before the LORD. And, behold, the LORD passed by, and a great and strong wind rent the mountains, and broke in pieces the rocks before the LORD; *but* the LORD *was* not in the wind: and after the wind an earthquake; *but* the LORD *was* not in the earthquake: And after the earthquake a fire; *but* the LORD *was* not in the fire: and after the fire a still small voice.'** (74)"

"That still small voice is what I heard," Lance interjected. "Many times, it has helped and guided me, and when I've ignored it, I usually got into trouble."

"So, you've always been a Christian?" King Lot asked.

"Heavens no, but that's the great thing about God. He talks to everyone, because we are all his children, even when we don't know it. His thoughts and ways are perfect. If we don't rebel, our lives can be too."

"In this brutal world?"

"Even in this world, we are supposed to live in the kingdom of God. As it says in the Lord's prayer, **'And he said unto them, When ye pray, say, Our Father which art in heaven, Hallowed be thy name. Thy kingdom come. Thy will be done, as in heaven, so in earth.'** (75) Prayer brings us closer to God's will and allows us to live a life separate from mortal strife."

"Unless we are deceived like I was," the king uttered morosely. "I should have been smarter, and my queen would be alive."

"You didn't listen to God; you listened to a wicked, cunning wizard, thinking that he told you the truth. You can't blame yourself; he had many others convinced of his veracity, and here comes one of his former disciples now," as Percy and Gawain descended the steps.

The king straightened up and waved. "I want you two to meet our new teacher. Father Elam is from the monastery at Culross, where Thaney is staying with your new nephew," he said, grinning at Gawain.

"Really, she's alive?" the boy screamed.

"Yes, she is, and doing very well," Lancelot added as he noticed a flicker of relief in Percy's eyes. *Maybe he does have a soul.*

"Father Elam will teach us about Christianity, would that I had listened years ago," King Lot said with a wane smile.

"Better late than never, Father."

Elam interjected, "So, we have King Lot, Gawain, and Percival for our first class, anyone else?"

"These are special students. We should teach them as

a separate group, so their light shines clearly to show the Christ to others in the kingdom," Lance said.

"Very well, I shall start at the beginning, **'In the beginning God created the heaven and the earth. And the earth was without form, and void; and darkness *was* upon the face of the deep. And the spirit of God moved upon the face of the waters. And God said, Let there be light: and there was light.'** (76) In the first chapter of Genesis, God creates the world spiritually, the kingdom of God that mankind seeks."

Chapter 50

Stories Of Columba

Lancelot pulled back gently as he uttered, "Whoa," and slid off the horse by the monastery's stable. He handed the reins to a monk raking a stall, loosened the straps holding his staff, adjusted his satchel, and walked toward the dormitory. It had only been two weeks, but he was anxious to see Thaney and Mungo.

Servanus caught him at the door when he entered, "How was your trip?"

"Much better on a horse than by foot. The king was overjoyed to hear that Thaney survived and gave birth, and is enjoying his lessons from Brother Elam, thank you."

"Did you learn anything?"

"Elam and I talked a long while about Genesis. I'm still confused about the snake telling Eve to eat the apple," he confessed.

"Well, the turning point of the story had nothing to do with the apple."

Lancelot felt his eyes narrow, "No?"

"God created all things spiritual and perfect. Man was created in the image of God, then what happened?"

Lance shook his head, "I thought God made man from dust."

"That's what most of the world thinks, because they ignore one very important phrase, **'But there went up a**

mist from the earth, and watered the whole face of the ground.' (77) Do you remember?"

Lance shook his head.

"What does a heavy mist or fog do?"

"Limits and obscures your view."

"Yes, it distorts your perception of reality. So, what happened after the mist? **'And the LORD God formed man *of* the dust of the ground, and breathed into his nostrils the breath of life; and man became a living soul.'** (78) A false, material concept of the world now appears as real. The perfect world that God created is obscured behind the mist. Mankind now believes in material life that is a mockery, a false concept of spiritual Life."

Lance suddenly spoke, "That's why Jesus gave us the Lord's prayer, to tell us, **'Thy kingdom come. Thy will be done, as in heaven, so in earth.'** (79) We should experience his will, his perfection, his kingdom on earth."

"I believe that is what he meant, but we can only do that when we see the Truth that lies beyond the mist. Beyond material life. The real world that Jesus knew was comprised only of God and His perfect ideas. Are you going up to see Thaney?"

"Of course."

"I'll stop up as soon as I deal with some unruly students."

"See them as God made them."

"Wise words, my brother. I believe you understand."

"I hope so," he said before turning and running up the stairs.

"Lance, you came back," Thaney greeted him with a hug and a kiss on the cheek. "You look younger than the day I met you."

"I feel young. Knowing you gave me two reasons to start living again: my favorite princess and her little prince. Your father, Gawain, and even Percy send their warmest wishes. Even now, they are studying to be Christians."

"Amazing how the world changes so quickly. Mother would be really proud and happy. What do you carry in your satchel?" she said and pointed at the ragged leather pouch hanging from his shoulder.

"Only the essentials, knife, fire starter kit, some twine, and this copy of Martin's scroll that you gave me," he said proudly as he pulled it out.

"Oh my, it's practically destroyed."

"Well, it and I have had some hard journeys of late. I didn't tell you how many times I fell into the surf as I searched for you, and it rained on me twice on my return trip from Lothian."

"It's illegible, the water made the ink run," as she pulled several of the soggy pages apart.

"The ideas are still there, I just can't read them very well," he laughed as he moved over to Mungo.

"Maybe Ezra can pen you a new copy."

"Can he walk yet?" he asked as he gently patted the boy's belly.

"Of course not, he's too young."

"Too bad, I'd like to take him hunting with me."

"It'll be a number of years before that happens," she smiled. "What are you going to do now?"

"Wait a few years, I guess," he laughed again. "I told your father I'd come here and protect you two. I'll try to find some odd jobs I can help with around the monastery for a while. At some point, I might take a trip up to Iona to visit Father Columba, but not anytime soon."

"Why do you want to see him?"

"I've heard a lot of crazy stories about him. I'd like to know if any of them are true."

"Such as?"

"I heard when he was a young man in Hibernia, studying the scriptures, The church ran out of wine for the mass. He heard the ministers arguing, picked up a pitcher of water and changed it into wine."

"Amazing, any others?"

"Plenty, he spent some time among the Picts, preaching the word of life through an interpreter. A Pict heard him speak, and his whole household was baptized. A few days later, one of that man's sons experienced severe pain. The Pict wizards began to make folly of the one God, saying that their gods were stronger. By the time Columba heard about the boy's sickness and returned, the young man had already died. His parents were performing various death rituals for their son. Columba returned and asked to see the boy's remains. He was led to a building where the bishop entered alone. People heard him say, "In the name of Jesus Christ, awake, and stand up." He led the boy out of the building and into his parents' arms."

"That's wonderful."

"If it's true, but there is another story about the monastery that bothers me. I hope it isn't true."

"What?"

"Supposedly, when Columba tried to build a chapel on Iona, its walls would collapse each night, and they would have to start over every morning, repairing the damage. A mystical voice told Columba that the walls would only stand if a man were buried alive beneath the foundation. A monk named Oran volunteered and supposedly lies beneath the walls, covered with dirt by his friends."

Thaney's eyes grew wide, "That's horrible."

"Afterward, the walls stood, and they finished the chapel, but there's more to the story. Columba decided to check on his friend who had sacrificed his life and ordered the monks to uncover him once more."

Thaney's voice trembled as she asked, "What did they find?"

"As they wiped the dirt away from Oran's face, his eyes opened, and he spoke as he tried to climb out, 'There is no heaven or hell as men believe, those saved are not always happy, those in hell are not forever lost.' Supposedly,

Columba yelled for them to hurry and cover him with dirt before he finished talking."

"What do you think he was going to say?"

"Mind you, I won't believe the story until I speak with Bishop Columba. If I had to venture a guess, I think he would have added; until all become complete in God's Love."

"Sounds logical. We all need to grow closer to God, here or hereafter."

"At-one-ment with God is the ultimate treasure. Miracles come from glimpses of His Truth in our lives."

"Lancelot, you are the most multi-faceted man I have ever known."

"Thank you, I think."

"It's the highest compliment I can give. It's wonderful to have you back with us."

"You honor me, I'm grateful to share any time with you and your son. Where's Ezra?"

"He's been copying manuscripts for Father Servanus. Let's go see him, he's in the Scriptorium," as she began to gather Mungo into her arms.

"Could I," Lance murmured.

Looking up, she stepped back, beaming. "Of course, Uncle Lance."

He gently lifted the lad in his large hands as she led the way. They walked down the steps and turned into a narrow hallway that led back to a room where four monks sat and wrote on parchment pages with sharpened quills.

"Brother Lance?" Ezra stumbled from his bench with arms outstretched.

"My friend Ezra, you can't hug me, I've got a precious burden here."

"Mungo," the monk's smile widened. "Our fearsome man of action and adventure, cherishing a tiny infant. I wish I had a painting of you two."

"No one would believe it."

"I would," Thaney said with a smile, as she lifted her

son from Lancelot's arms. Ezra advanced and wrapped his arms around him.

"I've missed you."

Lancelot patted his back. "Apparently, what are you working on here?"

"Copying manuscripts to protect the ideas for posterity. Follow me, I'll show you. Brothers, this is Brother Lance that I've told you about." The other three nodded politely and went back to working.

"We copy mainly religious works, but also some other stories as a spiritual duty to preserve the knowledge. Brother Thomas and I copy the text. Brother Callum and Brother Rory add illumination to the religious texts."

Lance walked over to one of the illustrators, "Beautiful work."

"Thank ye," as the man finished painting an elaborate border, and scattered pounce across the page to dry the ink. "We do our best."

"It shows, sir," Lance added as he turned to leave.

"I'll see you at dinner," Ezra said as he remounted his bench.

"Looking forward to it," Thaney said as they walked out.

Chapter 51

Stories Of Benedict

"So, what made you become a monk after living a life of adventure and carnage?" Thaney asked as they walked back to the dormitory.

Lancelot shook his head sadly, "My life fell apart. Arthur was dead, Guinevere joined Amesbury Priory, and refused to kiss me when I last met with her. That tore my heart out." He let out a loud sigh. "She became so distraught that she swore that I would never look upon her face again in this life, and she made sure that I didn't. She wanted to find her salvation in a life of penance. I hope she did," the words caught in his throat, and it was a minute before he resumed speaking. "After Guinevere was lost to me, despondency overtook me. I drifted from town to town with no real purpose in life. One day, just by chance, I met Bishop Servanus as he was traveling through Camelot after leaving Rome. He told me how he was introduced to Saint Benedict in Montecassino Abbey, and I listened to him recount a number of the Saint's myriad miracles. Those stories convinced me that I desperately needed to try another vocation at that period in my life. So, I decided to try to become a peaceful monk. I thought a life of penance might take away a few of my sins, too."

"What did he tell you?"

"I remember the first story was unbelievable. Do you

know what a wheat sieve is?"

"Yes, like a screen to shake and let the wheat fall through."

"Right, well, someone borrowed a sieve made of clay, a very valuable tool. Well, by chance, it was carelessly left on a table, fell off, and broke in two. Benedict took the two pieces away and prayed. When he finished, the sieve was in one piece again and was used for many years afterward."

"Two pieces became one again. What else?"

"A man was trying to clear briars from beside a lake. As he worked with a hoe to dig them out, the head of the hoe fell into the lake and was lost in the water. Benedict came to the lake, took the handle from the man, and stuck it into the water. The iron hoe swam up and attached itself to the handle again."

"How?"

"I suppose the same way that the iron swam in the Jordan river for Elisha, **'But as one was felling a beam, the axe head fell into the water: and he cried, and said, Alas, master! for it was borrowed. And the man of God said, Where fell it? And he shewed him the place. And he cut down a stick, and cast *it* in thither; and the iron did swim. Therefore said he, Take *it* up to thee. And he put out his hand, and took it.'** (80) I thought about that a lot, but I doubt if I could ever swim in my old suit of armor." he laughed.

"Amazing."

"He told me many other stories, too. As his monks were building a new stone wall for their Abbey, it fell down and killed a child. The young boy was mangled so badly that they had to carry his body in a sack to Benedict's cell. He shut his door and within an hour, the boy was completely restored, and he sent him back to help the workers continue to build."

"Servanus told me a story that he heard when he still lived in Hibernia, of Saint Patrick resurrecting a boy who had been torn apart by a wild hog. Sounds much the same."

"Nothing is impossible to God, although mortal thoughts impede miracles for most of us. Benedict also provided food during a famine when only five loaves of bread remained to feed his twelve monks and himself. His monks were desperate for food, and he told them that the next day they would have plenty to eat. Two hundred bushels of meal were found in sacks outside his cell door the next day."

"How is that possible? No one saw it being delivered?"

"No one. There are other stories, too. He healed a boy of Leprosy after his hair fell out and his body swelled. Oh, and one of my favorites was almost like when the meal showed up outside the abbot's door. Benedict had given all the wealth of the Abbey away to the poor. They had no oil left, but a small amount in a glass in the cellar. There was an empty barrel nearby, covered with a lid. Benedict kneeled and continued in his prayers until the lid lifted, and oil spilled out across the floor. A full barrel of oil from nothing, and their needs were met once more."

"Like Elisha said unto the woman who had nothing to pay her debts:; **'What shall I do for thee? tell me, what hast thou in the house? And she said, Thine handmaid hath not any thing in the house, save a pot of oil. Then he said, Go, borrow thee vessels abroad of all thy neighbours, *even* empty vessels; borrow not a few. And when thou art come in, thou shalt shut the door upon thee and upon thy sons, and shalt pour out into all those vessels, and thou shalt set aside that which is full. So she went from him, and shut the door upon her and upon her sons, who brought *the vessels* to her; and she poured out. And it came to pass, when the vessels were full, that she said unto her son, Bring me yet a vessel. And he said unto her, *There is* not a vessel more. And the oil stayed.'** (81)"

"You're right. The oil was replenished just as lives are restored. There was another story of a peasant who carried his dead son to the Abbey gate, imploring Benedict to, 'Give me my son!' The abbot prayed, and the child began to tremble and pant. Then he took the child by the hand and presented him to his father, alive.

"Any other tales?"

"Yes, but I've forgotten some of the others. I think these were the best ones," he winked.

"Please, I want you to tell them to Mungo."

"I will enjoy that,. he smiled as they walked up the steps to the dormitory. "I'm glad I decided to become a monk. It's been a wonderful journey away from everything I once held dear."

"I see where it would require a completely different perspective than most people's experience. I'm certainly glad you became a monk, or I'd be dead by now," as she held his hand and looked into his eyes.

Chapter 52

Surprise Gift

The years passed, and Thaney could see that Lance's spirit was restless. Mungo was finally walking and talking now, but even hours of playing with him didn't relax the man. Finally, she confronted him as he sat on the floor, wrestling with the boy. "Why don't you take your trip to see Father Columba now? We are safe. Mungo will start school with Father Servanus soon. Go on your quest to Iona that you've put off for all these years."

"I guess I could do that now, although I will really miss this little guy. I'll make the request for a leave to Servanus," he said as Mungo squealed with delight.

"I already asked, and he agreed. You can leave tomorrow morning," she watched amused as his mouth fell open. "I have something for you, too. She walked over to a peg on the wall and lifted a leather thong with a cylinder hanging from it."

"That looks like your scroll."

She smiled, "Mine is safe, around my neck. This one is yours," as she draped it over his neck. "Well, open it." She noticed his hands shake a bit as he twisted the end and pulled it off.

He raised an eyebrow, "A scroll for me?"

"Go on, look at it."

He shook the roll of papyrus into his hand and began

to unroll it. "I, Martin, humble servant…, oh my. This is wonderful," he blinked back tears.

"Now you can burn those illegible pages you've been carrying, your new copy even has Saint Patrick's message added at the bottom."

"How did you?"

"I asked Ezra to help me make the parchment. He has trouble seeing small letters, so I copied it onto the papyrus. I made the container too. Ezra whittled the wooden plug to fit. I noticed that you didn't have trouble reading it, though."

"Yes, I like to think of my eyes as spiritual discernment, untouched by the years," as he shook his head, "You are a marvel. Thank you from the bottom of my heart," then he read aloud.

"I, Martin, humble servant of the one Lord, do hereby set my hand to this document with humble prayers for all of mankind. I have been blessed with a lifetime of service to others. I have healed many suffering from mental and physical ills, including the great nemesis of death. These were not miracles. They were the result of my conscientious and continuous communion with God. For prayer to work, you must look at the spiritual evidence hidden beneath layers of human thought and emotion and strive to understand God's perspective. Every one of my life's questions has been answered through a broadened spiritual understanding.

*What separates us from the eternal and everlasting spiritual reality that is God? What holds this conglomeration of material experience together for all people and creatures? I believe that it is a false sense of history, for in the sage words of the apostle Paul, **"For I am persuaded, that neither death, nor life, nor angels, nor principalities, nor powers, nor things present, nor things to come. Nor height, nor depth, nor any other creature, shall be able to separate us from the love of God, which is in Christ Jesus our Lord."***

(82)

The Lord is infinite, and the only history in an eternity is now. No before, no after, just now. In my own experiences, if a man truly realizes for a moment that he is not separate from the Kingdom of God, false historical images pass away, and he is healed.

If mankind would strive after this knowledge, perfection would become increasingly evident in all of our lives. With God realized as each individual's only father/mother, mortals would see God as their one true relative, the only creator. If you perceive everything and everyone as spiritual ideas, discrimination disappears. There is no gender, age, race, or human history to hate, all becomes Love.

When material history is seen to be a lie – all anger, resentment, and fear must pass into the nothingness that spawned them. Reality then appears as harmony, health, and purity, untouched by the lie of an existence separate from God. Remove this keystone of material history, and the façade of a limited life crumbles, replaced by limitless unfoldment. I can best illustrate this with a parable of two young boys:

Cain was raised with a belief in a material mother and father. He is continually exposed to fear, sickness, and death. He believes he is entirely separate from God and cannot fathom infinity. He sees mental and physical violence from his father, witnesses its marks left on his mother and siblings, and listens to stories of past violations heaped on his family by others. He becomes a bigot and spews hatred toward others of different faiths, skin color, and social status. Cain believes in a world driven by both good and evil, including people possessed by evil. Challenges to health, prosperity, intelligence, and joy have been handed down to him through generations of ancestors. It is that inheritance that he passes to his own offspring.

On the other hand, Abel was raised with an understanding that God was his father/mother. Speaking to God directly, with unselfish motives, he receives God's perfect ideas. He experiences growth in Love, Wisdom, and Harmony. Perceiving the spiritual reality that is obscured by the mist of mortal existence, he sees evil, the devil, as unreal because, as Jesus announced, it is a lie when he said, **"Why do ye not understand my speech? Even because ye cannot hear my word. Ye are of your father the devil, and the lusts of your father ye will do. He was a murderer from the beginning, and abode not in the truth, because there is no truth in him. When he speaketh a lie, he speaketh of his own: for he is a liar, and the father of it. And because I tell you the truth, ye believe me not."** (83)

Abel is victorious as our master, his disciples, and I have been at healing disease, fear, and even death, through an understanding of God's allness and the universe as spiritual – not material. God could not be omnipresent if evil lurks in any part of the universe. Otherwise, he would be a house divided against himself, as it is recorded, **"And Jesus knew their thoughts, and said unto them, Every kingdom divided against itself is brought to desolation; and every city or house divided against itself shall not stand: And if Satan cast out Satan, he is divided against himself; how shall then his kingdom stand? And if I by Beelzebub cast out devils, by whom do your children cast them out? Therefore, they shall be your judges. But if I cast out devils by the Spirit of God, then the kingdom of God is come unto you."** (84)

Abel's inheritance is peace, perfection, and an infinite

supply of spiritual ideas that he can demonstrate in his own life. He understands that God is All, and as a reflection of God, he is himself unlimited by any material laws or restrictions. Remember how our master walked on water? **"And when even was now come, his disciples went down to the sea. And entered into a ship and went over the sea toward Capernaum. And it was now dark, and Jesus was not come to them. And the sea arose by reason of a great wind that blew. So, when they had rowed about five and twenty or thirty furlongs, they see Jesus walking on the sea, and drawing nigh unto the ship: and they were afraid. But he saith unto them, It is I; be not afraid. Then they willingly received him into the ship: and immediately the ship was at the land whither they went."** (85)

Their two lives are opposites. Which one will prove to be true? Cain holds the tatters of ruined, limited lives and beliefs around him as he walks through a dismal existence with fleeting promises of happiness. Abel is free of mortal encumbrances and shares the unlimited joys of the universe with others. Which experience do you aspire to?

The latter legacy I intend to leave with my flock. It is the heritage of salvation for this world, as it is the Kingdom of God discerned by mankind. I have no material roots! I wish only to bless this world as an expression of the Love of God. **"And thou, child, shalt be called the prophet of the Highest: for thou shalt go before the face of the Lord to prepare his ways; To give knowledge of salvation unto his people by the remission of their sins, Through the tender mercy of our God; whereby the dayspring from on high hath visited us. To give light to them that sit in darkness and in the shadow of death, to guide our feet in the way of peace."** (86)

This verity pertains to all races, creeds, and creatures

upon this earth. As people struggle to free themselves from the lures and anchors of mortal reasoning, realization occurs. As beliefs in sin and materiality wash away, they find 'at one ment' with all the ideas of creation in the Mind of God. Mankind must see itself as not removed from God. With no material history to bind them, man and woman become free to discover their true origins. Earthly yearnings subside as they discover that they themselves are the perfect images and likenesses of God. Strive to perceive materiality through the lens of Spirit. Discern the Heavenly qualities expressed in corporeal ideas. Learn the opposite of what the world is teaching you. Study the Laws of God, which protect and guide. Heal yourself and others on this earthly plain. Be Deity reflected.

I humbly petition God daily to be a better example for others of freedom from material limits. A vocation that sorely needs to be nurtured in this coarse world. I am leaving copies of this document with a few of the receptive minds that I have encountered on my life journey. This knowledge is my most valuable possession, and I bequeath it to all generations that must follow. With people, there is always dissension. The only balm for this irritation is spiritual concepts. Mankind must understand that they have never fallen from God's grace, for God, being infinite, knows nothing opposed to himself. This is the only solution for harmony and healing in this world!

Awaken my children to the latent joy and power of Christianity. You are not mortals. You are spiritual creatures! Beauty lies beyond the Adam dream.

Humble servant of the one Lord,
Martin of Tours

Magnus,
One copy of this treatise resides with my relatives,

Conchessa of Kilpatrick, and her husband Calpurnius. They have promised to help protect and nurture these ideas with others. If you need assistance, contact them.

Go with God's Love and protection, my son.

I, Patrick, Bishop of Hibernia, and privileged bearer of this manuscript penned by St. Martin, do hereby signify that his extraordinary observations on the human race are true as recorded. Especially the pure Love it expresses for humanity. Each time I read it, God's Love fills my thoughts for the world and all the souls in it. My ministry on this island would not have survived nor thrived without the spiritual insights it contains. The concepts recorded in Martin's scroll, coupled with my knowledge of the Bible, have given me victory over all the barriers I have encountered throughout my ministry. God has protected me from harm. I have touched and converted many lives with its eternal secrets. I pray that future generations glean the grains of God and reality from it and learn to ignore erroneous mortal concepts. Then God's kingdom can truly claim victory over the lies of man's separation from God, and Love will rule in continuing miracles throughout this world. Miracles always have, and will forever exist, in pure thoughts from the one and only source of Life.

Patrick"

Words choked in his throat as he finished. "I don't know how to thank you for this."

She hugged him as she looked into his eyes. "You have protected me, fought for me, and I know that you have loved me as no other man in my life ever has. This is my way of thanking my big Brother Lance. Now you have your own scroll, you can add your own statement at the end of it for the generations that follow."

"I hope my words can be a worthy addition to those that are written."

"With your heart and courage, they could be nothing less. You may have started out as Cain, but now you are Abel."

"Well, be assured that I'll return from Iona as soon as I am Able. Thank you for everything," as he kissed her forehead.

"I will miss you, but I know you need to spread your wings for a while."

"Wings?"

"You're an angel. I want you to share your blessings with others."

Chapter 54

Lancelot Returns

Thaney sighed. It had been almost a year since Lance had left to visit Bishop Columba's monastery at Iona. *What could be taking him this long? He should have returned by now. I wish I hadn't sent him on that quest.*

"Mother, where is my tablet?"

"Where you left it. Under your bed."

"Thank you, see you later," Mungo said as he grabbed a couple day-old biscuits and ran out the door."

"Have a good day," she called as he ran down the hallway. She straightened up the room and gathered up dirty clothing into a basket. Hoisting it to her hip, she carried it out of the dormitory and down to a sparkling stream that ran beside the bishop's palace. There, she filled one of the washtubs with water and started scrubbing the clothes with lye soap on the washboard.

"Good day," one of the younger monks carried a basket filled with soiled habits and sat it down at a washtub beside her.

"Morning," she replied as she continued to scrub and rinse the pile.

"Your friend Lancelot hasn't returned yet from his journey. Do you think he got lost?" The man asked in a good-natured tone.

"No, I'm sure he is just taking his time."

"If I were him, I don't think I would leave a woman like you in a monastery filled with men for months at a time."

"Why?"

"Aren't you afraid that some of us are lonely for the touch of a woman?"

"You are wedded to the church; you must remember your vows to God."

"Seeing you every day makes remembering my vows seem like a lifetime ago," as he reached over to fondle one of her skirts.

"What are you doing, Brother Duncan?" Ezra challenged.

"Nothing, I'm just doing a bit of washing for the brothers."

"Then do it somewhere else. Leave Thaney alone, or I might forget my vows."

"Bring it, old man."

"Stop it," Thaney yelled as she shoved the wet clothes back into the basket. "I'll find someplace else to do my work."

Ezra reached down and held the basket, "No, princess, leave them. I'll wash them and return them after they are dry."

She watched Duncan avert his eyes and begin scrubbing again. "Thank you, Ezra," as she walked off.

As she walked back to the main buildings, she saw a rider approaching in the distance and changed her route toward the stables. She waited anxiously until Lancelot's horse glided to a stop.

"You are a sight for sore eyes," she called, and hugged him as soon as he slid out of the saddle.

"Hello, beautiful, I'm glad to know you missed me."

"I did miss you and your protection. One of the monks was feeling frisky this morning."

"Who? I'll pin his ears back."

"Now it doesn't matter, and I'm safe. I don't want you

to quarrel and get thrown out by Servanus.

"Me either," he smiled.

"So, how was your trip to the abbey in Iona? Did they actually bury that poor monk alive?" Thaney asked.

"I don't know, that was the one question everyone there refused to answer when I asked, so I have to believe it's true," he winked. "I even asked about what Oran said when they uncovered his head. Most of them turned pale and turned away. I did learn a lot about Columba, though."

"Like what?"

"Well, the story of him turning water into wine is apparently true. Just like Jesus did at Cana, it happened while he was still in Hibernia at Moville. When no wine was available to celebrate the Eucharist, Columba grabbed a pitcher, filled it with water, and prayed. They all said it became wine."

"Did he ever do that again?"

Lance laughed, "No, I guess they haven't run out of wine since then. The other stories about Columba seemed true also. They have a nice community there, the landscape is beautiful, but the weather is becoming harsh this time of year."

"Did you get to talk with Bishop Columba?"

"Not much. I was well received and treated with honor, but the bishop is a very busy man. I did tell him about Martin's scroll and the adventures it took to find it, but he seemed unimpressed, so I didn't even show it to him."

"That's surprising, I thought he would have been thrilled about its connection to Saint Patrick, since he was Irish too."

"I didn't have a chance to mention Patrick; some crisis came up among the local pagans, and he cut our discussion short."

"That's too bad."

"Not really, I needed the time to pray and reflect. They left me alone for the most part, so I sat by the sea and meditated most days, reading the scroll over and over. I feel much more centered now. Almost peaceful," he grinned.

"I find it hard to believe that Sir Lancelot could ever feel peaceful."

"Me too, it is a strange feeling."

Chapter 55

Redbird

Thaney thought time passed too quickly. *How had twelve years passed since my coracle ground to a stop on the rocky shoreline?* Lance had been gone for almost a month now, visiting other monasteries and churches founded in the northwestern areas populated by the Picts. *I miss him.* She stared at her bowl of barley porridge as she thought of the various duties awaiting her after Mungo left for class.

"Mother, I'm going to be late," Mungo whined.

"Fine, don't wait for me. Say hello to Bishop Servanus for me."

"I will," as the boy grabbed his satchel containing his wax tablet and ran out.

"Come straight home after school."

She saw him nod his head as he raced away. *I hope he doesn't have issues with the other boys today.*

———— • ● • ————

"Here he comes," a boy shouted as he neared the classroom door. "Teacher's pet is here," several others chimed in. As he stepped through the doorway, the biggest boy in the class, Fergus, blocked his way. "Why did you do it?" he accused.

All Mungo could muster was a questioning stare; his mouth went dry, as a cold chill ran up his spine, and he took a step backward.

Fergus lunged forward and grabbed his tunic. "Oh no, you aren't getting away from us. You're going to admit your guilt to the bishop."

"For what?" Tears were forming in his eyes, clouding his vision.

"You know what. You killed his pet redbird."

"I did not," Mungo heard himself squeak as he looked toward the windowsill where a dead, decapitated redbird lay. He suddenly pushed past Fergus and walked toward the window,

"Bishop Servanus is going to hate you for killing his pet bird. He loved that bird. Remember how it would sit on his head, lap, or shoulders? He is going to beat you to death," Fergus smiled as the other boys jeered.

Footsteps sounded as Servanus neared the classroom. "Bishop, look what Mungo did; he killed your redbird," Fergus pointed at the window.

Tears rolled from the man's eyes as he entered and hoarsely asked, "Is this true?"

"It is not true," Mungo said loudly as he continued walking.

"Why are you lying to me, Fergus?" the bishop hissed.

Fergus withered under the stern gaze of the bishop, "We didn't mean it. We were just playing with it and..."

"You killed it and were all going to blame Mungo."

When Fergus started crying and hung his head, the other boys did the same.

Mungo had reached the windowsill and gently gathered the little carcass and head in his hands. He pressed the head to the body. "Jesus showed us that God is eternal Life. Please God, restore to this little bird the breath of life and freedom to fly, so that your blessed name will be praised forever."

The bird immediately revived in his hands, took flight, and landed on Servanus's head. Tears of joy ran down the man's face as he spoke with difficulty, "You have all seen a miracle. **'Where *is* the wise? Where *is* the scribe? Where *is* the disputer of this world? hath not God made foolish the wisdom of this world?'** (87) My precious redbird is restored. I want you all to meditate on what you witnessed this morning. Vicious lies uncovered. Precious life resurrected. Class will be dismissed, but first pray to God for forgiveness for your treachery." Fergus was the first to kneel in prayer, and the others quickly did the same.

Tears were running down Mungo's face as he knelt. *Thank you, Jesus, for showing me God's kingdom, and the Truth about the redbird.*

———•●•———

Thaney heard three knocks on her door. "Come in."

Bishop Servanus and Mungo entered together.

Concern suddenly etched her face, "Has something happened? What did you do?"

"Something wondrous, I don't even have words for it." Servanus answered for him with a wide smile. "Your young man proved today that he is a chosen child of God."

"What did he do?"

Servanus related the whole story as Mungo stood silently.

Thaney could only say, "Oh my," when he finished.

"I have resurrected people, but I could not even attempt what you, son, did this morning. Not since Saint Patrick have injuries that drastic been erased by prayer. It takes a clear perception of God's Kingdom, where everything is created and remains perfect despite any material images presented, to demonstrate healings like this. He had the whole class lying, working against him, until they confessed their combined treachery. My little redbird was restored. It was marvelous."

Thaney couldn't think of anything to say as she knelt and hugged her son close.

"Mother, can I go play now?"

She nodded, and he ran down the hallway.

Servanus smiled and shook his head, "Oh, to be young. I would like you both to be my guests for supper tonight in my palace, and Ezra, too. I have a special surprise for you, but now it will be a celebration. I can't wait to tell him the story. I'm going to find him now."

"Thank you, your excellency, we will be there, Ezra is probably in the Scriptorium," she called after him. *My son is a miracle worker; wouldn't mother be proud.*

———•●•———

Thaney and Mungo arrived at the bishop's residence in the late afternoon. Ezra was already there and ushered them in. "Master Mungo, I was thrilled to hear about your miracle with the redbird."

"Me too," the boy grinned.

"Come in and sit down," the bishop's voice drifted in from the adjoining room. "Sit across from me with your backs to the door, please."

Thaney thought that was an odd request, but did as she was told. *Maybe they planned a surprise for Mungo.*

She heard the door open behind her, and Servanus stood up. "Please stay seated," he told them. "Welcome to our humble dwelling, gentlemen. Please announce yourselves."

"Daughter."

Thaney almost fell off the bench as she twisted around, "Father?" she cried as she stumbled forward into his embrace.

Another voice asked, "Remember me, big sister?"

She opened her eyes and stared at a man's chest, "Little Gawain?" She looked up into his handsome face. "Goodness, you've grown. What took you two so long to visit us?"

Her father answered, "I couldn't trust leaving the kingdom until I had someone trustworthy to maintain it. Father Elam brought all of us into the Lord's fold, even the guards and villagers. He offered to keep an eye on things during our visit here. Oh, and also my friend from Wales sent his son to visit me, and here he is, Prince Dyngad ap Nudd, he wanted to meet you after hearing of your many tribulations," King Lot grinned.

The gentleman bowed deeply with a flourish, firmly took her hand and kissed it so lightly. "It's the honor of my life to meet you, Princess Thaney."

Blood was pounding in her ears; her mouth went dry. "Thank you," she whispered, staring into his eyes.

"Are you my grandson?" the king yelled, breaking the spell.

Thaney nodded, "Hug your grandfather, he's come a long way to see us." She smiled and pushed the boy forward, while still gazing at the prince.

"This was going to be a surprise reunion, but today it became a celebration of life." Bishop Servanus announced, as he gleefully mentioned his precious redbird was alive. He then addressed the king. "God has chosen your grandson to join with him in holy works," he said as he raised his hands above his head. "Now let us all pray before our meal. Father, thank you for this joyous reunion of a family that has suffered so much. May they all be blessed as they share the stories of their lives with each other and the friends who are here. Bless Mungo in all his future efforts to provide your kingdom on earth in wonderous ways as he did with my little redbird today. Bless this food which you have provided from your bounty. Now let us eat this fine feast that Father Munice has prepared for us. He is the treasured head of our kitchen, and able to turn our simple foods into mouth-watering delicacies."

"What did Mungo do?" the king demanded.

"Sit next to me, your highness, and I'll tell you all about it," the bishop winked. Everyone ate quietly as the bishop once again related the story of the redbird.

Prince Nudd sat next to Thaney. Once in a while during dinner, his knee would touch hers, and she couldn't hide a smile. Ezra saw it and winked; she blushed.

Of course, Mungo finished first and begged Ezra to play with him. As he was leaving, he nodded and shot her a smile. "I'll make sure he gets to bed, and I'll stay with him until you come in."

"Oh, I won't be long."

"Don't make promises you don't want to keep." The prince breathed into her ear.

"I try not to, but it's hard…" she whispered, touching his leg.

Chapter 56

Divine Fire

Mungo was waiting for class to start the next day. The other boys sat away from him. They chatted amongst themselves and, once in a while, turned to stare or make faces at him. Even he had to laugh when Fergus turned and stuck two index fingers in the air beside his head like a devil. "You look like your father," Mungo yelled.

"I'm not a devil," he shot back.

"You sure looked like one," as the other boys started laughing.

"What? Let's see how your prayers save you from this," and Fergus swung his legs over the bench with his fists clenched.

Mungo closed his eyes, ***"And God said, Let us make man in our image, after our likeness: and let them have dominion over the fish of the sea, and over the fowl of the air, and over the cattle, and over all the earth, and over every creeping thing that creepeth upon the earth."*** (88) *Fergus is acting creepy.*

"Fergus. What are you doing out of your seat? Sit down." Servanus commanded.

Mungo opened his eyes in time to see Fergus make an abrupt U-turn and slink back to his bench.

Bishop Servanus continued, "I'm glad I arrived when I did," he winked at Mungo. "There will be no bullying allowed if you wish to finish school. Is that clear?"

The boys dutifully nodded.

"And I am adding a new responsibility to your studies. In addition to classwork, each of you will be required to prepare the lamps in the mornings for the church and school rooms on a rotation," he held up a schedule sheet. "I think his recent success with healing the redbird warrants Mungo to have the honor and be first on our list to light all the lamps tomorrow morning."

All eyes turned on him, and Mungo felt animosity fill the room as the boys slowly faced the front again. *Oh well, God will sustain me.*

As he filed out of the room after class, Servanus stopped him. "Don't worry about the others, they will grow up and out of their petty jealousies eventually."

Mungo nodded and walked on. *Some people never grow up.*

Before he heard a cock crow, Mungo jumped out of bed in the morning darkness and ran to the church. He had slept in his clothes to make sure he had plenty of time to light all the lamps, but there was no fire anywhere. He felt inside each of the oil lamps, and they were all empty. *My classmates did this.* He clenched his fists and started walking away from the monastery. *I'll leave. I won't be around for them to make fun of.*

As he walked past a hedge, he stopped and tried to clear his thinking. *No, I can't run away from my duty. No matter what, I have to try somehow to light those lamps. Lord, what should I do?* He reached out and broke a leafy green branch from the hedge. "Dear Father, enlighten my path in this dark world. Provide me a lamp to put to nought the efforts of those who would shame your servant and pervert and diminish the good expressed by others." He raised the branch and breathed on it. Immediately, fire sent from heaven engulfed the branch, and he walked back to the church. He found a pitcher of oil and filled and lit all the lamps, one by one. As he approached the last one, Servanus stepped from the shadows.

"Good morning, Mungo, I see the other boys gave you quite a challenge this morning," he stuck his fingers into the last lamp. "Hardly damp, they poured out the oil."

"Did they? Good thing my Father in heaven didn't notice your excellency, or he might have filled them for me."

Servanus smiled and shook his head, "And what wonderous torch do you hold there? I see it burn, but it is not consumed," he extended his arm to feel the heat.

"My Father's torch, the same one he showed Moses," he waved it in the air, and it flared. **'And the angel of the LORD appeared unto him in a flame of fire out of the midst of a bush: and he looked, and, behold, the bush burned with fire, and the bush *was* not consumed.'** (89) See, it doesn't stop burning."

"Well, fill and light this last lamp, and we'll see if it survives a barrel of water."

Mungo stood on his toes and tipped the pitcher of oil into the lamp. Then, backing up, he waved the branch over the lamp's spout.

"Beautiful, the fire of the Lord." Servanus gazed at it with fascination. "One more gift you've given me, my boy. Now, let's find a barrel of water before that Holy Fire burns my monastery down."

They walked together to breakfast, and then back to the classroom, where the boys had already started to arrive. "Good morning. Welcome to class, boys." Bishop Servanus stood outside the doorway and greeted each child individually. Mungo sat silent in his usual spot, noticing the stares from his classmates.

Servanus took his place at the podium. "Yesterday, I told you that bullying would not be tolerated in this classroom. Today, I am expanding that dictum to include aggravation, pranks, and slander among you all. If I find that any of you persecute another one of your classmates, you will be expelled. Is that clear?"

The boys stared at the floor with a few heads nodding.

"Is that clear, Master Fergus?" Servanus slammed his hand on the desk, and Fergus squirmed. "Last night, some of you took it upon yourselves to make Mungo fail to light the lamps throughout this edifice. You tried your best to stop him from doing a task I assigned to him. You extinguished and poured the oil out of all the lamps. Did you notice when you entered that they are all lit?"

Heads nodded around the room.

"Do you see this branch, all green and leafy? Do you boys think it will burn?" Mungo was the only one who nodded in the affirmative. "What if I told you this branch burned and lit all of the lamps this morning."

"How?" a small boy in the front ventured.

"With the fire of salvation. God's own flames. I saw it blaze as Mungo lit the lamps. I myself extinguished it in the rain barrel outside this classroom. I couldn't believe it either, until I saw it with my own eyes. Mungo prayed, and that prayer brought a solution, just like it did with the redbird. I wish I could explain clearly how you need to see Spirit, instead of this world, Love instead of hate, to find Christ who supplies healing through inspired thoughts. I'm hopeful that all of you are going to gain those higher levels of spirituality at some point. Mungo already has. You need to listen to him, rather than torment him. I promise, if you ever torment him again, you will be expelled. Once again, I want you all to pray and meditate today on what I said. Class dismissed. Fergus, you light the lamps tomorrow morning."

Mungo watched a red-faced Fergus scowl at him before walking away.

Chapter 57

A Proposal

Lancelot urged his horse forward. He enjoyed traveling, but he was anxious to see Thaney and Mungo again. He topped a hill and paused to view the monastery spread out below him with the waters of the firth glistening in the distance. Then he gently pushed his heels into the horse's flanks as it began walking again. *I wonder if anything has changed since I left.*

Thaney and Prince Dyngad walked along the rocky beach for hours, watching the waves crash over the boulders. "Looking at this restless sea, I can't believe you didn't drown riding in that coracle. Your father showed me the cliff where you were thrown off on our travels here. It's over seven hundred feet tall. You should have been killed."

Thaney wiped some of the salty mist from her face as she licked her lips and tasted the salt, "Believe me, I agree with you on both counts. My only answer is that God preserved my life for Mungo's birth. I had him over there beside those rocks. Then shepherds found us and took us to the monastery."

"They should build a shrine there for you."

She laughed, "No, I'm no saint."

He grabbed her wrist and spun her around as he dropped to one knee, "In my eyes, you are. I made this journey just to meet you, in the wild hope that you could find it in your heart to marry me."

She felt her mouth drop open, and she covered it with her other hand, "But you know nothing about me, I'm damaged goods, I…"

"You are perfect in the eyes of the Lord, and that's what I want. Your father told me all the stories about you, and I had to meet you." He hesitated and looked down. "Do you share your heart with another?"

"No, it's just a shock. I have never thought about anyone wanting to marry me, after what happened."

"Why? You're beautiful, and you have humility and compassion for others. You're everything I need in my life. Will you give me your answer soon?"

"I will, but first I want to talk to Mungo and my friends."

"I trust that God will lead you to the right decision, dear Thaney," as he leaned forward and kissed her hand.

She noticed shivers running up her arm as her mouth went dry again. "We should head back now," she rasped as he stood up.

"As you wish, fair maiden, lead on," his hot breath whispered in her ear, and she felt herself blush.

They were nearing the buildings when she suddenly darted forward. "Come on, I know that rider, it's Sir Lancelot.

"The knight?" she heard him say as he jogged alongside.

"He's a monk now, but he's got a lot of knight left in him."

They ran up to the stables and paused to catch their breath just as Lance turned a corner and saw them. "Thaney," he urged his horse into a gallop and slid to a stop within a few feet of them. With a

flourish, he hopped down and buried her in a hug. "Thaney darling, you are a sight for these sore eyes."

"Father Lance, I'd like you to meet Prince Dyngad ap Nudd. He is visiting with father and Gawain."

"Prince, is it? Welcome, young man, to Culross," as he buried the prince's grip in his calloused hand. "So Thaney, your father finally made the trip? Where is he?"

"Probably with Bishop Servanus."

"I'm going to find him and report on my trip to Lochquaber. I'll see you and Mungo later."

"Ask the bishop about Mungo's miracle," the prince added.

"A real miracle?"

"Just ask him," Thaney said with a smile.

"I'll be sure to," Lancelot said as he picked up the reins to lead the horse. "Where is Ezra?"

"Probably in the scriptorium."

Lancelot smiled and walked away toward the stable.

"He's a big one," the prince whispered.

"With a heart to match. Let's find something to eat," she clasped his hand and led him toward the kitchen.

"Father Munice, do you have a few morsels of food for two hungry souls who missed breakfast?"

A white-haired monk smiled a greeting. "I'm sure I can find something good. Sit down, and I'll be right back. He returned with two bowls of porridge. "It's a little cold, but sometimes I like it that way. Let me know if you want something else."

They ate for a few moments in silence. "I'm sorry it's cold. We should have waited for our walk," she said.

He reached forward with a smile and brushed a speck of food off her chin. "It's delicious, I

may just eat it cold from now on," he grinned.

"Why are you so nice?"

He contemplated a moment before answering,

"Because I'm in love, it makes everything nice."

"Will you always be in love?"

"Yes," he shot back. "If you spurn me, I will still always love you," as he shoved more porridge into his mouth.

She cocked her head, "Are you serious? No matter if I say no?"

He stopped chewing, stared at her, and swallowed hard. "No matter your answer. I just pray you say yes," with a sincere smile.

"Still hungry? Father Munice asked from the doorway.

"No, I couldn't eat another bite. Thank you."

"Let me take those bowls back," the monk leaned down.

Where did you learn to cook?"

"My dear Gael mother taught me most of what I know, quite a few years ago."

"You certainly make delicious meals; would you consider moving south to Wales?" Prince Nudd asked.

"Thanks for the kind offer, your highness, but I need to remain with Bishop Servanus." He picked up the bowls, but suddenly, the old man sank to his knees.

"What's the matter?" she cried as Prince Nudd sprang forward and steadied the man from falling.

"I don't know, it hurts. Tell Bishop Servanus someone else may need to cook dinner tonight."

"Can you walk?" Prince Nudd wrapped one of the man's arms over his shoulders and lifted him

slowly. Munice moaned with pain but stumbled forward.

Chapter 58

Congratulations

The prince was sitting by Brother Munice's bedside when Thaney returned with the bishop.

Servanus bent low and felt the man's forehead. "Brother Munice, what's wrong?"

"I don't know your excellency, I have pain."

"I'll have the brothers assemble and pray for you at once."

"Thank you, your, Ahhhh," Munice cried and moved into a fetal position.

"Stay with him, I'll be back as soon as I can."

Thaney sat down next to Prince Nudd and slid her hand over his, "Thank you for helping."

"I live to serve," he said. "I always try to help wherever I can, that's why I'm trying to learn more about the Christian faith, to help this world awaken."

Thaney felt her heart open to limitless possibilities. *This is a real prince among men.* She lay her head on his shoulder.

Several monks came into the small cell. "Please, let us watch with him," one of them said and gently ushered them out.

"Now what?" the prince said.

She hesitated before she answered. "Can you spare me some time to talk to my friends? Maybe you could do something with Gawain this afternoon."

His eyes narrowed, "Are you trying to get rid of me?"

"No, actually it's the opposite of that," she smiled and tilted her head back, he seized the opportunity and kissed her, lingering for a long moment.

"Well, try not to take too long," he grinned as he backed away.

"Why should I hurry?" but she knew her wide smile betrayed her, and suddenly his arms were around her, and his lips found hers once more. Someone cleared their throat.

"Lancelot, I was just going to find you," she stammered.

"Funny place to search," he said gruffly, although his eyes sparkled with glee. "What did you want?"

"I need your advice."

"From what I saw, you don't need my advice. You're doing great on your own."

"No, not that, I mean…" she felt flushed.

"I'll see you later, Thaney, good seeing you again, sir," the prince waved and walked away.

"Well? I'm waiting."

Thaney took a deep breath and rubbed her cheeks, "Well, there is a prince who seems to be interested in me. He says he loves me, and I don't know what to do."

"Do you love him?"

"I don't know, this never happened to me before," she felt herself smile and cry at the same time.

Lance opened his arms and gently enveloped her in a hug. Holding her close, he said, "Just judging from appearances, it looks like you're in love with him."

"But what should I do? Do you like him?"

"It doesn't matter if I do or don't. What do you feel?"

She pursed her lips and blinked.

"I see the battle is lost. For what it's worth, I think he's a fine young man. What does Ezra think?"

"I haven't asked him yet. I'm worried about Mungo,

though. I'd have to leave him here for his education."

"From what I hear, he's a wise man in a child's body. Servanus told me all about the little redbird and how he lit the lamps with a divine flame. I think he'll be fine staying with Servanus. He'll need his guidance for the next few years. Let's find Ezra and see what he thinks."

"Divine flame? When did that happen?"

"This morning, you didn't know?"

***

Thwack. The arrow pierced the target just to the right and a bit below the center. "Darn, pulled it again," Gawain muttered as he fitted another arrow to his bow.

"Prince Gawain, your father told me I'd find you here. Impressive shot."

"Not for me, I'm usually much better. Would you like to try?" handing the bow to Nudd.

"Sure, I would." He took the bow and tested its pull. "You have a strong bow here."

"It's taken a number of years for me to be able to hold it steady. Usually, I can. Go ahead, take a shot."

Prince Nudd grunted as he pulled the string back. Then he eyed along the arrow as he dropped it toward the center of the target and let go.

"Bullseye," Gawain shouted. "Great shot."

"Lucky." Nudd smiled.

"Where's Thaney? I haven't seen you two apart in some time he chided."

"She had some things to do and told me to find you."

"I'm glad she did," as he shook his free hand and handed him another arrow. "Let's see if you can do that again."

———•●•———

Thaney and Lance found Ezra in the Scriptorium. "Ezra, can you spare a moment to talk with us?"

Ezra paused and rubbed his eyes, "I could use a short break, but I want to finish this manuscript today."

As they walked into the hallway for privacy, the words jumped out of Lance's mouth, and he smiled. "What do you think of Prince Nudd?"

Ezra rubbed the side of his head. He seems all right to me."

Thaney opened her mouth, but Lance spoke first, "He wants to marry Thaney."

"What, our Thaney is getting married?" Ezra's toothless smile broke wide.

"Yes."

"Wait," Thaney held up her hands. "Don't I have something to say about this?"

Mischievous glances suddenly passed between the two old monks until they shouted, "No," in unison. Then they linked arms and pranced in a circle singing, "Thaney's getting married."

Thaney felt a chill run up her back as she stared at two insane monks, but then the cold melted into joy, as it did in her heart, and she extended both arms to hug them both.

"Congratulations."

"Yes, congratulations, Thaney."

"Thank you both," she said and cried.

"By the way, this is way too much excitement for me," Lance added, kissing her forehead.

Chapter 59

A Passing

Mungo ran into the room, "Mother, I'm back."

Thaney dropped the doily she was crocheting into her lap and reached out to him, "How was school today?"

"Fine, can I go play now?"

"Not yet, I want to discuss something important with you. Do you think Prince Nudd is a good person?"

"I guess so, he smiles a lot. Why?"

"He asked me to marry him."

"Honest? That would be great."

"Really?"

"You need someone to care for you. I won't always be around, and for now, he's young enough to help me learn to fight and hunt like Lancelot does when he's able."

"Well, that's an issue. If I marry him, I will need to go and live in his castle in Wales. It is a long way away, but you'll have to finish school here."

"So, you'd leave me?" his face clouded over.

"I haven't said yes yet, that's what I want to discuss."

"No, I don't want you to leave."

"Why?"

"Because I love you."

Thaney wrung her hands together. "All right, let's leave it there for now. Go ahead and play, but be back in time for dinner." She watched him run down the hall and shook her head.

A light knock sounded on the door, and she looked up into the prince's eyes.

"No luck yet?" as a thin smile played across his lips.

"I'm afraid not, he wants me to stay here, but he does like you."

"I'm glad he likes me. I'll continue to pray about it; I have a feeling everything will work out for us."

"I hope so. I do love you," she said and stood up.

He advanced toward her, gently wrapped his arms around her, and kissed her. "That's the music I've wanted to hear." He rose to close the door.

"No, leave it open. Propriety, you know."

He sat down and smiled, "You are right, princess, we don't want scandal to touch us."

———•●•———

"No, Brother Munice, wake up, don't leave us," Servanus cried as he ran into the cell and knelt beside the man's bedside with his hands clasped tightly. Other monks stood silently as the bishop continued, "Pray, all of you pray. This is not God's will," as he bowed his head to the floor.

One of the monks spoke up softly, "Bishop, we have prayed all day, but he passed and has not returned. Normally, Brother Munice would have been cooking for an hour now. Should we start dinner?"

Servanus didn't move, but he answered, "Yes, to your regular tasks, leave me, let me pray."

———•●•———

A dirty Mungo pranced into the room and stared at them.

"What have you been doing?" Thaney demanded.

"Just playing in the stables, hide and seek," he grinned.

"You'll have to have a bath before dinner. You stink."

"I don't."

She crossed her arms, "You do and you will, young man."

Prince Nudd gave a small laugh and headed out the door, "I think I'll excuse myself. Until dinner, then?"

"We'll see you there," she said without breaking eye contact with Mungo.

"I don't need a whole bath. It's cold out, can't I just wash with the basin and pitcher?"

"All right, but wash everywhere, even your hair. I'll be back in a little while," she slipped into the hallway and closed the door. *I hope Father gives me his blessing.* She headed between the buildings for the guest rooms attached to the bishop's palace. Knocking on the door, she heard his gruff voice answer, "Come in."

"I need to speak to you, Father."

"Daughter, this is a pleasant surprise. Is it about your impending marriage to Prince Nudd?"

She gasped, "How did…"

"The prince stopped by a little while ago and asked me for my blessing concerning your marriage to him. He told me you said you loved him. Is that true?"

She blushed and nodded.

"Well, I'm glad I gave him the right answer. I'm so happy for you, darling. I pray none of the trials and challenges I brought to my wife are visited on you. I like him. I don't think they will be, but if he ever mistreats you, send me a message."

"He's been wonderful so far, Father, but I promise I will stay in touch, just in case," as she hugged him.

"Thaney, the Lord is wonderful. He protected you from Oberon, the cliff, the ocean, even me and my misguided sense of right. He will bless your marriage."

"I am just wrestling with having to leave Mungo; he

wants me to stay," she blurted.

"Morgan couldn't stay with me, though I pray she had, but then again, I may never have changed from my disgusting former beliefs if she had. It's been a hard experience and journey, with marvelous healing in the end. I'm sure Mungo will change his mind soon. He won't want to be tied to his mother much longer."

"I know, I think that's why I resisted at first, I treasure my moments with him."

"Aye, but you need to spread your wings so others can spread theirs. Otherwise, there's no room for anyone to fly," he let loose a booming laugh, and she joined in.

"Shall we go to dinner now, princess?"

"We shall, after we get Mungo. Hopefully, he's clean by now."

Chapter 60

Burial

Thaney could hear hushed voices among the monks as they walked toward the dining hall. *That's odd, they are usually silent before the evening meal.*

Lance and Ezra joined them in the throng. "Why are there voices?" Ezra asked with wide eyes.

"We don't know, something has happened, though."

They entered the main door, walked up to the bishop's table, and sat down. Soon, the princes entered and joined them. Kitchen staff brought bowls of thin, tasteless soup and bread that was burnt. Lance stopped one of the servers and asked, "Where is Bishop Servanus?" but only received a slight shake of the head.

"The food is terrible tonight. What was Brother Munice thinking?" Ezra asked as he tried to chew on a blackened piece of bread without teeth.

"I need to find Servanus," Lance announced as he suddenly left the table. A low hum of complaints about the food rose louder and permeated the room.

"I can't eat this. It's vile," the king whispered to Thaney.

"Brother Munice wasn't feeling well this morning, but I hoped he had recovered," she replied.

A few minutes later, Lance and Bishop Servanus stepped from behind the kitchen doors, and the room fell into an uneasy silence as the bishop spoke. "I hear the food is not prepared well, and there is a reason for that. Our beloved cook, Brother Munice, has passed. Our prayers today for his return to this world have not been answered. I ask you all for a moment of silence and prayer for his life after death. We will hold a wake tonight in the main chapel. He will be buried tomorrow morning."

"He didn't die," Mungo announced before raising his soup bowl and drinking more.

Thaney and the others stared at him.

After dinner, they waited in the line leading to the church. As they entered, they saw Munice's body ringed with candles. Someone was reading passages in Latin. One by one, they knelt and made the sign of the cross.

That night when she lay down, she asked, "What did you mean when you said Brother Muncie didn't die?"

"Just that. He didn't."

"What do you mean? They are going to bury him tomorrow."

"That's not him."

She sat up in bed, "All right, if that isn't him, who is it?"

"Mortality, a counterfeit of the real man."

"I know, his soul left it, right?"

"No, if God is everywhere, he is the Soul of man. Man can't have a soul separate from God."

"But he died," she shot back.

"Did Jesus die?" he asked.

She wrestled with that for a few moments, "He seemed to."

"Yes, he appeared to, but he never did, just like the rest of us who won't ascend first," he laughed. "Life is infinite, because God is infinite. Jesus said: **'Your father Abraham rejoiced to see my day: and he saw *it*, and was glad. Then said the Jews unto him, Thou art not yet fifty years old, and hast thou seen Abraham? Jesus said unto them,**

Verily, verily, I say unto you, Before Abraham was, I am.' (90) He was saying that Life is infinite."

"Did he mean the I AM that Moses spoke of?" **'And God said unto Moses, I AM THAT I AM: and he said, Thus shalt thou say unto the children of Israel, I AM hath sent me unto you.'** (91)"

"Yes, 'I AM' is the one true omnipresent God in whom we all live. Jesus was at one with God and tried to teach others Truth. **'Then said Jesus to those Jews which believed on him, If ye continue in my word, *then* are ye my disciples indeed; And ye shall know the truth, and the truth shall make you free.'** (92) He wanted men to live free from the bondage of this word."

"And that includes the bondage of a belief in death?"

"Of course, one of mankind's greatest fears. He said, **'Verily, verily, I say unto you, If a man keep my saying, he shall never see death.'** (93)

Thaney yawned, "How have you learned so much so soon?"

"I don't know. It all just makes sense."

"Not from man's point of view," she laughed.

"But it does from God's point of view. It answers all the world's questions."

"Well, thank you, I'm glad to know your grandmother and great-grandmother still live, although I sure miss them."

"We all live in God mother, because God is all," Mungo yawned and was quiet.

Thaney couldn't sleep for quite a while. *How in the world does he know so much about God?*

"Your son knows about God, because he is at one with him."

"Cynde, is that you?"

"No, dear, did you forget my voice?"

"Mother?"

"Yes, dear, I'm proud of you. Keep striving to listen for God's thoughts. I love you."

"Mother, I have so many questions. Should I marry Prince Nudd? Mother, are you there? Mother?" Thaney came awake, hearing her own voice calling out. *Listen for God's thoughts, thank you, Mother.* As she closed her eyes once again, she felt her mother's love.

"Get up young man, or we'll be late for breakfast and the cemetery service," she gently prodded him.

"Jesus said unto him, Let the dead bury their dead: but go thou and preach the kingdom of God." (94)

"What?"

"Oh, never mind," he said as he rolled out of bed, rubbed his eyes, and pulled on his trousers.

They left the dormitory with other groups of monks headed to the refectory. The meal was a thin gruel, but slightly more edible than the previous night's offering, she decided.

After that, they hiked up a small hill next to the church. "Why do they bury people so early?" Mungo moaned.

"Shush, respect," she whispered as Bishop Servanus began the burial service. She watched her son's face as a stream of foreign words flowed from Servanus. *He understands everything. I guess I should have learned Latin too.*

After the service, Prince Nudd clasped her hand as they descended the hill. "Any plans for this afternoon?" he smiled.

She shrugged and smiled.

"Thaney," Lance called behind her. "Bishop would like a word with you."

"Me, why?"

"It's important," Lance said. Looking at the prince, he said, "Sorry, but his excellency needs her assistance now."

The prince gazed at her, shrugged, and kissed her hand before saying, "Fine, I will seek you out later."

Her father said, "Go ahead, Gawain and I will take care of Mungo," as he reached over and clasped his grandson's hand.

"All right, thank you," she added before she followed Lance toward the church.

Bishop Servanus was on his knees praying when they arrived. Thaney noticed the deep circles under his eyes; he looked terrible.

Lance offered his hand and lifted the man to his feet. "Thaney, thank you for coming. I have a favor to ask of you."

"Anything, your excellency."

Tears began to drip from the man's eyes as he bowed his head and said in a broken voice. "Will you implore upon your son to raise my friend Munice?"

"Brother Munice?" she spurted, "But he was just covered with dirt."

His eyes were shut tight, but tears streamed out as he nodded vigorously.

Lancelot touched her arm to guide her out. "I will ask," she promised. As they left, she saw the bishop slowly sink back onto his knees.

Thaney and Lance walked out into the sunshine. Thoughts were spinning in her head. "Why does he want Mungo to try now? Munice is buried."

Lance shook his head, "You saw how tired and strained he is. He tried to resurrect Brother Munice all day and night, but failed. Now he is grasping at straws, anything that might bring the man back."

"I can't imagine my little boy could do it, but I will ask."

"His understanding is great. Servanus's pet bird is a clear testament to that. Servanus also told me that he summoned divine fire to a green branch and lit the lamps in the church and school yesterday. If anyone can, he can," Lance smiled.

"What?" Thaney felt her eyes widen, "I forgot to ask him to tell me about that."

"Well, you have been preoccupied with a certain

prince." Lance chided.

They walked together over to the waters of the Firth. Each was lost in their own thoughts.

292

Chapter 61

Growing up

"I'm finally growing up, rather than chasing childish urges," as Lance picked up a stone and flung it toward the firth.

She put a hand on his shoulder and stopped him, "I'm glad you waited to stop being childish, or I might have never known my mother was murdered, and no one else would have searched the coast to find out whether I was dead or alive either."

"I'm glad I waited too. You're precious.I had to search for you. Despite all the anguish and treachery I've encountered after meeting you, it has been the most rewarding period of my life. You've given me more blessings than I can count."

"I hope that was a compliment," she laughed.

"The highest possible," he winked.

"At least I kept it interesting for you."

"Intriguing would be a better word. I never knew what to expect. Now, your son continues in your footsteps., I certainly don't know what will befall him next."

She was suddenly serious, "If I do leave with the prince, promise me that you will stay and protect Mungo."

He stopped short and stared into her eyes, "You didn't need to ask."

"I had to, a mother's fears, you know."

"I wonder how deep they buried Brother Munice?"

"Why?" she asked.

"At the monastery in Iona. I heard they buried Brother Oran the height of seven men deep, if the story is true."

"Why so deep?"

"I have no idea, maybe they were afraid that he'd dig himself up, sounds like he might have if he spouted off as soon as they uncovered him," he chuckled. "No, I was wondering about poor Brother Munice."

"What made you think of that?"

"It's been quite a while since I dug much dirt. I sure hope that ground is soft."

"Of course it is, they just buried him this morning. I just hope Mungo is successful. I'd hate to have him fail. It might hurt his faith."

"I don't think his faith can be shaken by any setback."

"I know you're right; no one could reattach a bird's head and have it take flight immediately, unless he sees it spiritually."

"I believe you are learning," he beamed.

"I'm trying my best, but it's complicated, so much to understand."

"Much to unlearn about this convoluted world. Understanding God becomes simple after that."

"My mother came to me in a dream the other night. She told me to always listen for God's thoughts."

"I remember you told Mungo that, too. Next time, tell her hello for me."

She nodded, and they walked on toward the dormitory in silence.

Chapter 62

Resurrection

When Thaney and Lance entered the king's guesthouse, they saw Prince Nudd and Mungo sitting cross-legged on the floor playing Tabula. "I win again," Mungo shouted, while the prince shook his head. "Who's next?" he asked as he looked around the room.

"Mungo, I need to talk to you."

"Mother, the prince just taught me this game, and I won twice."

"That's fine, but I need to talk to you alone, right now."

"I need to lick my wounds right now anyway. You two go and talk," the prince motioned him away with a grateful smile.

Mungo and Lance followed her outside to a shady spot next to the building. She lowered her voice, "Bishop Servanus wants me to ask you a favor, and I know you can do it."

"What?"

She whispered, "He wants you to resurrect Brother Munice."

"But he just buried him," he blurted.

"Shush, keep your voice down," she motioned with her palms.

Mungo began again in a hushed tone, "He just buried him, why should I try to bring him back?"

"Because they were friends, and he struggled all night to bring him back to no avail. You should see him. He looks awful. It would be a kindness to him."

"Why didn't he ask me himself?"

"I don't know. Maybe he is ashamed that he couldn't do it himself. Remember all the kindness he has poured into our lives. At least try to repay him with this additional challenge."

"I will try. Lancelot, will you come with me and help dig him up?"

"Certainly."

"Then let's go, goodbye, Mother," he said as they marched away.

As they left, a hand sought hers, and she squeezed hard. She and Prince Nudd watched them walk away toward the cemetery.

— • ● • —

"We need to stop by the cemetery garden shed and borrow spades," Lance said, and Mungo nodded. There was one monk still smoothing out stray footprints as they walked up and startled the man. "Bishop Servanus sent us. We need to borrow two spades."

The man's eyes narrowed, "What for?"

"We need to dig up Brother Munice. He borrowed a copy of the Lord's Prayer from me and never gave it back. Problem with that?" Lance scowled.

The man's eyes widened in fear, "Naw, sir. Here take this one, another is in the shed," as he hurried away down the hill.

"Looks like we have three or four more hours of daylight left. We'd better get started. You run over to the shed and get another spade." Lancelot walked up the hill while Mungo ran over to the shed. By the time he got back, Lance had a large hole dug in the soft dirt. In a few more minutes, Lancelot's shovel hit something soft. "We're here. Throw your spade out; we mostly dig by hand now." They clawed handfuls of dirt and rock out and were finally rewarded with a view of the carcass wrapped in cloth. "All yours, Mungo, although I will be praying too," as Lancelot clambered out of the hole.

Mungo settled himself and straddled the legs of Munice. The damp ground was starting to chill him. "Lord God of Jesus Christ, hear my prayer. You are the Life of all things. You exist in everything, everywhere. Wake up your faithful servant Munice, so that he can once again minister to your followers. Wake him from his sleep so your Holy name will be blessed forever."

He concentrated on how much the people enjoyed his food. How welcoming and orderly he was in everything he attempted. *He was a wonderful person.* In a few minutes, he felt something touch his leg. An instant later, Munice coughed.

"Where am I? It feels damp?" he croaked.

"You're fine, Brother Munice. Let me help you up, and we'll go back to your kitchen."

"Who are You?"

"I'm Mungo, and Brother Lance is here too."

"Mungo, the miracle worker? You brought me back from the dead? I was in a place of judgment, and someone said, 'Mungo, the beloved of the Lord, is praying for this man.' Then I remember a being, streaming in golden white light, leading me back to my body."

Mungo lifted Munice's arm to Lance, who grabbed the monk's wrist and helped him climb out of the grave and walk down to the kitchen. Mungo then fell to his knees in the soft dirt. "Thank you, Lord God, thank you," as his tears fell in a torrent of gratitude.

Twilight was encroaching, and Mungo was just shoveling the last clumps of dirt back into place, when he heard his mother cry out for him. He wiped a filthy sleeve across his sweaty face. "I'm here, Mother."

"Are you all right?" concern etched in her voice.

"I'm fine, but I fear I have a few new blisters." As he steadied himself with the spade he grimaced.

"Well, stop digging and come down to the refectory, Brother Munice wants to thank you."

"He should be resting in bed."

"He says he rested too much already today, come on."

Mungo gave the spade one last strong thrust and left it standing on the empty grave as he walked down the hill.

Mungo hesitated as they drew nearer. "I need to wash first."

"Son, don't listen to my words of advice anymore. Only listen to your Father from now on. What is he telling you?"

"To go inside," he smiled and opened the door to cheers.

"Quiet, everyone, quiet," a beaming Servanus announced. "My friend would like to share a few words with Mungo and all of you. Brother Munice, you have the floor."

"First of all, I have this young man to thank for my return to this world. I was in a place where the Highest Court of Judgment was deciding on my fate, but Mungo, the beloved of the Lord, was praying for me. They said that, I remember clearly." He pointed a finger in the air. "In gratitude, I wanted to bake something special. So as soon as I removed my grave clothes, my kitchen staff and I began cooking sweet corn bread for all of you. The first piece I cut for Mungo," as he carried a plate forward and bowed.

Mungo looked at the golden cake and then at his mother, who nodded. He took the cake and bit into it, smacking his lips and swallowing. "Much better than last night's dinner," he announced as the hall erupted with applause.

Chapter 63

A Boy's Blessing

"Morning hero."

"What?"

"Wake up, it's nearly seven o'clock. I brought you some breakfast that Brother Munice made especially for you."

"He did? Why?"

"I declare, you don't understand how grateful he is for life restored. We all are grateful for his return."

"He makes good food," he said as he ate.

"That's one way he expresses love to others, but he is good in many other ways, too. That's why Servanus cares for him so much. He wants you to stop by and see him this morning."

"All right."

A knock sounded on the door. "May I come in?" Prince Nudd asked.

"Sure," Mungo answered.

"I wanted to talk to you, son, about your mother and me. I want to marry her."

"I know, and she deserves a good life as a queen after the sores she's borne because of me."

"Don't say that. You weren't the cause of my challenges; it was people, it was me trusting the wrong people. I only survived by trusting God," Thaney cried.

"I know, that's how we all survive and thrive in this world. Regardless, Mother, I have grown to see more multifarious forms of Spirit in the last few months than ever before. I have grown, and have an appreciation for others' situations, now more than ever. I think you should marry Prince Nudd, Mother."

"Really?" she said, feeling tears fill her eyes. "But it means that I would need to leave you here for your studies with Servanus."

"Mother, I am grown in Spirit, if not in body. If it is right in God's eyes, I will see you again in this world."

"So be it," his mother whispered. When will we leave?" she asked.

"Tomorrow," Prince Nudd smiled and kissed her hand.

"I need to tell Lance and Ezra," Thaney said, "Mungo, go tell the bishop now."

"All right, Mother," he stopped to shake the prince's hand on the way out, "Congratulations, you have gained the most wonderful woman in the world."

"Thank you, but I already knew that."

"I just pray you always remember," as he walked out the door.

Thaney felt the prince's arm wrap around her shoulder as he said, "Your son is incredible."

"God knows," she said, squeezing his hand.

———•●•———

Mungo knocked on Servanus's door.

"Come in," a cheery voice answered, and then, "Ow."

"What's the matter?"

"Nothing, my hands just hurt sometimes."

"Mother told me you wanted to see me, sir," the boy said as he entered.

"That I did, Master Mungo. Please sit down and be

comfortable. I'd like to understand more about how you perform your resurrections."

"The same way you did with those two brothers, I guess."

Servanus walked around his desk and offered honey and oat bars to the boy. "Brother Munice made these today. I hope you like them." Mungo took two and said thanks. "You're welcome, if you want more, help yourself," he said as he set the plate down on his desk. "I resurrected those two a number of years ago, but I'd like to know what you did yesterday."

"I told him to wake up," he said, licking a sticky finger.

"That's all?"

"Well, I thought about God being in all things, including Brother Muncie, and if God was in him, he was still alive."

"But we buried him…"

"God doesn't care where he is. You told me, **'For I am persuaded, that neither death, nor life, nor angels, nor principalities, nor powers, nor things present, nor things to come, Nor height, nor depth, nor any other creature, shall be able to separate us from the love of God, which is in Christ Jesus our Lord.'** (95) You told me we could never be separated from God.

Servanus's eyes glistened with tears, "You are correct, sometimes I forget."

"How could you forget? God is ever-present, always available. If I twist an ankle or have a cold, I look at my image in Him, feel His Love for all, and I am healed. He made us in His image, not the image of man."

"Of course."

"So, His image is spiritual, not material. You aren't subject to the ills and concerns of this world when all you see is God's world."

Servanus sighed, "Mungo, you are no longer a student, but a better teacher than I am. **'But Jesus called them unto** *him,* **and said, Suffer little children to come unto me, and forbid them not: for of such is the kingdom of God. Verily I say unto you, Whosoever shall not receive the kingdom of God as a little child shall in no wise enter therein.'** (96) Sometimes the images of this world are hard to ignore as you grow older, and I forget."

"How can you grow old? You are one with God, you are timeless through the ages." Mungo grabbed another oat bar. "These are really good."

"I am growing old, I see you with your whole life ahead of you. I envy you and your expansive understanding at such a young age."

"Are you growing old, or do you just imagine you are? **'Jesus said unto them, Verily, verily, I say unto you, Before Abraham was, I am.'** (97) He was at one with the Father throughout all time, along with you and me and everyone," as he licked the honey from his lips. "Can I go play now?"

Servanus chuckled, "Yes, go and play. Once I've digested some of your ideas, I may come out and play hide-and-seek with you."

"They aren't my ideas, they are God's," as he ran out the door, he stopped, "Oh, and Mother is marrying Prince Nudd, they are leaving tomorrow for Wales."

———•●•———

Bishop Servanus sat with his elbows on his desk and his hands over his eyes. *Forgive me Father, for I have sinned...* Then he noticed that his hands weren't hurting anymore.

Chapter 64

Celebration

Everyone was seated in the refectory before dinner when Bishop Servanus and Brother Munice entered. Servanus addressed them. "Greetings, brothers and honored guests. We will be served one of Brother Munice's finest feasts in a few minutes to honor the impending wedding of Prince Nudd and Princess Thaney." Clapping started, but he raised his hands to stop it. "We were extremely sorry to hear today that they will be leaving us to travel to their kingdom in Wales tomorrow, but we all understand how the weather may become an issue this time of year. Tonight, we celebrate their future of wedded bliss along with recent miracles brought to us by Thaney's son, Mungo. First, the resurrection of a bird, then a divine fire, and also the return of my dear friend Munice, who has cooked a delicious meal for us all this evening."

"Will Mungo go with them?" Brother Munice asked loudly.

"No, I have it on his mother's authority that I will be able to continue to tutor her son, although I fear he is teaching me more about the Almighty than I can ever teach him." Polite laughter filled the room. "Let us pray. Thank you, Lord, for this bounty you have blessed us with, for our friends who have shared their love with us, and, of course, the miracles and the return of our dear Brother Munice from death's grave embrace. In God's name we pray. Amen. Please, Brother Munice, have your staff start the dinner service."

Tankards of mead and ale were brought to the tables, followed by platters of meat, fish, and local produce, including cabbage, turnips, carrots, peas, onions, and beans. Mungo's belly must have been full before he tasted half of the offerings. "Mother, I can't eat anymore."

"I know, darling, just sit back and enjoy seeing everyone happy. This is our last night together for a long while," she said, and hugged him. "I'm going to miss you so much."

"God is omnipresent, we reflect him. We can never be parted from each other."

"I'll still miss your face."

"I'll certainly miss you, Miss Thaney," Ezra chimed in. "I've never felt like I had a family before we started on your quest for the scroll. At least I'll still have Mungo here. I may take him to see Caleb someday."

"That would be wonderful, Ezra, say hello to Caleb for me when you do," she laughed.

"I feel the same," Lancelot's deep voice rumbled with emotion. "I fear I would have passed on by now, if it weren't for the adventures you provided in my life, and the terrors, fears, life and death struggles, sleepless nights, pains…"

"All right, we all get the pictures you so eloquently painted in our minds." Thaney held up her arms in submission, "Excuse us for a moment, please." As Thaney clasped Lancelot's hand and pulled. She saw Prince Nudd's mouth fall open. "I need a few moments alone with this former knight. We'll be back soon."

Thaney led him out into the moonlit cloister and over to a nearby bench. "I wanted to tell you that I am going to miss you the most of all the people in my life," as they sat down.

"And I'll miss you more than any other person besides

my dear Guinevere."

"It's going to be a hard change for me. My life here has been pretty sanguine. Not much to worry about for these many years."

"You are up to the challenge. The prince seems like a wonderful fellow and is very interested in following Christianity. I hope you can develop a little support group for yourself in Wales, like your mother had here."

"I will try, thank you."

"But never forget that Christianity is not just fellowship, its primary purpose is to destroy the works of the devil."

She blinked, "Like sin and sickness?"

"And death," he continued. "Being a Christian is fighting the works of the devil, the lies of mortality. We are spiritual creatures, like Saint Martin wrote in his scroll."

"Once a knight, always a knight. You've gone from fighting regional battles for kingdoms to fighting for Truth and the revealing of God's Kingdom on earth."

"I never thought of it that way."

"Obviously, Mungo knows that from his recent successes, too," she smiled. "And you and I know it from reading the scroll. That's why I made you a copy to hang around your neck."

"The most precious gift I ever received," as he reverently touched the leather cylinder.

"I'm just grateful that you'll always have 'Sir Lancelot's Scroll' to guide you after we separate."

"Sir Lancelot's scroll?" he looked shocked.

"Of course, Saint Patrick added his thoughts to make it his, and I left room at the bottom of it to add your thoughts. I wonder where our scrolls will end up?"

"Or if they'll survive," he added. "I do hope God gives me great ideas to declare."

"I'm sure he will feed wonderful Truths to both of us in the coming years that we will be able to add to them," she paused. "Before we go in, I want to say that I love you, Brother Lance," as she leaned forward, kissed him on the cheek, and lingered.

He blushed as he held her hand silently for a few seconds, "You know I love you too, princess, and always will."

"I know you didn't get to kiss Guinevere the last time you saw her. Do you want to kiss me?" she said quietly.

"You mean until we meet again?"

"Yes", as she leaned forward and their lips touched as their arms wrapped around each other.

Lance finally pulled away with a contented smile. "Thank you. We'd better go in before people start to talk."

"I'm sure it's too late for that," she said, standing. "But I really don't care, do you?"

"Not in the least," as he led her to the doorway and back into the dining hall.

Chapter 65

Lancelot's Scroll

Mungo felt someone shaking him awake as dawn started to emerge from the horizon. We're leaving now, darling. This room is all yours from now on."

"Why are you leaving so early?" Mungo asked, rubbing his eyes.

King Lot spoke up, "The days are shorter now, and we need to travel in the daylight. It's safer than riding at night."

"I guess so," Mungo said as he stood up. Thaney and the prince hugged him first, then the king and Gawain as they all said their goodbyes.

"Any last words for us?" Thaney asked as her eyes glistened.

"The only way to still the upheaval in this world is to live in the kingdom of God," as he hugged his mother once again, and saw the shocked look on her face.

The king spoke up, "Where is His kingdom?"

"Within each of you."

"Where did that come from?" she asked.

"God told me that just before you woke me up."

"Remember what I told you?" She kissed him on the forehead.

"Yes, Mother, I need to only listen to my father, now you know I am," he smiled.

"Yes, you are, and so you always will. I hope you come

and visit us when you finish your studies."

"I will try, Mother, safe travels to you all," as the travelers filed out of the room.

Mungo turned toward the window and saw the first rays of the sun striking trees in the distance. He sat and watched until he saw the small caravan thread its way out of the monastery grounds onto the cart path winding away beside the firth. He finished dressing and wandered down to the kitchen. A few monks were busy with various chores. Brother Munice smiled when he entered. "Mungo, welcome to my culinary domain. Why are you up at this hour?"

"Mother and the others left to travel south this morning. This is my first morning alone."

"You should know better than anyone that you are never alone."

"That's true, but He doesn't talk as loud as she did," he grinned. "Can I help you with anything?"

"Would you mind mixing this bowl of dough? Just keep stirring it until it is smooth through and through.

Mungo took the wooden spoon and started trying to work it through the thick mixture quickly.

"No, slow down, you'll either tire yourself out or you'll break my spoon. Take your time. Don't fight it, love it," he smiled.

Mungo looked up, "All right," as he slowed his movement and swirled the mixture around.

"Wonderful, I may ask bishop Servanus if I can keep you as my protégé. That way, if the meal tastes bad, you could heal it," he laughed.

"What's this?" Lance asked as he walked in with Ezra, "Do we have a new cook?"

"No, just helping until I can get something to eat. Did you see everyone off?"

"I did, one of the hardest things I've done in my life is to say goodbye to your mother, but I think it's for the best," Lance said as Ezra nodded silently.

Mungo just nodded and set the bowl down, "I think it's done."

"Marvelous, you did a fine job. Now you three sit down and eat, here are bowls of porridge and some bread," Munice demanded.

They ate in silence for several minutes until Mungo asked, "So, are either of you going to leave soon?"

Ezra responded, "I'm not, I promised Thaney that I would wait and take you to Kilpatrick to meet my friend Caleb when you finish your schooling."

Lancelot finished eating and wiped his mouth. "Nope, I'm bound by a promise to your mother to watch and protect you. Does that surprise you?"

"No, but God is my protection if you need or want to leave."

"I know, but I am constantly entertained around you. A redbird's head reattached, buried people coming back to life, green branches burning with divine fire, I wouldn't want to miss any of it."

Mungo grinned, "Thank you. I still want both of you in my life. Now I have to go to class, or I'll be late," as he hurried away.

"I'm off to the scriptorium. I'll see you later, Brother Lance," Ezra said.

— • ● • —

Lance took his time walking back to his small cell where he sat down at the table. He fumbled with his robe, pulled the leather thong over his head, and carefully shook the small roll of paper out of its leather cylinder. He started reading it from the beginning and finished with the words of Saint Patrick. Then he sharpened a quill feather, dipped it into an ink well, and began to write.

I am Brother Lance, a poor and humble servant of the Lord who has been honored to witness and aid in a multitude of extraordinary miracles, all of them beyond the comprehension of mortal men. Saint Martin's precious words ring true in my life experiences. My early life was filled with carnage, hatred, and madness. People knew me as Sir Lancelot, a knight of the Round Table. I demanded respect and followed all of my carnal desires that only provided small fragments of fleeting pleasures. I see now that they only contributed to my lingering guilt and pain in this material world.

After renouncing my former life of violence, and taking my solemn vows as a monk, I have begun to see the visions that John saw, ***"And I saw a new heaven and a new earth: for the first heaven and the first earth were passed away;"*** *(98) My selfish ambitions have been replaced by a life of service to others.* ***"as the truth is in Jesus: That ye put off concerning the former conversation the old man, That ye put off concerning the former conversation the old man, which is corrupt according to the deceitful lusts; And that ye put on the new man, which after God is created in righteousness and true holiness."*** *(99) This world has become a new, bright place to me, filled with possibilities and an overflowing sense of Love. It has given me freedom to act and reflect God's spiritual qualities, along with the humility needed to bow to His will in all judgments. It provides a clear perception of God's Kingdom on earth and I begin to understand what Divine Love is. Love is the key component in all the miracles I have witnessed thus far.* ***"God is love; and he that dwelleth in love dwelleth in God, and God in him."*** *(100)*

Brother Lance

To be continued…

Epilogue

"But if there were a man who had sufficient force, he would shake off and break through, and escape from all this; he would trample under foot all our formulas and spells and charms, and all our laws which are against nature: the slave would rise in rebellion and be lord over us, and the light of natural justice would shine forth."

**Callicles -
Greek Philosopher
(c. 484 – late 5th
century BC)**

Callicles sounds like he was speaking about Jesus and his followers. They destroy the concepts and restrictions of this world. The weak become strong. Wisdom of this world is found to be false. Sickness, sin, and death are destroyed without the use of matter remedies.

"It is the spirit that quickeneth; the flesh profiteth nothing: the words that I speak unto you, they are spirit, and they are life." (101)

Primal Christians measured success through the healing of sickness, sin, and death. What do today's popular religions promote? Usually, only fellowship and the removal of some sins. Churches should seek the whole of Christianity. Rid yourselves of the belief that you are living a life apart from Christ. Obey the precepts of God. Live in His spiritual kingdom, free from the world of mortal pain and imagined pleasures. Healings and resurrections are still occurring through the ages. How? Seek the ultimate Truth about Life with your whole heart, and I pray the knowledge will be revealed to you.

"Rabbi, we know that thou art a teacher come from God: for no man can do these miracles that thou doest, except God be with him. Jesus answered and said unto him, Verily, verily, I say unto thee, Except a man be born again, he cannot see the kingdom of God." (100)

Be born again in the perfect, spiritual image of God. Reality is revealed as the mist of human perception clears.

Citations

1)	I Corinthians 2:9 *Eye,* 10
2)	Matthew 5:1-12
3)	Matthew 5:14-16
4)	James 5:14
5)	Genesis 1:27
6)	Matthew 6:9-13
7)	I Peter 2:9
8)	John 18:36
9)	Matthew 23:9,10
10)	John 3:24-29
11)	Matthew 8:5-10,13
12)	Matthew 18-23
13)	Isaiah 7:14-15
14)	Matthew 2: 1-6, 9-11
15)	Philippians 14:3
16)	1 Corinthians 2:12-14
17)	Matthew 6:9,10
18)	Matthew 6:10
19)	John 8:29
20)	Matt 1:18
21)	Proverbs 30:5
22)	Psalms 59:1

23)   Matthew 16:23
24)   John 6:63
25)   Romans 8:13
26)   Matthew 6:12
27)   Psalms 8:2
28)   Leviticus 19:31
29)   James 3:16
30)   I Corinthians 14:33
31)   Matthew 12:50
32)   Acts 10:28
33)   I Peter 2:9
34)   Luke 12:2
35)   Jeremiah 33:8
36)   II Samuel 12:1–5,7
37)   Luke 1:30, 31, 33–35
38)   Isaiah 33:22
39)   II Kings 6:16
40)   Luke 22:42
41)   Acts 9:17
42)   Matthew 6:9, 10
43)   Genesis 1:27
44)   Genesis 1:31
45)   Genesis 2:6
46)   Genesis 2:7
47)   Psalms 59:1
48)   Psalms 89:18
49)   John 4:24
50)   Titus 3:3, 4
51)   Acts 20:9,10,12
52)   Luke 12:2
53)   Luke 22:42
54)   Psalms 91:2–5
55)   Exodus 10:17
56)   I Timothy 2:5
57)   Luke 23:34
58)   Psalms 91:12

59)	Matt 28:18,20
60)	Romans 13:1
61)	Mark 12:29
62)	Psalms 106:1
63)	John 8:44
64)	Matthew 4:8–10
65)	I John 4:8
66)	John 4:24
67)	1st John 4:1
68)	1st John 4:6
69)	1st John 4:6-9,11
70)	I John 4:12
71)	James 4:4
72)	Luke 12:11, 12
73)	Numbers 22:26–32
74)	I Kings 19:11–13
75)	Luke 11:2
76)	Genesis 1:1–3
77)	Genesis 2:6
78)	Genesis 2:7
79)	Luke 11:2
80)	II Kings 6:5–7
81)	II Kings 4:2–6
82)	Romans 8:38
83)	John8:44
84)	Matthew 12:28
85)	John 6:16-21
86)	Luke 1:76-79
87)	I Corinthians 1:20
88)	Genesis 1:26
89)	Exodus 3:2
90)	John 8:56–58
91)	Exodus 3:14
92)	John 8:31,32
93)	John 8:51
94)	Luke 9:60

95)	Romans 8:38, 39
96)	Luke 18:16, 17
97)	John 8:58
98)	Revelation 21:1
99)	Ephesians 4:21, 22, 24
100)	John 6:63
101)	I John 4:16